WHEN TH

BY FRANK MALLEY

FCM BOOKS

2nd Edition

Copyright © 2025 Frank Malley

First published by Whisper Publishing in 2020

Frank Malley has asserted his rights under the Copyright, Designs and Patents Act 1988 to be identified as the author of this work.

This book is a work of fiction, and except in the case of historical fact, any resemblance to actual persons, living or dead, is purely coincidental.

A CIP catalogue record for this book is available from the British Library.

This book is sold subject to condition that it shall not, by way of trade or otherwise, be lent, resold, hired out, or otherwise circulated without the publisher's prior consent in any form of binding or cover other than that in which it is published and without a similar condition, including this condition, being imposed on the subsequent purchaser.

For Carole and Michael
and in memory of Mum

Laughter may be a form of courage. As humans, we sometimes stand tall and look into the sun and laugh. I think we are never more brave than when we do that.

Linda Ellerbee (US TV journalist)

Cover art: Sarah Moore

FRANK MALLEY

PROLOGUE

Dan didn't like Mondays. It was the only thing he had in common with Bob Geldof.

In an idle half-hour, he calculated that he'd experienced 2,514 Mondays in his lifetime and couldn't remember one that had been memorable for the right reasons. Today was another – a bad, bad Monday.

What had his mother told him? 'Breathe, Dan. It's just a bad day, not a bad life. Like the rest, it only lasts twenty-four hours.'

That morning, Dan had remembered his long-gone mother and taken deep breaths when visiting the dentist. *Root canal treatment.* Even the words made him shiver, conjuring up visions of mechanical diggers dredging with sharp implements and finding rusty, old supermarket trolleys and dead dogs. Inside his mouth. That's why he always demanded the maximum dose of anaesthetic. *Go on. Give me another shot. I can take it.* Consequently, Dan had left the surgery after an hour of dredging with a numb face, frozen jaw and fog for a brain. On the way home, he'd popped into a newsagent for a copy of *the Daily News*.

"Jelly Newsh, pleash."

"What?" The woman behind the counter

looked puzzled.

"Jelly Newsh."

"Jelly Babies?" she asked, taking pity, she thought on a customer with an obvious affliction.

"No. Jelly Newsh."

"You'll have to speak clearly. I don't understand."

Dan asked again, this time raising his voice.

"I said clearly, not louder."

Dan gave up talking. He pointed to a stand behind the woman, where the paper sat between two other local dailies.

"Oh, *the Daily News*. Why didn't you say?"

Dan handed her a £1 coin, took his paper and received a free gift of an exasperated look.

He'd told himself he should stay in that night with a good book, a warm drink and his feet up. Instead, he was at a posh hotel with ornate chandeliers, and waiters balancing trays laden with Krug champagne. It was not Dan's scene. He was more at home dodging Molotov cocktails and stray bullets or drinking beer. Strong beer. Flat. Straightforward. Honest. He swiped a half-pint of ale from the bar – a sound decision considering his jaw still throbbed, and he'd been popping painkillers all day.

Dan returned the nod of Paul Dankworth, editor of *the Daily News* and his boss for the past ten years.

"Going to be a great night," said Dankworth.

He was standing no more than five yards away but still had to raise his voice over the din of the crowded banqueting suite at the Hotel Café Royal on London's Regent Street.

For the occasion, Dankworth had donned black tie and dinner suit, and, with his growing paunch and diminutive stature was a dead ringer for Danny DeVito in *Batman Returns.*

What a muppet Dan thought although his natural polite demeanour conveyed a warm, welcoming smile before mouthing, "Smart suit."

Dan had also made an effort. An elegant Pierre Cardin navy jacket hung from broad shoulders, and he'd chosen his lucky blue and white polka dot tie. The one he'd taken on assignments to Afghanistan, Iraq, and Syria, although, not surprisingly, had never found an occasion to wear.

Tonight was the night the British press gathered to salute its finest writers and most fearless reporters. There were more than 400 guests in total, every national daily and Sunday newspaper plus a variety of broadcasters all taking tables of ten. The Journalist of the Year category included three of Dan's dispatches from Damascus, the accompanying newspaper cuttings mounted on a presentation board lining one side of the banqueting suite. Still-life exhibits in an art gallery.

Krug champagne? There were occasions in the Syrian deserts when Dan would have given his life savings for a bottle of mineral water. As he scanned the array of news clippings and photos, the memories of fear and rising panic flooded Dan's brain. A trickle of sweat ran down his spine, the back of his throat catching spontaneously. Dry, pasty. The taste of dust. *I'm getting too old for this.*

Dan took a seat at a table hosted by Dankworth. The dinner was the usual sumptuous affair. Smoked salmon starter followed by rare fillet steak served with a perfectly thickened blue cheese sauce. Conversation flowed as freely as the wine until three trumpets sounded, heralding the start of formal proceedings. A television news presenter, famous for his reports from foreign parts, stepped into the role of Master of Ceremonies and the awards began. The usual format – journalists selected from a shortlist with the winners invited on stage to say a few words after receiving his or her trophy from a former chat show celebrity.

News Reporter of the Year, Young Reporter of the Year, Fashion Journalist of the Year, Science Correspondent of the Year. There was even a Best of Humour award, won by a man from *the Times.* Attempting to justify his victory, he took the microphone and with a deadpan delivery, said, "Some cause happiness wherever they go – others whenever they go."

He scurried off stage in mock haste, greeted

by loud applause, despite not attributing his witticism to a citation he'd read in a book of quotations the previous day. *A thief in the night.*

Last up, the most prestigious award in the profession: Journalist of the Year.

Dankworth glanced at Dan. With a wine-induced leer and a fist pump, he growled, "Come on, my son!"

On stage, the Master of Ceremonies introduced the shortlist of six candidates. As he named each one, an image appeared on the big screen behind him. Dan was last on the list. As the MC announced his name, Dan's picture appeared, and Dankworth rose to his feet, put his fingers to his mouth and launched a piercing whistle. The rest of the table joined in.

Dan sat. Tight lips. Aching gums.

The MC began. "In third place and commended by the judges for his vivid imagery and considered analysis, Mark Hogan from *the Times*."

There was a collective whoop from Hogan's table – equal measures of disappointment and delight.

"In second place, Katy Merrick."

This time, the announcement generated a more enthusiastic response from *the Observer* table. Shouts of, "Well done Katy," resounded around the room before the paper's editor, James Ledwith, slobbered a kiss on her cheek.

"Now, for the big one." The MC boosted

anticipation.

Dankworth pumped another fist in Dan's direction.

"Before we reveal the winner, let's hear an example of what makes this writer the undisputed champion when it comes to reporting from home or abroad. Comfort zones or war zones."

An awkward Dan shuffled his feet.

The chat show celebrity approached the microphone, took a slip of paper from his inside pocket and proceeded to read Dan's most recent dispatch from Damascus. A personal reflection, heralding an unlikely ceasefire and genuine hope for the first time in months.

"'Today, for the first time since I can remember, I was awakened by birds singing rather than a dawn chorus of howling jets, exploding bombs, and wounded children screaming for their mothers. Today, for the first time in this brutal, bombed-out ruin of a city, I felt alive.'"

The room hushed to reverential silence as everyone listened to Dan's tale of appalling atrocities, individual heroism, and the routine suffering from the vile use of chemical weapons. So graphic was the chronicle, the stench of cordite was palpable, rising from the page to fill the reader's nostrils – a heart-wrenching example of stirring reportage. With a studied pause, the chat show star concluded with a poignant line.

"'Today, among the dead, the dying, and those clinging to survival in this square mile of a real-life Dante's Inferno, I feel truly alive.'"

A man bearing more than a passing resemblance to Danny DeVito rose to his feet, turned to face Dan, and began clapping.

The rest of *the Daily News* table followed Dankworth's lead. One by one, people stood, at first in twos and threes, then in 10s and 20s, until Dan was the only man sitting. *A standing ovation.*

Never one to underplay good news, Dankworth then cheapened the mood by sparking the chant, "There's only one Dan Armitage."

Cutting through the commotion, the MC walked up to the microphone. "The winner, the Journalist of the Year, is Dan Armitage."

Dan's immediate thought was he wished he'd spent more time, any time in fact, on preparing a speech. *What the hell was he going to say? Why do good intros prove elusive when needed most?*

Reluctantly, Dan got to his feet. Foreign news editor and good friend Cathy Wheeler pulled him close. Straining on high heels, she kissed him on the cheek, whispering in his ear. "No one deserves this more than you."

Dan weaved his way through the crowd, shaking hands, sharing the odd awkward high-five, thanking friends, colleagues, and strangers for their good wishes. He bounded up the half dozen steps onto the stage, the spotlights tracking him as he strode over to accept the trophy. This was the pinnacle of his career. A journalistic Oscar. A Gary Oldman moment. Everything he had worked for – his finest hour. The TV celebrity offered his hand and Dan muttered his thanks. As Dan turned to face the crowd, the big screen flashed up a picture of him in the desert, in a jeep flanked by a man with an array of cameras around his neck. Wearing a wide grin, another man with a bandana around his head sat at the steering wheel. Three more men sporting headscarves and holding rifles sat in the back.

Oblivious to the crowd, Dan stared at the image. Beads of sweat gathered on his forehead, and the back of his throat became constricted. He coughed, his breathing quickened, hands began to shake, and legs went numb. Almost stumbling, tears came to Dan's eyes. He reached for the microphone and tried to speak, but nothing came.

As the MC led him from the stage with a concerned look and an arm around his shoulders, all Dan could hear were his mother's words.

'Breathe, Dan. It's just a bad day, not a bad life.'

1

She looked in the mirror, rearranging the lock of hair that formed a fetching kiss curl on the side of her forehead. Elton John played on the radio, but she wasn't listening – too intent on making everything right.

A spray of perfume onto her left wrist, hitch of the cuff to prevent staining. A rub of the wrists to infuse scent from left to right, a check of the teeth. Next, a contoured dab of lipstick and a smack of her lips. The silver sheen must be uniform. *Perfect.* Today of all days, she wanted to put on her best face. Her brave face.

The doorbell rang. Flicking back the troublesome lock of hair, she pulled on a brown jacket and stood up. *Wow! I didn't expect that.* Her head was swimming, palms hot and clammy, weak legs trembled, and little black floaters darted back and forth in pale blue eyes. She leaned against the wall for a second, then swung a handbag over her shoulder and took a few tentative steps down the hallway towards the front door. Slow. Sluggish. Like trudging through Glastonbury's infamous festival mud to watch The Rolling Stones. Grabbing the frame to steady herself, she swung the door open.

"Jasmine Sharkey?" Complete with a dodgy

photograph, Dan Armitage held up an identity badge hanging awkwardly around his neck.

The woman nodded, voice faint. "Call me Jaz. Everyone else does." Jaz's eyes slid upwards and sideways then she was gone. Her knees buckled, and she slumped towards the stone step.

"Wotcha." Dan instinctively fell to one knee to catch Jaz with his right forearm, feeling his arm lock into place under her left armpit. *Thank God.*

Jaz was petite, around 5ft 4, and small-boned, but Dan couldn't hold her dead weight. He managed to break her fall, enough to ease her to the ground and prevent her head from slamming into the step.

"Are you okay?" Dan asked, immediately awarding himself star prize for the most redundant phrase of the day.

Jaz said nothing. Dan held her up, right arm around her shoulders, steadying her to a sitting position.

"My juice," she gasped.

"What?"

"Juice."

Without turning her head, Jaz raised her right hand and pointed behind her to the hall table. Dan followed her finger and spotted a carton of blackcurrant juice, the type with a straw in cellophane stuck to the side.

Dan stood, keeping one hand on Jaz's right shoulder while stretching over to the table with the other. He couldn't quite reach. For safety,

Dan knew he should have laid her down flat on the hall carpet. Why he took the Mr Bean route, holding her up by jamming his left leg and knee against her back and stretching sideways was a mystery. Dan strained, managing to grab the carton as Jaz rocked backwards. He lunged to his left to break her fall once more. *Two saves in two minutes. Not bad goalkeeping, Mr Armitage.* Dan inserted the straw in the carton and put it to Jaz's lips. She sucked hard. Her mind cleared. Lowering her head, she took deep breaths then sucked on the straw once more. A pink hue returned to her ashen face.

"I'm sorry," she sighed, "this happens sometimes. I am stupid. With getting up early and everything going on, I missed breakfast. I've had lots to think about. I'll be all right, really I will."

"Are you sure? Maybe it would be a good idea to take you to A&E to get checked out."

"It's low blood sugar. I know what to do and how to manage it. I forgot with everything else going on. Honestly, I'll be fine. Give me five minutes."

Dan gave a nervous chuckle. "Thank goodness. I'm not used to women falling for me so quickly. It usually takes a day or two. Must be my dodgy photo."

"Yeah, I noticed. It is pretty bad," Jaz giggled. "What's your name again?"

"Dan. Dan Armitage."

"Thanks, Dan."

"All part of the service."

The pair walked to Dan's car and, true to her word, Jaz seemed fine.

"Jump in the front," said Dan. "I have another three passengers to pick up, but they can squeeze in the back."

Jaz slid into the passenger seat and tugged at the seatbelt. Dan didn't turn the ignition key. He was running late but another two minutes to assess whether she'd fully recovered wouldn't harm. He looked at Jaz as she smoothed shoulder-length hair with her fingers. His question was direct if a tad clumsy.

"Is it your own? Your hair, I mean. Sorry, it looks great, but I noticed it slipped a bit when you fell."

Jaz smiled, fingers still teasing the flowing locks. "No, it's all wig. Cost a fortune but the best thing I've bought in years. I'd recommend to anyone going through this."

Her heart was no longer racing from the fainting episode, and full colour had returned to her cheeks. Jaz seemed willing, eager even, to explain her condition. She told Dan how she'd received a breast cancer diagnosis six months earlier, the week after losing Bentley. The labradoodle had been Jaz's constant companion for ten years and was the love of her life. *Doesn't life stink.*

Jaz had cursed, sworn and cursed again as

she struggled to digest the doctor's words. There were tears. Not tears of self-pity, she insisted – angry tears at the invasive presence intruding on her life. Hospital appointments, scans and a course of chemotherapy followed, which sucked the energy from her core and stole her beautiful long hair despite wearing an ice cap.

As if deliberating, Jaz paused and drew in a deep breath. She decided to continue. "The hair loss was the worst thing, starting with a few wispy, manageable plugs in the shower each morning then out it came in clumps. I'd wake up, and my pillow would resemble the nesting material of a family of magpies. No point in lying, I was upset, but the doctors warned me it would probably happen. I'd prepared myself."

Dan shifted in his seat half-wishing he'd kept his mouth shut.

"I used to throw my hair in the pedal bin." Jaz's tone was matter-of-fact.

Dan couldn't think of a more hideous symbol of a woman's suffering than having to discard her pride and joy with the rubbish each morning.

"I considered wearing a cap or scarf, but after spending an afternoon in front of the bedroom mirror trying different styles, I decided I'm not suited to hats or scarves. I looked like a country and western singer, and there are few things I detest more than country and western."

"Why is that?" said Dan, immediately bringing to mind several country artists he admired.

"Too repetitive. Too depressing. Too many songs about love gone wrong. I could do without that and opted for the wig. If I say so myself, the shade's close to my natural colour. Honey blonde. When I look in the mirror, I feel better somehow. Younger and stronger. I know it's an illusion, but it works for me, and I'm up for anything that helps right now."

Dan turned the key in the ignition and swung the silver Ford MPV into the line of traffic on Meadow Drive, noticing a subtle, fresh fragrance permeating the vehicle. Roses, lilies, and marigolds. A hint of jasmine too. *Or was that wishful thinking?* The car passed a bunch of schoolboys in navy blue blazers with rucksacks slung over shoulders, each one fiddling with a mobile phone. Dan slowed to avoid a teenager in school uniform, performing a wheelie at a crazy angle. Bumping up and down the kerb from road to pavement, to impress a group of giggling girls milling outside the local newsagent.

"Whoever said education was wasted on the young was bang on," Dan said. "You don't see pensioners at the retirement education centre in town doing wheelies on their way to the classroom. They pay attention in class, never miss lessons, do their homework and pay up on time for the privilege."

Jaz smiled. "Why, are you a pensioner? You don't look old enough to—"

"No, I'm not even fifty." Dan gave an indignant splutter, a tad hurt that he could be considered a contemporary of the silver foxes he'd seen pitching up at the retirement centre, despite his mini-rant being of the flat cap, park bench, 'It was better in my day' variety.

As the journey unfolded, Dan explained that his job as a charity transport driver for the Honeycomb Hospital Service was voluntary. Allocated four patients who would undergo radiotherapy every weekday for a month, today was his first day.

Jaz listened intently, before interrupting. "George Bernard Shaw."

"What?" Dan wore a puzzled frown.

"He said education was wasted on the young."

"Are you sure it wasn't Oscar Wilde?"

"I'm sure it was Shaw."

"That's easy for you to say," Dan chuckled breaking into an impression of Sean Connery's James Bond, with 'shs' in pertinent places in a doctored line from *You Only Live Twice*. "Japaneshe proverb shay, 'Bird never make nesht in bare tree.' Jashmine proverb shay, 'I'm sure it was Shaw.'"

"Idiot." Jaz laughed at Dan's impressive impersonation.

Dan wore a wide grin, wondering how long it had been since anyone called him an idiot. A long time, which was a pity because he was surprised how much he enjoyed it.

2

Heading out of the pretty market town of Lexford, Dan Armitage turned left at the next set of traffic lights. He glanced at his passenger list. *Mr Bob Murphy – number fifty.*

Dropping through the gears, Dan slowed the car to a crawl in the narrow street, sliding past numbers 38, 40 and 42 and fast-forwarding to the next line of houses. He computed number 50 was the imposing Victorian property at the end of the row. Pulling into the kerb, Dan killed the engine and walked around the front of the vehicle. A honeycomb-shaped brown motif on the bonnet made the car easy to spot.

SHELTERED ACCOMMODATION FOR VULNERABLE ADULTS OVER 60

Dan clocked the blue sign by the front gate and reached the grass verge, when a tall, well-built man, wearing a cream jacket, casual trousers and a wide, flat-brimmed beige hat adorned with a brown ribbon stepped out from behind a tree. A pair of rimless spectacles dangled on his chest from a lanyard around his neck. The man had a bleached complexion, grey beard and long, grey-white hair curling up under his hat. With an unhurried demeanour, he smiled at Dan then gazed at the blue sky and lifted his arms, palms upturned.

"What a beautiful morning. I'm Murph," the man said, in a voice so calm Dan wondered if medication or intoxication had induced the serenity. "I'll be back in five minutes."

Murph shuffled inside the house, and Dan waited patiently leaning against the car. Minutes later Murph returned and eased into the back seat. He explained that his condition meant he could no longer rely on his 'personal plumbing' – in past months, an hour-long car journey had become a lottery. A pained expression turned the wrinkles on his brow into deep furrows.

"Sometimes the plumbing's fine, other times, like a loose washer on a rusty old tap prone to the occasional leak. And I never get much warning. It's what you might call a fluid situation. A bit embarrassing, to be honest."

The requirement to drink a litre of water before each treatment didn't fill Murph with confidence – *anything might happen.*

"Don't worry, Murph," said Dan, "I'm sure you'll be okay. If needed, there are plenty of lay-bys on the way."

Dan eased through the traffic to his next pick-up. No mystery man behind trees this time. Instead, a woman in her forties, maybe fifties – difficult to tell through all that makeup. Wearing faded blue jeans and a white top, a purple and yellow floral silk scarf wrapped around her head, she teetered on high heels. Ridiculously high heels.

She slid along the back seat next to Murph, high-pitched voice, nervous giggle. "Hello, I'm Trish. "Is everyone all right? Can't say I'm looking forward to this, but you have to look on the bright side, haven't you? We're all still breathing, aren't we? It can't be that bad, can it? We're not dead yet, are we?"

Dan glanced over his shoulder and smiled. "That's five questions in one breath, Trish."

"Oh, sorry. I do go on." Trish covered her mouth and little beaked nose with her hand. "Ignore me," she giggled.

"Just one more gentleman to pick up," said Dan, pulling out into the suburban road and accelerating, only for a motorcyclist to hurtle past on the outside, exceeding the speed limit. Undertaking on the inside the biker weaved behind the car in front, firing a spit of exhaust and thunder of revs.

"Stupid prick!" Trish raised her right middle finger and jabbed it in the biker's direction.

Murph cupped his ear in protest to Trish's shrieking, while Dan made a mental note. *Ignoring Trish for the next month wasn't going to be easy.*

"Sorry, if it's a bit of a squeeze in the back, but the hospital's no more than forty minutes away. Hopefully, it's cosy," Dan said.

There was no need for Dan to get out of the

car at his next pick-up. Bill Murdoch, a small man of compact, well-balanced stature, waited on the doorstep of his bungalow. He gave the thumbs-up on spotting the Honeycomb motif emblazoned across the side panel of the car. Trish squirmed across to the middle seat to make room.

"Sorry we're late, we should've been here at eight-thirty," Dan smiled.

"Why? What happened at eight-thirty?" said Bill, in a matter-of-fact comic delivery enhanced by the sound of Lancashire, a county renowned for flat vowels and earthy tones.

Within two minutes, and before they'd reached the dual carriageway leading to the Barrett Bailey hospital, everyone learned Bill was a retired car salesman hailing from near Bolton. He and his wife Jean moved to the area 12 months earlier to be near their son, daughter-in-law, and two grandchildren.

"But I can't talk too much," said Bill. He leaned back against the headrest, sighed and closed his eyes.

"Why not?" said Trish.

"I've got a bit of a hangover."

"A few too many last night?"

"No, it takes only one drink to get me drunk."

"Really?"

"The trouble is I can't remember if it's the thirteenth or fourteenth."

Dan and Jaz chuckled, Trish looked bemused,

and Murph stared out of the window watching the flat plains of the Lexfordshire countryside roll by. As if the silence was challenging Bill to perform, he asked Trish if she went to see the doctor often.

"No. Only since I've had this." She pointed to her head and explained a scan detected a tumour in her brain some months before. Radiotherapy was a precaution following surgery. "What about you, Bill?"

"I had to go with a hearing problem once."

"What did the doctor say?" said Trish, checking to see if Bill was wearing a hearing aid. There was no sign of one.

"He asked me to describe the symptoms."

"What did you say?"

"Homer's a fat bloke, and Marge has blue hair."

Dan and Jaz looked at each other and giggled, not so much at the corny, old joke, more at Bill's smooth delivery. Trish was a moment or two behind, but when the punchline registered, she let out such a raucous cackle, Dan had to grip the steering wheel until the explosion subsided. Trish then sucked in a gulp of air with a wheeze and a trailing high-pitched whistle, which had the same effect as reloading a gun.

Out came another cackle, high-pitched gulps of oxygen in between. "Oh, Bill, what are you like? You are funny. How does your wife put up with you?" Trish spluttered.

Such comments were a gift to Bill, and he

wasn't going to let the offering go unrewarded. "You don't know my wife." Bill's tone was sombre. "Only this morning she said to me, 'If you won the lottery, would you still love me?'"

Bill paused and Trish looked at him open-mouthed, trying to work out whether he was serious.

"And?" Trish beckoned the answer with the palm of her hand.

"I said, 'Of course I would. I'd miss you, but I'd still love you.'"

Trish exploded again. Not as frenzied as before but enough wheezes and whistles that prompted Dan to tell her there was a small oxygen cylinder and mask in the boot if required. He was only half-joking. Under Dan's probing, it transpired that comedy was Bill's passion and had been since childhood. Bill had watched many a Laurel and Hardy film on crisp winter weekend mornings, sitting with his back to his father's chair in front of a roaring fire. He felt the glow of that fire now, and the safe, comfortable warmth of his father's company and paused for a moment to savour the memory.

Bill's father had also introduced him to the humour of American stand-ups, Bob Hope and George Burns, as well as the zany Marx Brothers. In the 1970s, he'd become a devotee of *Monty Python*, and *The Comedians,* a TV show in which a line of stand-ups would perform quick-fire routines. He never missed a programme and years later bought the DVDs. All 81 episodes! Each night, after watching the half-hour show, Bill would stand in front of the mirror in the family bathroom and pretend to be the next act.

"Never if it was in bad taste, though. I wasn't into racist stuff that some comics choose. That is everything a comedian shouldn't be. Cruel and bigoted, giving British comics a bad name."

Bill preferred clean, sharp, uncontroversial jokes. When asked by Dan to tell his favourite, he agonised before choosing two. One he'd heard from American TV host, Ellen De Generes and another from British comedian, Tommy Cooper.

Bill affected a high-pitched female tone. "My grandmother started walking five miles a day when she was sixty. She's ninety-seven now, and we don't know where the hell she is."

Trish went off again, wheezing and whistling. Bill's delivery had an infectious, engaging quality. Even Murph had taken his eyes from the window and stopped counting lampposts to listen to Bill's story.

"Go on then, tell us the Tommy Cooper one," said Dan. "You know you want to."

Bill indulged his talent at family weddings, and once when he'd won a competition in the local paper for a five-minute charity slot at the Comedy Store in London. He'd never indulged professionally and said the others would have heard the joke. That didn't matter though because in his opinion it was the best simple joke ever told. Clear. Concise. No clutter – perfectly formed.

"Like Lennon and McCartney's *Yesterday*," said Bill. "Perfectly rounded. Pop songs don't get better or simpler than that."

In his enthusiasm, Bill gave the show, the channel and the night on which he'd first heard Cooper's joke. He doubtless would have gone on to explore every avenue of its history if Dan hadn't cut in.

"For the love of Mike, Bill, tell the joke!"

Bill cleared his throat, put his arms out at chest level and turned to face Trish and Murph, assuming the gravelly tone of the man many regarded as one of Britain's greatest comics.

"I backed a horse today. Twenty to one. Came in at twenty past four."

He followed the punchline with a passable rendition of Cooper's famous laugh. Dan and Jaz groaned, Trish and Murph smiled.

"Oh, please yourselves," Bill said in a mock tone of indignation.

"We're here." Dan turned into the pick-up-and-drop-off car park of the oncology department at the ultramodern Barrett Bailey hospital. Specialising in the latest cancer care, Bill christened it the 'Old Bailey'.

"We can't be here already, it only seems like ten minutes," said Trish.

The car slowed to a halt outside the entrance. Bill opened the passenger door and pretended to tumble out, accompanied by a couple of ostentatious staggers. He stood upright and straightened his jacket. "Doesn't time fly when you have cancer."

This time he wasn't joking.

3

The trip back home was not so uproarious. Within minutes of leaving, Bill had his eyes shut, dreaming of headlining the Royal Variety Show in a stand-up slot at the London Palladium, while Murph snored in contentment. Cancer does that. Sucks the energy, kicks the legs from under its victims. Having had copious warnings, the group knew fatigue was the main early side-effect of radiotherapy. A double blow – if cancer doesn't get you, the treatment will.

Jaz was thinking the same. "Funny, isn't it? Our government chases Russian agents using radiation-dipped umbrella tips, cups of radiation tea or door handles smeared in radiation gel. Yet, we're happy to let hospital staff pepper us with it every day."

"I don't eat bananas anymore," said Trish.

"What have bananas got to do with the price of fish?" Dan asked.

"They're full of radiation."

"Fish?"

"No, bananas."

"Are you sure?"

"That's what I read in a magazine."

Dan glanced at Jaz. "I haven't seen any Russians running around Lexford with bananas at the ready, have you?"

Trish didn't respond. She was struggling to hear over Murph's snoring. However, Jaz, who wasn't scientifically qualified, unless GCSEs in physics and biology counted, had done her research. She'd read the radiotherapy warnings – the entire list of possible side effects. She realised the dangers inherent in frying the human body but also knew radiation naturally occurred in many avenues of everyday life. In the air and the ground. From space and the sun. In our food chain. In Brazil nuts and other foods rich in potassium, such as bananas.

"So, Trish is right," said Dan.

"Yes and no. She's right in saying bananas contain radiation, but she'd have to eat millions to receive a lethal dose. The article I read said you're more likely to die of potassium poisoning first. You'd need to eat one hundred and ninety-five in one sitting."

Dan was impressed. "Were you a boffin at school?"

Jaz shook her head, laughing as a memory surfaced. A flashback from her schooldays. She'd never regarded herself as the prettiest in her fifth-form class. Or the tallest. Or most stylish. She wasn't the smartest – definitely not the smartest. Not in those days.

To one mock exam history question, 'What did Mahatma Gandhi and Genghis Khan have in common?' Jaz had answered, 'Unusual names', half-convinced she was right. She was, but not in the way the examiner intended.

Jaz had always possessed a natural charm, quick wit and bubbly personality. The sort girls admired, and boys warmed to. She allowed the Gandhi memory to linger for a few moments until Dan asked how the treatment had gone. There was nothing she could fault. Jaz told him how impressed she was by the efficient procedure that involved undressing to the waist and having the affected area lined up using indelible 'tattoo' markers on the skin. Ten minutes later, she was heading back to the car.

"And the staff?"

"Wonderful! The nurses were warm and welcoming, and the machine operators so helpful. It's as if they'd all had a caring gene blood test before being hired."

With its constant need for cash and resources amid ever-increasing pressures and demands of an ageing population, The Health Service often received criticism. Damned for the way it lost sight of patients' hopes and fears. Not from Jaz. Not at the Barrett Bailey. Not in the oncology department, even when dealing with some of the most delicate, embarrassing aspects of the human body and psyche.

Engrossed with Jaz in conversation, Dan cruised along an isolated, hedge-lined section of the route when he felt a tap on his left shoulder.

"Any chance we could stop somewhere soon,

old chap?" said an anxious Murph. "I doubt I'll make it all the way home."

Dan knew what he meant. *When you gotta go, you gotta go.*

Dan estimated the café they'd passed on the way out – *Lord of the Fries*, boasting 'The Best Breakfast in the Country(side)' – was around five miles away. By the worried look on Murph's face that was five miles too far. Dan's quick search of the hedgerow to his left revealed an opening and a gate to a field beyond. He braked hard and pulled into the cramped clearing, easing the car out of the potential path of any following traffic.

"Is here okay, Murph."

It wasn't a question, more a statement. Dan knew full well it had to be here or he'd rue not packing that can of air freshener in the boot along with the essentials. Bandages, sick bags, first aid kit, traffic cone were required paraphernalia he must carry as an ambulance car driver.

Murph held onto his hat with one hand and opened the door nearest to the five-bar gate with the other. He clambered out and considered opening up and letting nature take its course but remembered Jaz and Trish. *Not gentlemanly in front of the ladies.* Stepping over the long grass, Murph avoided a patch of nettles in front of the gate. He slipped the metal catch and shuffled into the field beyond, turning right along the hedgerow where the others couldn't see him.

Turning his back to the field, Murph began watering the hedgerow as others might have done down the decades when caught short.

The stop had awakened Bill from slumber, and he was chatting to the others, agreeing that the treatment that day had been painless and reassuring. He told Dan about one long-standing patient who'd stopped him on his way out as they passed each other in the corridor by the treatment room.

"Leave your dignity at the door on your way in, mate, and pick it up again on your way out."

Bill had nodded, in the mode of a young soldier after hearing words of advice from a seasoned veteran, before inevitably having the last word. "The body, mate, achieves what the mind believes." He spoke with mock gravitas.

Bill was proud of that little one-liner. He was sure he must have read it somewhere before, but it was impromptu as most of Bill's pronouncements were.

Trish was telling her tale of the nurse with the warm smile and cold hands who shared the same star sign of Gemini. Halfway through, a commotion on the other side of the hedgerow arrested Dan's attention. A combination of a drum and a growl followed by a hissing gasp of air. A pause then it came again. Drum, drum, hiss, hiss, this time accompanied by a scurrying sound. *A clutch of excited hens scratching their way across wooden decking?*

Then Murph's voice filled the county air, his usual serenity abandoned. "No, no, no! Get back. What the … you stupid, stupid thing. Oh, dear. Go away. Go away. Now."

The drumming, growling and hissing intensified. Dan looked at Jaz, whose door was half-open. She jumped out to investigate. In the time it took Dan to inch his way around the front of the car, Jaz had climbed onto the second bar of the gate. She leaned over to see what was happening, letting out a roar to rival Trish's earlier cackles.

"Come on, Dan, it's like Swiss Family Robinson!" Jaz yelled.

"Swiss Family what?"

"You know. That film where a family get stranded on a desert island."

Dan didn't have a clue what she was talking about, but all became plain when he craned his head over the gate to see Murph, back to the hedgerow, held prisoner by two emus. Every time Murph made a break for the gate, the creatures launched, drumming and hissing, necks raised, so they stood six feet or more. Resembling a dog's hackles the birds' feathers plumed, displaying the emu sign for, 'Bugger off out of our field'.

Murph grew more anxious by the second. Forced back against the hedgerow, he'd suffered third-degree stinging to his hands. He'd lost his hat, which lay crumpled in a bed of nettles, and the chance of wounding by a thrusting peck increased as the angry birds became emboldened by Murph's apparent fear. His strategy of cowering one moment, then attempting to shoo them away with flailing arms the next wasn't helping.

Dan climbed the gate. "Don't worry Murph. I'm coming!" He hadn't a clue what he'd do when he arrived but knew something must be done. Fast.

Tottering on her heels, Trish reached the gate with Bill trailing behind. "Come on, Bill, hurry up, there's a couple of ostriches in the field."

"Emus," said Jaz, grabbing Dan's leg to stop him straddling the gate. "Stay there. I have an idea."

Jaz ducked down on all fours until her head disappeared underneath the hedgerow. Seconds later she emerged clutching a big branch, gnarled and curved at one end.

"Hold this above your head and follow me closely." She gave the branch to Dan and pushed open the gate.

"What are you going to do? Hold the barking birds while I smack them?" said Dan, wielding the branch like a baseball bat, bewildered by Jaz's choice of weapon.

"No, idiot, just do what I say and hold the branch high above your head."

That was the second time in a few hours Jaz had labelled Dan an idiot. Not the ideal time to mention that fact, he concluded.

Jaz stepped into the field and placed herself between Murph and the birds. Raising her right arm in the air and arching it at the elbow and wrist, she pinched her fingers into the shape of an emu's head. With her other hand, she pulled Dan close and hissed at him to hold the branch high in the air. There were now two simulated emu necks on show, both towering over the angry birds. Suddenly, the emus were confused. Walking sideways, then backwards, then in a circle, they tried to compute what was happening.

"Okay, Murph, walk behind us towards the gate," ordered Jaz, stomping at the emus and swinging her illusionary neck.

Bemused yet fascinated by the surreal encounter, Dan muttered, "Holy mother of Moses," following Jaz's lead.

The birds backed away, dipping their heads, neck plumes slowly receding. Murph was now beyond the gate doing up the zip of his trousers with Trish fussing around him.

"They're vicious bastards those ostriches, said Trish. "Another ten seconds and they could have had your eye out."

Meanwhile, Jaz and Dan walked backwards towards the car, keeping the emus covered with one bent arm and a branch. Jaz scooped up Murph's stranded hat and stepped beyond the gate, pulling it shut behind her.

"Where the hell did you learn that trick? Do you work in a zoo?" Dan said.

"No, I work on the check-out in a supermarket petrol station," said Jaz. "I came across emus after college when I spent a year working on a farm in New South Wales. At times, they were real brutes. They can be soft and cuddly creatures but rile them, and they come out fighting like Tyson Fury. I still have the bruises to prove it."

Dan couldn't decide whether the most astonishing part of Jaz's sentence was an A to Z understanding of the emu or that she knew the name of a British heavyweight boxing world champion.

Everyone clambered back into the car. Down the road, they saw a sign on the left-hand side:

EMU AND OSTRICH SANCTUARY
VISITORS – PLEASE, STAY IN YOUR VEHICLE

"Are you sure they weren't ostriches?" said Trish. "They look the same to me."

"Both birds are ratites," Jaz explained, "emus come from Australia, ostriches from Africa. Ostriches are bigger and run faster, up to forty-five miles per hour.

"As fast as we're going now," Dan intervened. That was about as helpful as he could be on the subject.

"What's a ratite?" asked Trish.

"A rodent that doesn't get a round in," Bill

piped up.

Jaz ignored the interruption. "Ratites are flightless birds. As well as emus and ostriches, there are kiwis, rheas and giant moas from New Zealand. Australian farmers can't get enough of the emu, particularly in recent times. The meat is a rich, lean source of protein. Emu oil is an expensive delicacy, said to be ten times richer in healthy vitamins than fish oil."

"Wow," said Dan. "You know your stuff, Miss Attenborough, but they must be pretty thick if they go weak at the knees when they see your arm and my stick."

"That's the whole point, Dan. They are thick. The ostrich's brain is the size of a walnut. It has the biggest eyes of any bird on the planet and can see minute detail two miles away but can't always work out what's in front of its nose. The emu isn't much better."

"They thought we were real emus?" Dan sounded dubious.

"Almost certainly they did, at least for a few moments. They're like any other creature in this world. Don't like taking on something or somebody bigger than themselves unless they have to. Make yourself as big as possible."

"That makes me the alpha emu," said Dan, preening himself just a tad in the rear-view mirror.

"No, you were assisting the alpha emu," said Jaz.

"Is that where birdbrained comes from?" Bill asked.

"No," said Jaz, taking a sharp intake of breath and beginning to wish she'd never started.

"Parrots can talk and imitate people. Pigeons can perform all sorts of complex cognitive tasks to receive food. They have small brains, too, but they're packed with front-loaded neurons, in some cases as many as the great apes who have bigger brains. For their size, lots of birds are intelligent. It's difficult to generalise, but the emu is not the brightest."

"How many neutrons in an emu's brain then?" said Trish. That was a question she didn't envisage asking when leaving home a few hours before.

"Neurons," Jaz corrected with a kind smile. "About one billion."

"And how many in Murph's brain?"

"About one hundred billion."

"Funny old world," said Trish. "Murph is a hundred times cleverer and yet he's the one full of nettle rash."

"Don't worry, Trish, I'm fine."

The car slowed at the roundabout by the Lord of the Fries café.

Bill couldn't resist. "Hey, Murph, from now on you are Lord of the Flies Down."

Everyone laughed, especially Murph, although, for the rest of the trip home, Dan was quiet. He'd heard all he needed to know about emus for one day. Something else was on his mind concerning Jaz. How had it happened? This woman who knew Hemingway from Wilde, neurons from neutrons, emus from ostriches. Who spoke with eloquence and knowledge as well as act with absolute authority at a moment's notice. How had she ended up as a cashier in a petrol station? An enigma wrapped in a paradox topped with a stunning blonde wig.

Dan dropped his passengers off in reverse order. Bill first, followed by Trish who offered a cheery wave as she clambered out, slammed the door then opened it again to remind Murph to put some calamine on his nettle rash.

"I swear by that stuff," said Trish. "Works bloody wonders."

Murph nodded. Five minutes later he was back in his flat where he made do with running his nettled hands under cold water. Medication on tap – calamine had never featured on his shopping list.

Dan pulled up outside Jaz's house and was about to reiterate how impressed he was with her handling of the surreal happenings when she took him by surprise.

"Thanks, Dan."

She looked into his blue-grey eyes, fascinated by the multitude of cracks and creases around them, the consequence of squinting into the sun and straining too often at distant objects in foreign lands.

"I can't believe it, but I've enjoyed today," she said. "I woke up this morning, not knowing what to expect. Yes, they give you a tsunami of information at the hospital. What to eat, what not to eat, what the side effects are. How sick you can get. How some people can handle the treatment, and some can't. I know they have to cover all bases, but some of it's scary. You lie awake at night wondering all sorts of stupid things. Have they drawn the tattoo marking in the right place? Will it burn? Will it work? What next if it doesn't work?"

"Yet all I'll remember about today, apart from giving you the shock of your life when I opened my door and fainted, is the look on Murph's face as those emus tried to take him prisoner. It's a long time since I've laughed as much."

"I can't believe that."

Jaz did what his much-missed wife Annie would have done. Before easing herself from the car, she gently touched his forearm.

"See you in the morning, Dan."

4

"Hey, Dan, are you that guy I read about in the Lexford Journal a month back?" The unexpected question came from Bill in the back seat of the MPV.

"Which guy would that be?"

"The one who won an award, Journalist of the Year I think, then nearly fell off the stage. He was all over the paper. I thought you looked familiar but couldn't place your face. Was that you?"

Dan admitted he had been the subject of a few stories and pictures in the national and local press following the ceremony at the Café Royal. The Lexford Journal had gone to town. As Dan had started his journalist career there, and local newspapers loved chasing a local line on a national story, they devoted four pages.

"So, you're famous and a journalist. How exciting," said Trish.

"Not exactly. I just happened to have a bit of a funny turn in the wrong place at the wrong time."

"How exciting," Trish repeated.

"Go on, tell us what happened." Jaz was intrigued. "You can't leave it there."

Dan accepted the challenge and by the time they reached the Barrett Bailey he'd surprised himself how much 'Oh, so private Dan' had revealed.

"I worked for *the Daily News* as a foreign correspondent. My editor entered some of my articles in the annual press awards. It wasn't my idea. I don't like those back-slapping affairs, but judges shortlisted the pieces in the main category of Journalist of the Year. I had to turn up – would've been rude not to."

"What sort of pieces?" said Trish.

"Oh, stuff from Syria – the war, sacrifices of ordinary people and all they had to endure. Shootings, bombings, chemical attacks, genocide – common in twenty-first-century warfare. Man's inhumanity to man, as someone once said. That sums it up."

Trish's mouth dropped open, and she stared at the back of Dan's head, the mop of unruly black hair waging its own battle against a sprinkling of fine silver lines and losing.

"Did you get shot at?"

"Not directly, Trish, but on occasion, I had to dodge the odd stray bullet or take cover from yet another bomb."

Dan admitted that on the morning after the awards ceremony, he'd done something he'd usually avoid. Joined hundreds of other commuters in cattle class at Lexford rail station and headed into the London office. On the way, he'd tuned in to Radio Four through headphones. His award had made the final item on the news, although he was thankful the report had skated over his funny turn.

Bill had no such intention. "What the devil happened, Dan? Was it because you remembered all that death and destruction?"

Dan licked his lips and took a deep breath. "I don't know – probably alcohol mixed with painkillers I'd shovelled down all day after major dental work. I went all hot and woozy. They wanted to ring an ambulance and get me checked out, but once I had some fresh air, I felt fine. I caught a cab and took the next train home."

Bill shrugged, "It's one way of getting out of giving a speech, I suppose."

Jaz took a packet of mints from her handbag and offered them around. Dan declined and continued his story, telling his passengers that after his train pulled into King's Cross, he decided to walk to *the Daily News* office. Not for the exercise, but to give him more opportunity for considered deliberation.

"I'd had a terrible night, couldn't sleep. It was unsettling. All these dark thoughts were going through my head."

"Such as?" said Jaz.

"Dreams of bombs exploding. Visions of maiming and death in Syria, Iraq, Afghanistan and any place a war correspondent finds himself."

Dan had sauntered, and by the time he arrived at work, he was sure. Heading straight to the office of editor Paul Dankworth, his boss for the past ten years, Dan told him he needed a break from dodging bombs. He was taking a six-month sabbatical.

"What did he say?" said Jaz.

"You can't do that, that's what he said, although I don't think he was thinking clearly at the time. He had a jackhammer hangover from the night before and was pouring painkillers down his throat. It was quite flattering. He said, 'You're on top of your game, the best bloody writer in the business. Journalist of the Year. You're the man, Dan. You can't jack it in.'"

Jaz interjected. "Oh, that was nice."

"That was what I thought. Then he said, 'Oh, for fuck's sake, why does everything always happen to me?'"

Everyone laughed as Dan gripped the steering wheel with one hand and put his other to his forehead in a cradling motion to mimic Dankworth's theatrics. Dan confirmed Dankworth relented, but it had been a close-run thing.

"What clinched it?" Jaz asked.

"I don't know. I think deep down he's a decent guy under a lot of pressure. I convinced him I'd been under more, reminding him I'd done the job for twenty years. Caught in crossfire, taken prisoner by rebels in Afghanistan, nearly blown up in Iraq, seen many kids die in Syria. I needed a break. It felt good to receive the award, but sometimes you just know when enough is enough and when a photo flashed up on the big screen, I realised most of the people were no longer alive. It felt as though time, *my time*, was running out."

There was a grimace on Dan's face that only Jaz in the front seat could see. His voice faltered as if a surge of emotion had taken him by surprise. For a second, Jaz thought he was going to cry.

Dan coughed to clear his throat. "Anyway, I finished by telling the editor I was taking a break whether he liked it or not."

"What did he say to that?" said Bill. "Get your coat, and I'll call you a cab?"

"No. For the first time, I detected a weariness, a sort of melancholy in his manner. It could have been the hangover, of course, but he said, 'Okay, Dan, take six months, then come back and see me,' and that's what I'm going to do."

"Did you have a leaving party?" It was a question only Trish could have asked.

Dan laughed. "No, I walked out of the office. Didn't speak to anybody – not even my mate Cathy."

Dan hated fuss. Wasn't keen on emotion. He'd slipped down the side stairs and onto the street, leaving the frantic churn of news behind.

"If I'd been Humphrey Bogart in *Casablanca* I would've lit a cigarette, took a long drag of calming nicotine and stared into the middle distance, leaving cinemagoers to absorb the enormity of my situation," he quipped.

"But you're not Humphrey Bogart," said Jaz.

"No, and I don't smoke unless you count the lungful of polluted London air I sucked in on my way to Moorgate tube station."

"Wow! And I thought you were just a taxi driver, Dan," said Trish as the MPV turned into the Barrett Bailey car park.

"That's nothing, I thought he was a pensioner," said Jaz.

"No worries. You were both wrong – there's life in me yet. I decided to give a bit back and experience some peace and normality driving with Honeycomb for six months, helping patients who are going through a lot more than I have. I'm going to enjoy the break, and after six months I might return to the paper. Or I might not. I don't know yet."

Everyone clambered out of the car with a renewed respect for Dan. For the second day running, the treatment couldn't have been smoother. By contrast, the journey back to Lexford wasn't as revealing. Bill, Murph, and Trish fell asleep in the back and Dan thought he'd said enough for one day. As the car approached the outskirts of Lexford the back seat stirred, and Trish asked Murph how long he'd lived in his accommodation. She'd noted the sign outside, promoting the property as a sheltered haven for vulnerable adults over 60.

"Nearly two years. I have a room with an en suite bathroom, and the meals are wonderful. I'm happy there."

"How do you qualify for a place?" said Trish.

It was a tricky question, especially as Murph showed no apparent signs of physical or mental compromise.

Bill wasn't one to skirt around such delicate issues. He dived straight in. "There's a test, isn't there, Murph?"

"What do you mean, Bill?"

"I've heard a doctor comes in and fills up a bathtub. Then he offers the prospective resident a teaspoon, a teacup, and a bucket to empty the bathtub."

"Oh, I see. A normal person would use the bucket because it's bigger than the spoon or the teacup," Trish said.

"Wrong!" Bill chuckled. "A normal person would pull the plug. Do you want your bed near the window, Trish?"

Dan stopped the car, and Bill eased out of the back seat.

"The window's fine," said Trish, pulling the door shut as Bill waved farewell. "That way, I can see you coming."

5

Heavy rain fell as Dan swung the car into the petrol station at Hendos supermarket, Jaz's workplace. She'd been on extended leave since starting treatment.

Filling up with petrol after each shift, courtesy of a fuel credit card supplied by the charity, was part of Dan's new job. He'd used less than half the car's fuel capacity that day, but protocol decreed that each shift should start with a full tank. He topped up with the cheapest unleaded fuel, easing the hose out a little as the automatic cut-out kicked in, only for a splash to spurt over his right hand. Dan hated his hands smelling of petrol, yet it never stopped him trying to squeeze in that extra drop every time. It was a man thing. A meaningless challenge. Like revving up and being first away at traffic lights.

Replacing the petrol cap, Dan wiped his hand on a paper towel from the dispenser then jogged to the kiosk head down to avoid the deluge. There was a queue. A petrol war was waging in Lexford between the supermarket big players and Hendos was undercutting them all. *Never underestimate how far people will go to save 2p on a litre*, Dan thought. Minutes later, he reached the counter.

"Hi, pump number six, please." Dan handed his fuel card to the attendant.

"Twenty-nine pounds." The lad looked mid-twenties, sported long, lank hair and a nasty case of acne. He had an awkward demeanour and the robotic voice carried a nervous tremble.

Not unlike a Dalek, an unusual combination to put front of house Dan thought, signing for the fuel. He took his receipt from the lad, whose nametag read Jordan alongside the firm's smiley logo.

"How's Jaz?"

"Erm, she's fine," said Dan, taken aback at the question as this was the first time he'd used the petrol station here.

"Good. We've missed her."

"I'll tell her you were asking."

"No, don't do that. Wouldn't want to worry her."

Dan saw an anxious frown on the lad's face and thought it was an odd thing to say, but let the matter go as he jogged back to the car. He had two more stops to make before returning to his apartment and a cold bottle of his preferred craft beer.

Dan's first stop was the printing plant of *the Daily News*. Five years before, and at a time when newspapers were desperate to cut costs to survive, the printing of the paper switched from its original printers in London's West Ferry. By chance, the new plant was six miles from

Dan's home. It made sense. Forty miles outside London, rental prices, wages, and living costs were all considerably lower than in the capital. Many of the print workers had made a move or chosen to commute. The many included a few Dan knew from the old days when invariably they enjoyed a drink in The Bell or the Cheshire Cheese in Fleet Street.

One of them was Pete Wilson – Wizz to everyone who knew him. Naturally warm, Wizz wore a permanent smile, and his eyes had a constant glint of enthusiasm regardless of whether he'd won or lost on the horses that day. Wizz was a gambler. Not a mad, hopeless punter, the sort who spend hours in front of slot machines mindlessly sliding cash into a hunk of metal in the hope three lemons will line up.

Wizz studied the racing form with a passion. He knew the horses, jockeys, trainers, the importance of the going – soft or heavy – the nuances of a right or a left-handed track. Wizz knew every aspect of the game. He didn't bet often, but when he did, he bet big. At least big for a print manager in the suburbs. That meant £2,000 or sometimes £5,000 a time, always betting odds-on favourites where he'd calculated a minimal risk of losing. Of course, he did lose on occasions but overall made a tidy tax-free living to augment his wages. Dan had always respected Wizz's canniness and discipline, as well as enjoying the carefree nature of his company.

When Dan pulled into the car park, he saw Wizz chatting to one of the lorry drivers before breaking away from the conversation to give a welcoming wave when spotting the ambulance car.

"Any good tips?" said Dan, sliding out of the driver's seat.

"Yep. Don't go back to dodging bombs for a living."

"Excellent, Wizz. I'll try to remember."

Apart from *the Daily News* editor, Wizz was one of the few people in the business who knew the full extent of Dan's misgivings over prolonging his career. They went back a long way. A few days after the award ceremony, Dan had shared a couple of pints with his old mate and confided in him. Ever since, Wizz had stayed in touch every week and recently, Dan had advised Wizz's 17-year-old son Mark on how to write his CV in his search for a job.

"I've brought the DVD I promised Mark," said Dan, reaching back into the car and pulling a slim cellophane packet from the glove box. He handed the package to Wizz.

One Hundred Ways to Impress Your Interviewer. Wizz's tone was mildly sarcastic when reading the title on the front cover. "It's not a load of baloney about not having a limp wrist and a sweaty handshake, is it?"

Dan raised his eyebrows and smiled. "No. There are some good ideas in there. It's all about conveying positive attitudes and selling yourself. There's a bit about how to turn your answers on skills and achievements into anecdotes about yourself. Managers, even ones like you, Wizz, remember the interesting people, especially if there are upwards of a hundred people applying for the job."

"I'll take your word for it."

"Just give it to Mark and tell him good luck with his interviews. If he lands a job, you can consider it payment for the papers." Dan was referencing the bundle of *Daily News* copies Wizz left at the gate for him to collect each morning. Mates rates, which in this case meant no rates. Free. Considering Dan had risked life and limb for the company for the past 20 years, he thought that was only fair.

It had become something of a ritual for Dan when he was home. Up at 5 am and a 20-mile cycle along a circular route, taking him past the print plant to pick up the papers. He would pop a few through the doors of his neighbours, take a quick shower then head off for the day. If his patients required a distraction or had waiting time to kill, it might be a good idea to leave a few copies in the car in future. He mulled over that thought as he slid back behind the steering wheel.

"Look after yourself, Dan," said Wizz.

Dan nodded and headed off for his final port of call. Ernie's car wash. The Ford didn't need much cleaning, save for a few spots of mud clinging to the undercarriage and wheel hubs courtesy of the field housing the emus. The back window had a small blob of pigeon crap splattered in such creative fashion Dan reckoned it resembled Edvard Munch's *The Scream*. Still, overall the car was clean and tidy.

Dan's charity training manual decreed that whenever possible, the vehicle gleamed at the start of each day. Some of the drivers took the protocol to obsessive lengths washing their cars with the hand hose in the ambulance bay on arrival at the Barrett Bailey as well as Ernie's car wash at the end of the shift. Twice in one day. That wasn't Dan. There'd been times on assignment when he'd been lucky to wash twice in one week. *Beam me up Scottie* went through his mind whenever he saw one of the twice-a-day brigade in action. Life was too short and far too uncertain for indulging in pedantic traits. Few knew that better than Dan. He was half considering hanging one of his fridge magnets from the Ford's dashboard. *A dirty car is a sign of character. Wait till you meet the character who drives this one.*

It took ten minutes to reach Ernie's. Dan swung the car through the tight opening designed to calm the speed of reckless drivers and joined the lane leading to the automatic car wash. Two cars were waiting. Directly in front, a black Volvo, driven by an elderly man with wispy silver hair, handlebar moustache and horn-rimmed glasses. He flicked through a copy of *the Guardian* laid out flat on the passenger seat. The lead car, a white Porsche Cayenne enjoyed a pre-wash by two lads, one who looked no older than 14.

One lad blasted off oil and dirt with a high-pressure hose. The other, sporting a cheeky smile and a jaunty walk, wore his blue and red FC Barcelona baseball cap back-to-front. He wielded a long, soft-bristled brush that he dipped in a bucketful of bubbles before smearing it across the Porsche's windscreen.

Fascinated, the boy and girl in the back of the Cayenne watched as the lad fashioned funny swirls and shapes on the windscreen and windows. In the driving seat, the children's mum laughed along with the kids. Encouraged by the children's interest, the lad increased the soapy content of the water and daubed the window where the little boy sat, so much so that the smears obliterated the child's view. With the forefinger of his right hand, the lad drew a smiley face in the soap making all three occupants giggle.

Dan was half-watching this quaint cameo while studying the carwash menu on a large totem sign. Should he order the headline basic wash for a ludicrous 99p, the intermediate for £2, or go for the works, which would cost the charity £5.50? Dan decided the basic version would suffice when, in his peripheral vision, he glimpsed the figure of a man striding from a small lean-to that served as the car wash office.

The man wasn't tall but thick-set, with a wide neck. Unshaven, he had an untidy mass of black, greasy hair and heavily tattooed, muscular arms. While his paunch suggested he'd let himself go in recent years, he covered the few paces from office to car with surprising agility.

Amid the hum of machinery and splashing water as the previous vehicle neared the end of its cleaning cycle, the young lad's first clue to the man's presence was the meaty palm of a calloused hand connecting with his right ear. The lad staggered to his left, went down on one knee and cupped his ear. It was ringing and hot and felt fat and squidgy. He stared at his Barcelona cap lying in a murky puddle of mud and detergent, his senses momentarily stunned by the unexpected blow delivered with a full sweeping arc of the man's right arm. The boy shook his head and, with a look of childlike bemusement tinged with terror, faced his attacker. The man mouthed obscenities in an incomprehensible East European accent.

"No, Gheorghe, no," the lad half-screamed, half-whimpered.

The man, whose name as far as Dan could make out began with an H and rhymed with corgy took another swipe, this time landing a solid, glancing fist to the side of the boy's head.

The lad went down on all fours in a cloud of soap suds. Gheorghe followed with a kick to the midriff, so savage the lad's body lifted into the air and landed with a sickening thud.

Gheorghe smiled. A leering, callous smile. Clearly, he enjoyed this type of work. Reaching behind, he picked up an old broomstick, minus the brush, leaning against a wall of the car wash. The stick wasn't there by chance, but rather as a handy weapon in case of trouble. Most customers were civil, but the odd one could turn nasty, accusing the wash attendants of scratching or damaging their vehicle.

With a smooth, practised swing, Gheorghe raised the stick, ready to bring it down on the lad's back as he cowered in a murky puddle. A piercing command sliced through the red mist and water spray.

"Stop! Right now. Stop. Put the stick down. Now. Down. Now!"

The voice was one of authority, firm and urgent, the meaning, clear and direct, irrespective of nationality or language. The sort of tone used by a SAS soldier in a hostage situation when time was critical and lives were at risk. The voice was Dan's. He'd bolted from the MPV and strode to where the beating was taking place. He knew he wasn't a physical match for Gheorghe, but he couldn't sit and do nothing. Heaven knows, during his time in Afghanistan and Iraq, Dan witnessed many beatings, not all of them perpetrated by the enemy. It hadn't been uncommon to see friendly troops beat seven bells out of prisoners or the harbourers of insurgents, especially when roadside bombs maimed or killed comrades.

Wrong but understandable. However, this was plain wrong. This was a boy going about his work and taking time to make his customers happy – service with a smile.

The intervention had the desired effect. Gheorghe, dark eyes under an impressive monobrow paused at the top of his downswing. Smouldering, he threw a venomous look at Dan.

"Down, or I call the police!" ordered Dan, pointing to the ground where he wanted to see the broom handle.

Inside, Dan's heart hammered. His mouth was dry, his stomach so tense he could have thrown up on the spot. Outside, Dan resembled a member of the Special Weapons and Tactics Team who he'd trained alongside in New York ten years earlier for a special feature in *the Daily News*.

"Fuck you," Gheorghe growled.

"Down. Now!"

Dan used the phrase learned from SWAT, up there with 'Hands Up!' as the most effective command when requiring immediate compliance to cut through confusion and diffuse an armed situation. He had knowledge gleaned from countless conflicts down the years, primarily from Operation Entebbe in 1976 when Israeli commandos famously rescued 102 out of 106 hostages held by pro-Palestinian terrorists. Put simply, when the commandos launched their rescue mission at Entebbe airport, they ordered everyone to 'Get Down Now!' on the assumption hostages would immediately comply. Terrorists would stand defiant, thus identifying themselves. It was a high-risk strategy, but it worked.

To be fair, none of that was going through Dan's mind. He was operating purely on instinct and half expected Gheorghe, who was more terrorist than hostage, to charge at him, stick twirling, fists flailing. To Dan's amazement, and more pertinently his relief, Gheorghe threw the broom handle to the ground. He marched around the back of the lean-to muttering and aiming but missing a parting kick at his young victim.

The lad got up, clutching his stomach and limping on one leg where his ankle had twisted but didn't appear seriously injured. He snatched up his soaked Barcelona cap and hobbled off in the opposite direction without even a nod to his rescuer.

A voice often associated with a tweed jacket, elbow patches and a mouthful of marbles rang out. The older, moustached man had wound down his window, craning his neck in the direction of the action. "Can everyone stop messing about, please. I'm in a frightful hurry."

6

Dan didn't sleep well that night. He'd downed a couple of beers and thrown together a chicken stir fry before going to bed at 10 pm, exhausted from what had turned into a long, action-packed day.

The confrontation at the car wash persisted in Dan's mind. Even though, when questioned, the older attendant had brushed off the incident and busied himself giving the MPV a meticulous clean the 99p fee barely warranted, Dan was worried. Dan didn't know the younger lad's name so nicknamed him Barcelona Boy because of his baseball cap.

Was the boy hurt? Where had he fled to? Was he old enough to be working? Did Gheorghe mete out beatings regularly? Was the boy safe?

Dan was unconsciously pondering the possible answers when his Big Mouth Billy Bass fish alarm clock chimed. *Don't Worry, Be Happy*. Christ, that fish was annoying, but his wife had bought Billy in a moment of holiday madness 20 years before, and Dan couldn't ignore it. The fish did the job each morning with infuriating yet dependable efficiency minutes before 5 am.

The last thing Dan wanted to do was 20 miles in the saddle, but he knew he owed his current strength and fitness to a daily regime of stretching exercises and cycling. The extent of his obsession might have tested men half his age. He took his usual course along the meandering country lanes of south Lexfordshire, with its long lines of hedgerows, thatched cottages and flat terrain. Once in the saddle, he cherished this summer morning routine. A new sunrise, barely a car on the road. Peaceful, serene. Rabbits, scattering as he passed and an appreciation of landmarks of genuine historical significance such as the 14th-century church of St Anne's with its turreted bell tower in the quaint village of Broughton Conquest.

Every time Dan passed that church, he promised himself he would return one day at a reasonable hour to look at this unheralded monument to ancient Englishness. He was always too busy to get around to it. A few minutes later he turned south before pulling into *the Daily News* printing works outside the market town of Watthill. As usual, Wizz had left half a dozen papers sticking out of the wooden post box attached to the railings at the front gate.

Kicking out of his cleats, Dan took a paper from the bundle and stuck the rest inside his rucksack. Out of a habit forged from decades in the newspaper business, he searched first for the byline on the main story on the front page: *Special investigation by Cathy Wheeler*, placed under a headline:

POLICE HUNT SLAVE GANG

A puzzled frown set on Dan's perspiring face – he wondered why his office-based mate and occasional confidante was writing the front-page splash. Cathy was the foreign news editor but, to Dan's recollection, she'd written nothing of note with byline attached for more than ten years. Dan scanned the first four paragraphs on the front page before the article turned to a two-page spread on the inside. Two thoughts occurred. One was that in all his career, he could think of no more than a handful of stories that couldn't contain all the salient facts in the first four paragraphs. The other, he must give Cathy a call.

The story identified a series of networks across the United Kingdom, forcing as many as 10,000 British and foreign children into modern slavery. Many, sexually exploited, some used as mules to spread the drug supply from urban centres into rural areas. The majority, channelled as cheap labour in nail bars, fruit and flower-picking farms and illegal trades including cannabis farming and prostitution. Most of the victims were vulnerable British children, as well as Albanian, Vietnamese and East European nationals. Applying the fact that youngsters were not on police radar and would receive more lenient sentences if caught, gangs targeted care homes.

Dan's eyes darted to a quote by Luke Vernon, a senior official of the National Crime Agency.

'*The number is shocking. There isn't a region in the UK that isn't affected. Many of these kids suffered horrendous journeys escaping war zones. Now violent, sadistic, ruthless individuals are exploiting and abusing them when they get here. A despicable, evolving crime.*'

Violent, sadistic, and ruthless. If he'd still been a reporter, that's how Dan would have described Gheorghe at the car wash. He would probably have thrown in cocky, cowardly and careless for good measure. Gheorghe looked like a gangster. Not an Al Capone, more a grimy, unwashed, poor man's version of Tony Soprano. He had the manner of a child abuser, wielding a stick with the brutal aplomb of a practised bully. *Could Dan have stumbled across the nexus for the networks described by the NCA at Ernie's car wash?* Whoa! Slow down, Dan chided. Too many journalistic careers crash and burn while hitching a ride on wrong assumptions. He parked the thought for later investigation, stuffed the crumpled paper into his rucksack and snapped on his cleats.

Back at his flat, Dan pushed three of the papers through neighbours' letterboxes, kept one for himself and placed the rest on the front doormat as a reminder to put them in the ambulance car. By 8 am, he was pulling up outside Jaz's house. She had spotted him turning into Meadow Drive from her bedroom window and was on her pathway before Dan had cut the engine.

"Hi, Dan." Jaz gave a cheery smile, slid into the passenger seat and planted her red handbag in the footwell.

"Morning, Jaz. By the way, Jordan sends his regards."

"Jordan? Jordan from the supermarket?" Jaz sounded surprised.

"That's the one. The lad with a face like a pepperoni pizza."

"Don't be cruel. He can't help having acne scars – he's a sweet lad."

"Sweet on you maybe. He seemed a bit surly to me – told me not to tell you he was asking about you."

"But you did, anyway. How did Jordan know you knew me?"

"No idea. Maybe saw you getting into the car yesterday."

"I don't think so. He lives on the other side of town."

Dan shrugged, pulled out into the traffic and picked up the rest of his passengers in the same order as the day before.

Popping his head inside the car, Bill greeted the others with, "Thought for the day, boys and girls. If at first, you don't succeed, skydiving's not for you."

He edged onto the back seat beside a giggling Trish, who informed him she'd told her friend all about him last night. "I said you were a bit like Ken Dodd, always telling jokes and making people laugh."

"Ken Dodd?" Bill snorted and affected an affronted tone. "He died not so long back."

"Did he?"

"No, Doddy," Bill grinned.

Dan and Jaz groaned. It was going to be another of those journeys.

At least it would have been if Murph, in an effort to join the conversation hadn't turned to Trish and asked, in a polite fashion, "Tell us, Trish, what's your story?"

All the excitement of the adventure with the emus and Dan's backstory had diverted attention away from Trish. Given her cue to take centre stage, she answered the call like any other Essex girl, with attitude and an earthy turn of phrase when required.

"My story, Murph?" She shook her head. "It's a fucking car crash."

Jaz, eyes wide and without turning her head, threw a sideways glance at Dan, who kept his mouth shut, jaw clenched as he tried to suppress a splutter. It wasn't so much Trish's use of the F-word that shocked. More the way she held on to the F, exhaling slowly between tooth and lip until the first syllable exploded in a shower of spittle. Like shrapnel.

"My goodness that was heartfelt," said Dan.

"Well, it's true," said Trish. "A car crash and

they're still sifting through the wreckage."

Trish went on to tell how life hurtled south three months before when, without warning, she'd suffered what appeared to be a fainting fit at the call centre where she worked. Oh, the irony.

"I was halfway through signing up a customer for health insurance," Trish said. "I'd reached the section explaining the prominent characteristics of a chronic condition. How it needed ongoing or long-term monitoring through consultations, examinations, check-ups, and/or tests when I keeled over. Thud. Head on the desk. Arms akimbo. Headphones askew. Mouth, dribbling.

"The only blessing? I was sitting down. I wasn't out long. Couldn't have been more than twenty or thirty seconds and the first aider was there in double-quick time. Not that she could do much. She was well-meaning but barely out of her teens. All I remember when I came to was my fascination with her blurry tattoo of Harry Styles, you know him from One Direction. I mean. Harry Styles!"

"What did she do?" said Jaz.

"Nothing, apart from ask me some questions."

"Such as?"

"Had anything like that happened before? Did I want a glass of water? Was I pregnant?"

"What did you say?"

"No, yes, and are you fucking serious?"

Jaz and the others chuckled as Trish explained

that after sipping the water, she'd insisted on calling back the customer to confirm why the line had gone dead. She'd convinced herself it was just a silly episode – one of those things – and went home, took two painkillers with a warm glass of milk, and returned to work the next morning.

"I was an idiot, a complete idiot. Only an idiot would ignore something like that, don't you think, Bill?"

Bill wasn't falling into that trap. He shrugged.

"What happened next?" said Jaz.

"Sirens, blue lights, you name it. Or so I'm told. I don't remember anything. I had a seizure and an ambulance took me to hospital, where staff gave me every test known to medical science. Or that's how it seemed. In the end, a doctor walked in and told me I had a brain tumour. I freaked. If he'd said I had a lump, I would have been okay, but I hate that T-word. It conjured up such fearful thoughts. Horrible images. Pictures of alien organisms invading my mind. I know it's daft, but that's what I thought."

Trish related how the oncologist pointed out the mass on a computer screen and how she'd asked the obvious question.

"How big is it?"

"About the size of an orange."

"Are we talking Jaffa or satsuma?" was Trish's typically pithy reply.

"I'm afraid it's closer to a Jaffa, probably after

peeling though, and Jaffas do have thick skins."

"That's all right then."

The doctor offered a sympathetic nod.

Ten days later the tumour, a primary grade two glioma, known as an astrocytoma, was gone. Or at least 95 per cent was gone, according to the surgeon who'd given Trish a capsule before surgery containing a fluorescent dye, which highlighted the border of the tumour, allowing greater precision when slicing out. The surgeon told Trish her tumour was the most common type of glioma in adults and children, and after surgery, prescribed chemotherapy tablets alongside the course of radiotherapy she was now undertaking.

"Because you are so fit and well we can fight it on two fronts," the doctor had reasoned.

"I don't feel fit."

"Believe me. You are, compared to many with your condition."

"How long have I got?"

The question was every cancer patient's elephant in the room. Some skirted around it as if sidestepping the question might somehow give them more time. That was not Trish's style. Trish was a hand grenade down the underpants type of interrogator. Direct. Urgent. She demanded answers, although the doctor explained it was impossible to put an accurate timeframe on cancer. By nature, the condition was individual and unpredictable. All he could offer was stark statistics taken from the National Cancer Intelligence Network of England. That suggested 50 per cent of people with Trish's type of grade two astrocytoma would survive longer than five years. Of course, that also meant half would be dead within five years. Sobering stuff.

Trish patted Murph on the knee. "So that's how I came to be here sitting next to you, Murph. And, before you ask, the customer never took out health insurance. I didn't even get my commission."

The car filled with laughter.

"Do you have a husband at home to look after you?" Jaz asked.

Trish let out one of her trademark cackles, with accompanying whistle and wheeze.

"I'll take that as a no," said Jaz.

Trish reached forward and squeezed Jaz on the shoulder before settling back into her seat. She said she and her husband had divorced ten years earlier and, until two months ago she lived with Terry, her partner of two years.

"What happened then?" Dan blurted, immediately realising in the circumstances there was no good answer to such a question.

"The bastard only ran off with my eighteen-year-old daughter."

The group didn't know whether to laugh or cry. They sat stunned before Murph, in a slow, considered whisper that somehow increased its effectiveness, found the phrase he felt Trish would most appreciate. "What a pair of pillocks!"

"Told you it was a car crash. I get smashed head-on, literally, by cancer and then shunted up the rear by my nearest and dearest."

Trish patted Murph on the knee again. Jaz mused that this car trip was weirder than the trashy daytime TV shows she'd become addicted to these past few months and, for once, an appropriate quip escaped Bill.

Dan swung the Ford into the car park at the Barret Bailey. His passengers alighted and disappeared along the corridor towards reception. Dan parked up, purchased a skinny latte from one of the hospital's coffee shops and strolled to the lobby at the back of the oncology department serving as a waiting room for drivers transporting patients that day. It was 9:15 am, and already the room buzzed. Professional ambulance personnel dressed in brown fatigues, commercial taxi drivers, some hired independently by patients, others provided by the health service at considerable cost. Many patients had travelled 70 miles or more.

Including Dan, there were six drivers from the Honeycomb charity in the waiting room, most of whom volunteered once or twice each week. Dan was the only one volunteering five days a week, even though he was the newbie and some drivers were old hands of more than ten years. The charity's bank of drivers fell into two main groups. Some had experienced the excellence of the health service in times of vital need and were eager to give something back. Others were retired men and women searching for good causes to fill their time. Then there was Dan, helping out while pondering his next career move.

All had undergone meticulous screening, expected to live up to the standards inherent in the Honeycomb motif. Dan had learned hexagonal shapes, such as those bees made to house the queen's eggs and store pollen and honey, fit together without space. The shape is renowned for strength and reliability as well as elegance. Throw in a caring nature, and you had the essence of the charity's transport service.

That didn't mean there wasn't the odd glitch. For instance, Ian had recently taken the wrong patient home. The woman had jumped in the back seat as the car pulled up outside the pick-up spot in foul weather. Ian's hearing aid was on the blink, and only when he caught a full view of her in the rear-view mirror some 20 miles down the road did he realise she was not the patient he'd brought.

"I thought we were going the long way around," said the lady. She had arrived at the Barrett Bailey from an entirely different direction courtesy of a private taxi, not dissimilar in colour and shape to the Honeycomb MPVs.

There was also the odd joker among the

drivers, such as Jeffrey. Known as 'the 'Brigadier' because of his military past, he insisted on taking new patients, apart from those in fragile physical shape, on a guided tour of the area's famous landmarks. The drive always took in a sweep of the country home of controversial local MP, Jonathan Pye. The Brigadier would park outside the gated driveway, wind down all the windows and shout with a questioning inflexion. "Steak and kidney pie?" He would urge his passengers to say yum, yum as if salivating at the thought of eating.

"Hot apple pie?" the Brigadier would continue, orchestrating another yum, yum from his passengers.

Then, the Brigadier would feign a look of disgust and shout the MP's name, stringing out the syllables for effect. "Jon-a-than Pye?" Retching and a loud yuk would follow, while the Brigadier encouraged his passengers to join in. Some did. Most giggled with embarrassment and squirmed in their seats. Such puerile behaviour was not on any consultant's treatment plan, but most patients accepted it as harmless fun.

Happily, for this day's patients, it was Jeffrey's day off. Martin was working – he was the driver who'd trained Dan. He was also one of the longest-serving volunteers after spending 20 years in the police force as a fast-response driver in London, and 15 years in the fire service.

He must have been over 60, had a friendly,

fresh face, a ready smile and composed demeanour.

"Hi, Martin, glad you're here," said Dan. "I wanted to pick your brains."

"That shouldn't take long."

Dan smiled. Having met only a handful of charity drivers, he would have bet a month of his journalist's wage that there weren't many as naturally streetwise as Martin.

"What do you know about Ernie's car wash?"

"What's to know? They're cheap as chips. I know that. How they do the basic car wash for ninety-nine pence beats me. I know you don't get any soap massage, sponges or windscreen attention for that price. Even so, a run through the water spray and revolving brushes is worth ninety-nine pence. I usually pay two quid and get the attendants to give the alloys a bit of a clean and ask them to brush the damn flies off the front mudguard. There are always lots of lads around. The place doesn't seem short-handed."

"Who owns it?"

"It used to be Ernie, Ernie Watkins. Nice old guy, getting on a bit. Ex-military I think. You knew he was there on top of the job because he always parked his car at the front. A bright red Mercedes, with a private number plate – ERN 1E. Gleaming and immaculate, like an advert to pull in the punters. I haven't seen it, or him, for months – don't know why. I haven't heard that he's sold up."

"What about the strongarm muppet with the big gut and foul temper who seems to be running the place now?"

Martin recognised the description. "You mean the guy who looks like he's eaten all the pies. He's got that mean glint in his eyes, too, as if he's spoiling for trouble. I wouldn't fancy meeting him in a dark alley, that's for sure."

"Or even a light alley."

"Why? Have you had a problem there?"

"Not exactly but I did witness the thug with the gut knocking around one of the car wash kids for fun. I don't mean a clip around the ear, Martin. The way he laid into him was brutal. Turned my stomach, and I don't think it was the first beating or the last."

"What did you do?"

"Told him I would call the cops. That made him stop, but I got the distinct feeling the kid would pay for it later."

Dan omitted his suspicions that the business was part of a national crime network. It was only his second proper day on the voluntary job, and he didn't want to appear melodramatic, especially to an ex-copper. Martin must have experienced hundreds of scraps and beatings in his career, but he looked concerned.

"I'll put out some feelers with my old mates. See if they've run into this fat guy with the fists."

"Thanks, Martin."

Dan stood up and strolled over to dump

his empty coffee cup into an orange bin for recyclables. When he returned, he caught sight of Jaz and Trish walking towards him, deep in conversation. It was only 20 minutes since he'd dropped them off, but as a general rule, radiotherapy treatment for ladies was quicker. The gents, especially those with prostate problems, often had to drink a few glasses of water before treatment began.

Thirty minutes later, Murph appeared, followed by Bill who reached the swing doors and held one open for two porters wheeling several helium cylinders down the corridor.

One of the porters nodded his thanks. Bill twitched his nose, motioned towards the cylinders and with a chuckle said, "It's going to be a helluva party."

The porters ignored him, and Bill let the door swing shut, accompanied by an "Oh, please yourselves."

7

Irritated, Trish fumbled with her seat belt, trying to click the buckle into its cradle for the journey home. Fastening the belt was always a struggle for the passenger in the cramped middle seat. A quick elbow in Bill's ribs did the trick. Trish had decided there was no way she was pouring out any more of her personal life. Not today, anyway. Too depressing.

"Stick some music on Dan. Something upbeat that we can have a bop to," Trish said.

"Bop in the back seat of a Ford with Murph and me? Good luck with that," said Bill. "Fancy doing the conga while you're at it?"

Trish ignored him.

"Have you got any ABBA? I love Mamma Mia and all that stuff. I've seen both films. Prefer the first one, though. Isn't Meryl Streep a good singer? Dancing Queen would do Dan, but if you—"

"Slow down, Trish, I think you're mistaking me for some DJ from your dancing days. I don't have any music with me unless you fancy a blast of Sixto Rodriguez."

"Who the hell's that? Sounds like an old tennis player from the sixties or early seventies."

"You've got the right era," said Dan, easing

the car away from the kerb while rooting in the centre console, "but I expect you're thinking of Pancho Gonzalez."

Most of the Fords no longer housed an old-fashioned CD player – newer models were digital, and music came from a pen stick in a USB port or via Bluetooth. However, the car Dan inherited was a few years older than the rest and still worked on old technology. So did Dan. He found the CD and handed it to Trish.

"I'm searching for *Sugar Man*," said Trish, reading the headline on the front cover featuring a Mexican man with long black hair. He wore black sunglasses and had an acoustic guitar strapped at a 45-degree angle across his back. "Never heard of him. What sort of music is it? Anything like ABBA?"

"Not exactly," said Dan, explaining the CD was the soundtrack to a film of the same name documenting what critics acclaimed, 'Rock "n" Roll's Greatest Untold Story'

The film was about a singer-songwriter discovered by two record producers in a Detroit bar. So struck were they by his melodies, the producers recorded an album they were sure would make him one of the most celebrated artists in the music industry. The producers believed his lyrics poignant and prophetic and said he was a better singer than Bob Dylan.

"I'm a better singer than Bob Dylan," interjected Bill.

"Fair point," said Dan.

"Prove it," said Trish.

Bill would have attempted to do so if Dan hadn't continued with his story.

"The album came out, received brilliant reviews then promptly bombed, and Rodriguez disappeared into obscurity."

"Why are we talking about him?" said Jaz.

"Because that's where the story gets intriguing. A bootleg recording of the album found its way into apartheid South Africa and took off. Rodriguez became the biggest-selling artist ever in that country, but for forty years he knew nothing about it. No one could find him. Eventually, two South African fans tracked him down, still in Detroit, in a modest house making a living as a painter and decorator with his family. The fans told him he was bigger than the Beatles back home. The film is all about the hunt to find him and his reaction when they do. It's one of the most uplifting films I've ever seen."

Dan reached behind with his left hand. "Give me the CD. I'll put it on, and you can see what you think."

A couple of prods later, and Rodriguez's rich, soulful voice rang out. Trish cocked her head to one side, listening for a few seconds. *Better give the music a chance.* A frown developed.

"Sorry. I've heard enough. I can't be doing with song lyrics that are just one long riddle. Okay, he's a good singer, but a bit depressing."

Dan hit the off button. "Songs can't all be like *Dancing Queen*, Trish," he said, bursting into a sarcastic rendition of one of the uplifting song's most famous lines.

"No, but I don't feel like being depressed right now if you don't mind."

"Fair point again."

In a bid to divert the conversation, Dan asked Jaz to name her favourite band of all time.

"That's difficult. There are so many. The Beatles, The Rolling Stones, and The Who. I saw The Who at Knebworth one year – can't forget that. At the end of the show, Pete Townshend set fire to his guitar, and Roger Daltrey's hair caught fire when he went across to take a bow and got too close. I like Pink Floyd, Duran Duran. Take That, Elbow, Muse—"

"It might be easier to tell us who you don't like," said Dan.

"How about the Bee Gees, do they float your boat, Jaz?"

Jaz let out the sort of noise Roger Daltrey might have done when he realised his locks were burning.

"Aagh! You've got to be joking. They always gave me the creeps. I couldn't stand the one with all the hair and medallion around his neck. Loved himself. Then there was the odd-looking one who always seemed in pain when he sang. The other one with the beard and the hat was all right. He was the one married to Lulu. Maurice,

I think. I just couldn't get into all that high-pitched singing. All that *Staying Alive* nonsense was odd. Weird. The Bee Gees? I used to call them The Jee Bees. As in heebie-jeebies. They freaked me out."

"They wrote some great songs, though," said Murph, who appeared to be asleep with his head lolled to one side against the window.

"You're not wrong, Murph," said Dan. "*Words. Massachusetts. Islands in the Stream.*"

"*Islands in the Stream?*" Jaz said in a mildly mocking tone. "That's not the Bee Gees. Dolly Parton and Kenny Rogers sang the song. Dolly Parton must have written that."

"Pure country music," agreed Trish. "You're right, Jaz. It's about the only country song I like."

"Bet you the Bee Gees wrote it," said Dan, smugness taking hold on his face.

The look stayed when Murph revealed he'd once played rhythm guitar in a band and *Islands in the Stream* was the preferred song to finish their show.

"It always got people up and singing. Never failed," said Murph.

"Hold on, Murph," said Bill. "You were in a band? You kept that quiet."

"Well. I've only known you for two days."

"What sort of band?"

"A five-piece. Rhythm and blues mainly with a bit of country and soft pop on occasion. We were semi-professional but played for beer money most of the time: weddings, birthdays, anniversaries, university bars, that sort of thing. We played one summer on a cruise liner. That was probably at our peak."

"What was the name of the group?" said Bill.

"Comfortably Numb. After my favourite Pink Floyd track."

"Go on then, Murph, let's hear a bit of *Islands in the Stream*," said Trish.

"It's been a long time," said Murph.

Trish gave him an encouraging nudge with her shoulder. "Come on, Murph, you never lose it."

"All right, but just the chorus, I can't remember the verses, and only if you lot join in."

Seconds later, a deep, resonant, authoritative voice reverberated around the MPV. A voice so rich in soul and rhythm that Jaz and Trish's mouths gaped, and Bill looked on in disbelief. In its way, Murph's singing was not unlike the moment Susan Boyle shocked and entranced eight million viewers with her first audition on Britain's Got Talent. Okay, Murph's audience was 7,999,996 fewer, but he still had a 100 per cent approval rating. The pitch and timbre of the notes were so distinctive that Kenny Rogers or perhaps Johnny Cash could be sitting in the back of the MPV.

"You've still got it, Murph," shouted Dan.

Murph milked approval. His voice grew stronger and louder, and Bill and Jaz started singing. Never one to be a party-pooper, Trish linked her left hand around Murph's right and her right hand around Bill's left and, for a minute or so, forgot that she detested country music. Dan joined in too, surprised at the harmony.

The three in the back began to sway, the pleasing rhythm transporting them to invigorating days of youth, while Jaz raised both arms and flung them from side to side as if part of a rock concert crowd. Murph was in the zone. He slid into another rendition of the chorus, the car revelling in a wall of sound and relentless motion of the 'stream'.

A blue light first alerted Dan. He caught the merest flash in his right-wing mirror, however, the warning sign utilised by the emergency services didn't fully register. The singing in his ears was disorientating. He ignored the flash. When he looked again, this time in his rear-view mirror, his heart sank. A 4x4 police traffic officer's vehicle, blue and yellow checks and orange chevrons, on his tailgate.

"Oh, shit!"

The police siren sounded, as did Dan.

"Shit, shit, shit!"

The singing stopped, and Dan hit the brakes just before a red neon stop sign illuminated. He pulled over in a convenient lay-by, praying that he hadn't exceeded the speed limit. They were on a country road, and there was little traffic, but in the excitement of Murph's impromptu concert, he'd lost sense of the national speed limit. *Did 60 apply? Or was it 50, the standard for short stretches in the area, often for no particular reason?*

The police car slowed to a halt behind Dan. The driver swung open his door, and Dan noted he was short for a police officer. Dan studied him in his wing-mirror as he veered to the driver's side of the MPV. Slicked, jet-black hair. Young. Cocky. Bit of a Tom Cruise swagger. He wore a high-viz yellow jacket, with blue police emblem, various metallic paraphernalia hanging from his belt.

Dan wound down his window and clocked the officer's collar number: 6749-3.

"Hello, sir, do you know why I've stopped you?" said the officer, twiddling with the controls on his radio to stem the static.

"Because you're a prick," was on the tip of Trish's tongue but she restrained herself and left the talking to Dan.

"Can't say I do, officer. I don't have a wonky brake light, do I?"

"No, sir. There are two reasons. One, there seemed to be a lot of waving and swaying going on in the car. Looked like a bit of argy-bargy from where I was sitting. A bit odd in an ambulance vehicle. Everything all right?"

"Couldn't be further from the truth. We had a sing-song – a bit of fun. Letting some hair down after treatment. *Islands in the Stream*, you know."

"Oh, yeah, who sang that?" asked the officer.

"Dolly Parton and Kenny Rogers, but The Bee Gees wrote it," said Dan.

Trish and Jaz silently fumed, beginning to realise, when it came to music, Dan was a tad infuriating.

The officer peered into the rear of the car. Murph had assumed his usual position lolling against the window. Bill pretended to be sleeping, and Trish held her head in her hands as if alleviating a splitting headache.

In the passenger seat, Jaz wore a coy expression.

"Okay, everything seems to be in order," said the officer.

"What was the other thing? Dan asked, immediately wanting to kick himself for his naivety.

"Do you know the speed limit on this stretch of road, sir?

"I thought it was sixty."

"No. It's fifty for a mile and a half on this stretch, and there are lots of signs indicating that. Four to be exact. I clocked you doing fifty-eight."

"Sorry, officer. I didn't realise, with it being so quiet."

"Hmm. What's all that about?" The policeman looked past Dan and pointed to the front-page headline of *the Daily News* lying on the centre console. "Police Hunt Slave Gang. First I've heard."

Dan handed the paper to the policeman. "On the house. All part of the service."

"Okay." The officer folded the paper like a truncheon, preparing to beat Dan and company over the head with an air of condescension. "Next time be more careful with your speed along here, look in your rear-view mirror and control your passengers."

Dan bit his lip and swallowed the admonishment. It sounded and felt patronising from someone half his age and minus virtually all his life experience. Still, Dan calculated there was no point in doing anything other than keeping quiet. Take one for the team. Avoid a fine and points on the licence. He nodded meekly.

By contrast, Trish made a miraculous recovery from her headache, gave the officer a cheery smile and called out as he turned to leave, "See you next Tuesday!"

Dan and Jaz turned in unison and threw Trish a curious look. The officer shook his head and swaggered back to his car.

8

That evening, Dan telephoned Cathy Wheeler at her London flat and spent a while reminiscing. Cathy had held a flickering torch for Dan since studying together as carefree 21-year-olds at journalism college in Sheffield.

"You were always going places – I didn't know those places would be full of death and destruction," said Cathy.

"There was a fair bit of beer and curry too."

Cathy chuckled. She had always been an out-and-out office girl while Dan was an out-of-office guy, but whenever they met or spoke, it was like pulling on a favourite jumper. Warm, casual, comfortable. A good fit.

"Yes, I remember. Too much beer at times," said Cathy.

The conversation moved on to old college mates, comparing notes on what became of the class of 1986.

Known for his ability to lunch daily on five baked potatoes smothered in a can of baked beans, John 'Spuddy' Rudd became show business editor for *the Daily Mirror*. Alex – aka 'Brains' – James, whose claim to fame was completing *the Times* crossword in less than eight minutes, went to *the Sun* as a sub-editor.

Lizzie Toogood worked for the Labour Party as a speechwriter. After several short-lived dalliances with prominent MPs, she'd been dubbed Lizzie Toobad.

"And what happened to Biffo?" said Cathy, remembering the infamously lewd Brian Laws, who was the chubbiest, brashest, but never the brightest student in their college class.

"Dunno, not seen or heard from him."

"He was quite a character, but I never knew why he was called Biffo. Was it something to do with Biffo, the Bear or more appropriately, Biffo, the Clown?"

"Neither," said Dan, suppressing a chortle as a sip of orange juice went down the wrong way. "He was BIFFO, as in Big Ignorant Fucker from Oxford."

"Oh." Cathy collapsed into a fit of giggles. "I do miss you, Dan. How are you? Be honest."

Dan assured Cathy he enjoyed his new role and for the first time in a long while felt he was helping others in their time of need rather than merely observing people in need. Cathy told him she had also moved on – she was no longer on the foreign news desk. There had been a radical shake-up at *the News.* A box of green tea in the office kitchen was now the longest-standing member of staff after a rapid turnover of journalists in the foreign department.

In the few weeks since Dan's departure, Dankworth had taken a new role as Editor-in-

Chief. He sat on the board, lunching and gladhanding, no longer responsible for the day-to-day running of the newspaper. A promotion? More like kicked upstairs. After several years trying to deny the demise of print journalism, the proprietors had surrendered to the internet tide, deciding to throw the last of their cash at digital in a thrust to survive. They were hopelessly late, but *the Daily News* was now online in a big way.

An arsenal of young guns, many fresh out of media college, ran the home and foreign news desks. Most posted text and pictures at lightning speed and were superficially impressive with their gung-ho headlines, creative ideas for listicles and snappy intros. Spelling words with devious double letters or sneaky silent letters proved more challenging.

The News was way behind the snappy digital operations pioneered by *the Guardian* and *the Daily Mail.* Still, there was round-the-clock energy and vitality, which meant Cathy was no longer comfortable in her role. Fortunately for her, new editor Glynn Morris valued experience as well as youth. His long foppish hair gave him the look of a Bohemian sixth-former rather than an executive in his mid-30s, but he was an astute Welshman. He recognised Cathy's worth as a meticulous, tenacious journalist, promoting her to special investigations editor, with a brief to delve behind the fabric of the biggest stories.

She could work alone, away from the youthful frenzy. The news would break online, and Cathy's in-depth analysis would grace the print edition.

"Go forth and multiply our most discerning readers," was how Morris had put it to Cathy.

Bullshit, Cathy had thought, albeit to herself. She was long enough in the tooth to realise that in journalism, there's no place for negativity. Not unless the perpetrator is prepared to find it used in evidence against them at a later date. So, she kept flashing those long teeth, at least when the editor was around.

"And that's how I came to be reading Cathy Wheeler for the first time in ten years," said Dan. "It was good stuff. You should have been doing that years ago. You always possessed the contacts and that knack of wheedling information out of people."

"Wheedling? That doesn't sound nice."

"Okay, make that charming."

"That's better."

"Tell me, how did you get onto this slave gang story?"

"Why do you want to know?" said Cathy, for the first time a little guarded in her reply.

Dan told her about his encounter at the car wash. Just a rough outline at first, but it was the detail that interested Cathy.

"How much were they charging?"

"Ninety-nine pence for a basic wash, two pounds for the intermediate."

"How many attendants?"

"Three, maybe four, five with the boss."

"And the violence? Was that provoked? Did it feel like a one-off incident or a routine beating?"

"Funnily enough, I haven't done a post-graduate thesis on car wash employees and their predilection to violent behaviour. It looked like the fat guy in charge was born to be a bully, if that's what you mean."

"Bingo! All the details add up to something unsavoury. How can any business with that many employees make a profit charging ninety-nine pence or two pounds? Problem is most people pounce on the low price rather than ask what's going on. At those prices, they'd have to wash about fifty cars an hour every hour to make a small profit. It doesn't add up – somebody is exploiting someone, for sure. It might just be a local thing. I don't know, but it could be part of something more sinister."

"Such as?"

"Don't get involved, Dan." Cathy's voice was soft but firm as she conveyed a prominent warning. "I've been investigating gangs involved in human trafficking for the past six months. The National Crime Agency and the Border Police are working flat out and are fighting a losing battle. Honest, Dan, there's a crime wave going on in the Channel right now. Two British men and a woman are due in court charged with ferrying four Vietnamese nationals across the

Channel in a speed boat. It was intercepted off the Kent coast and, thank God, happened as the motor broke down and they ended up drifting.

"Police mount daily raids in London. Earlier this month an undercover team unearthed half a dozen illegal cannabis farms in the suburbs, arresting a ring of young foreign nationals with no passports. They spoke limited English, yet my contact told me he'd never seen a better job of splicing into the national grid for a free, constant supply of electricity."

Cathy paused, but Dan was eager to learn more.

"How young are these guys?" he asked.

"It varies, but in the case of drug runners, some are as young as fourteen. They sell products in rural areas nationwide, from counties surrounding the capital and extending as far north as Carlisle. As I wrote in the article, the police know the problem is widespread. So far, no central control has been located, no one syndicate identified, no Mr Big fingered. At least not for public consumption."

"Who do you think's behind it?" Dan asked.

"Difficult to work out. There are so many copycat cells that have set up on their own after realising there's easy money to make. The network is too wide, connections too obvious, the money, some say as much as twenty billion, too vast for it not to be organised. It could be the biggest, most ruthless crime syndicate at work since Pablo Escobar ran drugs to every corner of the globe from Colombia."

"Wow! That will be a Pulitzer Prize exclusive if cracked."

"Remember, don't get involved."

"Don't worry. I'm sure a little car wash is not in that league, but do me a favour, Cathy. If you hear anything going on local to me, drop me a text or something."

"How about buying me a drink sometime?" said Cathy hopefully.

"Next time I'm in the smoke. Promise."

Dan ended the call and picked up a copy of *the Daily News* from the coffee table. His brow furrowed as three troubling words from Cathy's special report smacked him in the face. *Violent. Sadistic. Ruthless.*

9

Studying the crossword in *the Daily News* – heads together, scarf and wig touching – Jaz and Trish pondered the clue to 14 down.

Eight letters. Third letter T, sixth letter Y. *Perfidiousness akin to treachery.*

"What the hell's perfidiousness?" said Trish at a decibel level that invited the entire waiting room to join in. No one did.

"It means dishonest, someone who can't be trusted, someone who tells lies all the time," said Jaz.

"Like my ex-partner, you mean."

Jaz detected a snooty glance from a lady opposite and a snigger or two from her left.

"From what you've told me, he would seem to fit the bill. Thanks, Trish, the answer's just come to me." Jaz flicked the top of her blue biro and wrote BETRAYAL in the vacant squares.

"Be-tray-al." Trish explored the meaning of the word before surprising Jaz and the earwiggers with a thought of genuine poignancy. "The saddest thing is betrayal never comes from your enemies. It always comes from those closest to you."

Jaz looked up from the newspaper and touched Trish on the wrist. "Oh, Trish, such wise words."

The remark was probably the first time Trish and wise had occupied the same sentence.

Already, the two women were good chums. More than that. It was only their fifth day of treatment, but they'd formed a bond that glue manufacturers may have described as a *no-nonsense adhesive.* They could discuss anything, however dark, sticky or intimate.

Cancer finds a way of unlocking inhibitions and putting life in sharp perspective. Jaz and Trish's were different as was their treatment, but the pair were members of the same club, thrown together by fate and timing with the same hopes, fears and advice while under medical care. Don't eat shellfish or smoked salmon or sushi, which didn't bother Jaz, but Trish loved cockles, mussels, and jellied eels. Something to do with her Cockney ancestors.

The women used the same treatment room. Pale blue paint, clinical nature, chilly ambient temperature, allowing plenty of time to catch up as they waited their turn. Enough time to watch other members of the *club* as they came and went. They listened to Margaret – christened Lady Margaret by Trish – who lived alone in a six-bedroom mansion backing onto a fairway of the swanky local golf course. She had a redundant Rolls Royce in the garage, a gardener, and a handyman for occasional company.

David prattled on about his pension plans, two

years' severance pay and 40 years with the local council and, Oh, God, no, he's going on about his combination boiler again. They watched Andrew moved on by two security guards from the back door of the oncology unit. Approaching 60, Andrew looked ten years younger, due to his dark hair and gaunt, taut physique. He was 5ft 10 but weighed 7st 4 and rarely ate, but on the advice of his dietician, he was never without a white plastic bag full of protein drinks. On the advice of his flatmate, cans of high-strength lager kept the protein drinks company. His mate had been through many of the same life experiences. Heroin addiction. Methadone dependence. Multiple partners.

Despite his visible flaws, dubious drug history and physical shortcomings, Andrew was intelligent, polite, and personable. He suffered from emphysema and advanced-stage lung cancer, coughing and wheezing constantly but still insisting on popping out every five minutes for a cigarette. He stood at the back door in long, lingering clouds of smoke. Andrew would lean on the wall of the radiotherapy unit with the sole of his right foot pressed against the brickwork, reach into his bag and prise the ring-pull from a can of lager. When he started swigging, someone alerted the guards, who gently moved him on to the smokers' corner just off the main hospital site.

"What an idiot! He shouldn't be allowed to

come here like that," said the snooty someone in a half-whisper, but loud enough for those close by to hear. "What's the point of having treatment for lung cancer and smoking like a chimney? Ridiculous."

Trish bristled. "Maybe smoking's his only pleasure. Maybe he knows his time is almost up and a cigarette is his comfort blanket. For Christ's sake, he isn't hurting anyone except himself."

Jaz sensed the conversation was about to catch fire. It was time for a diplomatic full stop. "Live and let live. Who are we to judge him?" she said.

"Well said," a man sitting behind Jaz piped up in a gravelled Scottish accent straight from the Glasgow shipyards of yesteryear. "To quote Billy Connolly, 'Before you judge a man, walk a mile in his shoes. After that who cares? He's a mile away, and you've got his shoes.'"

Chuckling, Jaz turned to nod approval at the Scottish wit, and Trish let go with her trademark cackle. A hum of laughter spread around the patients in the waiting room. The snooty lady turned away, pretending to read the poster on the wall advertising 'The World's Biggest Coffee Morning' in aid of Macmillan Cancer Support.

Thirty minutes later, treatment complete, Jaz and Trish headed back to the drivers' lobby. Five down, 15 to go. Dan was waiting. With a flourish of his right hand, he invited them to take a seat. Neither Bill nor Murph had returned. Dan had checked on Murph, struggling his way through a pint of water. He was trailing up and down the corridor in a bid to allow gravity to assist in ridding his lower reaches of unwanted wind. Gas and radiotherapy do not mix. Go and blow for England was how Murph's nurse put it.

Dan was talking to Martin, his former policeman colleague, who'd been chuckling at Dan's description of his altercation with the traffic officer a couple of days ago.

"I loved pulling cars over in my day," said Martin. "Usually, it was just out of boredom, something to do. There was always someone who'd sound off, and I'd nick those who did. You were right, not getting involved in an argument, especially if you were doing fifty-eight in a fifty zone. We always worked on tolerance of ten per cent plus two, so he had every right to give you a ticket."

"Good God, I'm glad I never ran into you! Ever thought of becoming a bean counter?"

Martin smiled before telling Dan he'd spoken to one of his police contacts about Ernie's car wash. The business still traded under Ernie's name, and his car remained fully taxed and licensed. There had been no reports of disturbance or violence. As far as the police were concerned, there was no cause for concern. There had been one incident logged three months before. A 999 call from the landline at the premises: *Brief. Child's voice laughing.*

No request. Cut off after three seconds. The call formed one of a multitude of hoax or inappropriate calls made to UK police forces every year.

"Some of them are bonkers," said Martin. "We once received a call at our station from a woman who said it was her daughter's wedding day and her dress didn't fit. Could the police come around and help her get into it?"

"And you didn't send a car?" chirped Dan.

Martin grinned. "Funnily enough, no. Normally, when emergency callers don't ask for help, they're kids fooling around."

"Thanks for checking Ernie's out," said Dan. "With this wall-to-wall sunshine, I haven't called into the car wash for a couple of days but will keep an eye out for the fat guy with the temper just the same."

Bill and Murph popped their heads around the door, and Dan went to collect the car, passing Andrew on the way retracing his unsteady steps from smokers' corner.

On the way home, Trish turned to Bill. "Can I ask you a question, Bill?"

"You didn't give me a choice there, did you, Trish?"

"No, be serious Bill. I wondered, with you being a bit of a comedian and all, what were your thoughts when diagnosed with cancer?"

"To be honest, I just wanted things to be normal and hoped everybody would keep treating me as Bill, not the man with cancer. I didn't want sympathy. I didn't want attention, believe it or not. When the doctor told me it was cancer, I cracked a joke because that's what I do. 'Thank goodness. I need to lose some weight,' I said.

"The doctor humoured me and smiled, but I meant it, the bit about wanting everything to be normal, I mean. I've always hated the idea of people feeling sorry for me, but they don't hand out manuals on how to deal with cancer, do they? Everybody's different. Everybody has his or her way of coping."

Trish nodded and fiddled with the heart-shaped gold pendant hanging around her neck. Murph snored, head against the headrest, while in the front Jaz and Dan were deep in conversation about music.

"The one good thing is there's no such thing as the Big C anymore. Not in my head anyway. When my dad discovered his diagnosis thirty years ago, people didn't talk about cancer. As though the mere mention of the word was enough to invite the disease into your home. People were scared to hope, scared to let it out in the open. I know a lot of people are still like that.

"I was lucky. I received a routine letter from the NHS, inviting me to attend the local surgery for a health check for people aged between forty and seventy-four. I fell snugly into that age group. Because my father died from cancer, the

GP suggested a routine prostate examination. It was a bit embarrassing and uncomfortable, but not too painful. The blood tests revealed an elevated PSA protein-specific antigen reading of twelve. I had no pain, no tiredness, no symptoms, just a stark number suggesting everything wasn't normal and required further investigation.

"With modern technology and better survival rates, the Big C's becoming more of a little c. It's still scary, but treatable. Often curable. Cancer's a disease you can live with and manage. Lots of people still die, of course, they do, but they shouldn't pass in awkward silence. Cancer needs to become part of life rather than merely a cause of death. Too many forget to enjoy life. As awful as cancer is, you have to live and carry on. That's what I think."

Trish was beginning to see the real Bill, not just the old joke-telling, retired, amateur comedian. As with many comics, a sharp, analytical brain, serious nature and a myriad of life experience hid behind the mask of one-liners.

"Do you know what I did the day after I received my diagnosis?" said Trish. Her throat tightened, her tone intensifying as the memory screamed to the surface.

Bill shook his head.

"I cried, Bill. The moment I woke up, I cried. I cried all that morning and burst into tears at the oddest moments throughout the rest of the day. The postman rang the doorbell, and I burst into tears. My boss from work called and I ended up talking gibberish and wailing down the telephone. You could have filled a bath, honest you could. When I went to bed, I was still crying. Sobbing, you know, not just crying. I don't know why – I'm not a tearful person. I'm not soft, honest, Bill, I'm not soft.

"I asked myself so many questions. *How has my life come to this, why has it come to this? When did it all go wrong? What have I done? Could I have prevented this? Is it all over?* I couldn't find any definite answers. Maybe I was confronting my mortality I don't know. Perhaps I was alone, and everything came crashing down on me.

"Maybe I was feeling sorry for myself, but I felt as though I was stumbling around and around in a thick forest covered in mist not knowing where to turn. All I could think of was chemo and drugs and radiotherapy and survival rates and dark, dark thoughts. I was so frightened. I thought I would never find a way out. I couldn't see a future. Then the mist cleared."

Trish paused, took a deep breath and sighed, realising she was revisiting the epicentre of the shock that had thrown her life into turmoil. She became aware of the silence. Dan and Jaz broke from their conversation, entranced by the side of Trish, which thus far she'd hidden beneath a ditzy demeanour and sharp tongue. Murph no longer snored. He was awake and hanging on every word.

Trish let out a nervous, embarrassed giggle and smoothed down her yellow, floral-patterned blouse with the palms of her hands. "I remember waking up the next morning, and the tears were gone. Instead, I was spitting blood. Not literally. I mean, I was angry. Angry at this fucking disease. I was fuming that it could knock on my door, barge in and think it could take control of my job, my home, my life, like some alien debt-collecting service or something.

"No fucking chance, I said. I vowed there and then that I was not going to cower in the face of cancer. I was determined to carry on living, just like you said, Bill."

Trish squeezed Bill's hand. He turned to her. "Crikey, Trish, the mist has well and truly cleared from that forest."

She smiled, raised her shoulders and thrust her palms down onto her thighs like a little girl contemplating which doll to play with next. She shook her head, hardly believing she'd bared her soul to relative strangers. Then, without a join, she was back to the usual Trish, telling Bill about the snooty lady and the Scotsman's quip in the waiting room. Bill pursed his lips and turned his nose up when she mentioned Billy Connolly.

"Good storyteller and terrific performer on stage, but too much of his material involved bodily functions and the F-word for my taste.

Too much farting and fu— you know what, I mean. I preferred when he did wry observations, such as people saying, 'It's always the last place you look' when searching for something because it is. Why would you keep looking for something after you've found it? I liked his lists of pet hates, too – people pointing at their wrist when asking for the time."

They were still on the dual carriageway, trundling along at a sedate 40 mph as an articulated lorry had decided to overtake a petrol tanker on one of the few significant gradients in the county. The truck struggled to make headway and for a mile and a half had formed a rolling roadblock of dangerous toxicity, resulting in a growing line of frustrated drivers.

"Talking about pet hates," said Dan, "this is one of mine. Why clog up the road for everyone else when you can't get past? Even if you could, it would save around fifty metres at best. Chances are the lorry will give up and pull in before we reach the top of the rise. Just watch. Tenner on it."

Jaz pointed at the back of the tanker. "That's my pet hate."

"What?" said Dan.

"Inflammable," said Jaz, pointing at the word in capital letters alongside a placard identifying the dangers of a tanker carrying fuel oil. No smoking. No naked flames.

"What do you hate about that? All seems

pretty sensible to me."

"The fact that it says inflammable when it could or should be flammable. Both words mean the same. Why would you use the longer, more archaic style? English is full of words that sound as if they should be the opposite of each other but mean the same."

"Such as?"

"Invaluable and valuable, infamous and famous, loosen and—"

"Okay, I get the idea. Going on could get more annoying than this infuriating roadblock."

Jaz ignored Dan. "Loosen and unloosen. See, it's interesting. Oh, look, our discussion has roused, or should that be aroused Murph from his nap."

"If you don't mind, Jaz, I think you'll find that infamous and famous aren't quite the same." Murph polished the lenses of his dangling spectacles with a tissue. "You could argue they were opposites. Famous refers to good fame in the main, while infamous surely refers to bad fame. That's what I was taught."

"Is the sinking of the Titanic a famous event, Murph?" asked Jaz.

"Yes. Of course. Everybody knows about the world's most famous shipwreck."

"Is the sinking of the Titanic infamous?"

"Well, a lot of people died, and it was sailing too fast, and there weren't enough lifeboats, so I suppose so."

"I rest my case, your honour."

"Oh, no, you don't," said Dan. "Answer this. Is Mother Theresa famous?"

"Yes, of course," said Jaz.

"Is Mother Theresa infamous?"

"Dan, I think you should keep your eyes on the road. That lorry is slipping back towards us," said Jaz, attempting to avoid more interrogation.

"That's all, your honour, no more questions," said Dan through gritted teeth, trying to stifle a mischievous smile radiating across his face.

Trish, who'd been unusually quiet was still pondering her pet hate, a little too literally as it turned out. Like a child in primary school, she'd put up her hand. Dan caught sight of her animated expression in the rear-view mirror.

"Go on, Trish, what's your pet hate?" he said.

"People who pick up their dog's poo, pop it in a plastic bag and hang it on the branch of the nearest tree like a Christmas decoration. What's that all about?"

There was no answer, but everyone laughed.

The lorry accepted its limitations and shunted in behind the tanker, prompting Dan to put a hand in the air as if collecting the tenner from his imaginary bet. His foot pressed metal to the floor, the car surged forward, and Bill quipped, "Don't spare the horses, Dan, show Formula One how it's done."

The car left the dual carriageway and meandered through the hedgerows. Dan turned down the volume on the CD he'd put in the car that morning and announced an idea. As a rule, there was no treatment over the weekend, giving staff time off but more importantly allowing patients to recover from the frying effects of daily radiotherapy.

"I don't know how everyone's fixed, but how do you all fancy coming as a team to a pub quiz on Sunday afternoon at the local pub? The White Horse. A bit of fun with all the proceeds going to charity. I've had a meal there a few times and have always fancied joining in the quiz. Only a couple of hours so shouldn't be too tiring."

"A quiz? Me?" said Trish. "Are you sure you're not thinking of Trish from another planet, Dan. Jaz would be great, she's clever, but I've never been to a quiz in my life."

"You'll be fine," said Dan.

"No, I won't. I used to watch *Who Wants to Be a Millionaire?* and reached sixteen thousand once but couldn't remember who was the first man to stand on the moon. The answers went to fifty-fifty between Neil Armstrong and Alexander Armstrong, and I know this sounds thick, but I said, Alexander. Well, I wasn't born then."

"Dan's right, Trish, you'll be fine," said Jaz, who thought the quiz afternoon a splendid idea. "You need a real varied mix of knowledge in a quiz team, history, trivia, science and, most of all, general knowledge. I think we'll be okay, and it should be a laugh. If we come last, we come last, who cares?"

"I could pick everyone up in my own car," said Dan. "What about you, Murph?"

"Yes, I suppose so, as long as it's after two o'clock. I don't want to miss Sunday lunch."

"Starts at four in the afternoon, so you're in, Murph," said Dan.

Also in agreement, and as Dan intimated a full team consisted of six, Bill volunteered his wife Jean as the sixth member.

"That's it then," said Dan. "White Horse, Sunday, four o'clock. The more brains, the better."

Dan glanced in his rear-view mirror, and his heart skipped. "Not again. Not twice in a week." The blue flashing lights of a police car closed in and the red STOP sign illuminated.

"Have you been naughty again?" said Trish, a mischievous grin on her face. "You were clogging it a bit after passing that lorry."

Dan wound down his window and watched in his side-mirror as the officer eased out of his car. Shades, black hair, yellow jacket, Tom Cruise swagger, an air of condescension.

"You cannot be serious!" Dan half-whistled between his teeth as he recognised the familiar gait.

Had he been speeding? He was fairly sure he hadn't but couldn't swear to it.

The officer reached Dan's side, leaned his arm on the wound-down window and peered into the

MPV.

"Thought it was you lot. Do you know why I've stopped you this time?"

"No, not a clue," said Dan, an affronted tone replacing the appeasing manner of a few days ago.

"Any chance of a copy of today's *Daily News*?"

Dan picked out a paper from the central console and handed it over.

"Thanks," said the officer, leaving his parting words trailing in the breeze. "Have a nice day, everyone."

Dan looked across at Jaz, both mouthing in unison, "I don't believe it."

10

Like many pubs, the White Horse was dying on its feet only a couple of years ago.

Apathetic landlord. Tired décor and sticky tables. Average beer, dreadful food. Few customers, some nights, none. The atmosphere was so deathly locals had taken to calling it the White Hearse. Then, Jim and Joanne stepped in. The couple worked the cruise liners and knew a thing or two about entertainment and catering. Within a year, White Horse management and staff were galloping down to London to receive Pub of the Year prize at a brewery award ceremony.

Dan and company walked into buzzing conversation and laughter amid the clink of glasses. The lunchtime carvery, noted in recent times for succulent roasts, had shut up shop but the smell of cooked meat and mint sauce lingered, and many of the diners had stayed on for the quiz. Dan found a table for four in a convenient alcove, light enough, but not too noisy. Before he went to the bar to buy a round of orange juices and sparkling water, he explained that Bill and Jean weren't coming. Bill had called that morning to say he wasn't feeling well, probably side-effects after his week's treatment.

Dan debated for a moment whether to give the unpleasant details. *Why not? Bill would expect no less.*

"To be precise, Bill growled down the phone, 'my arse feels like it's been sitting on smouldering cinders all night and now it's leaking like a rusty old bucket. I'm shovelling down tablets and medications ending in odium, amide, and chloride like they're going out of fashion.'"

"Sounds like he's feeling crap," said Trish.

"Three times an hour at least," said Dan.

There was a collective groan.

"Dan, leave the jokes to Bill," said Jaz.

Dan pointed to landlord Jim fiddling with his tablet and the microphone settings on the pub's sound system at the opposite side of the room. His bald head shone in a shaft of sunlight. When he looked up, he revealed a neat brown goatee and a face radiating enthusiasm and energy, lined with rivulets of experience.

"Testing one-two-three. Testing one-two-three. Be with you shortly," Jim said into the microphone, adjusting the amplifier knobs to reduce the feedback. "As usual, two pounds each and team names must have a zodiac sign theme. Best name wins a tenner."

Murph took a tissue from his pocket to polish his spectacles, a sure sign he was musing on an idea. "What about The Topic of Cancer? That's what we all have in common now."

"Brilliant," said Dan. "The Topic of Cancer, it is."

Jaz and Trish nodded approval, although Trish looked perplexed.

"I know it's the Tropic of Cancer, not the Topic of Cancer, but what is the Tropic of Cancer? I've heard of it, but that's a strange name for a star sign if you ask me."

"It's simple, Trish," said Jaz. "The tropics are the only place on Earth where the sun can be directly overhead. Cancer is the most northerly latitude on Earth where that happens, passing through Mexico, the Bahamas, India, and parts of China. On the other hand, Capricorn is the most southerly latitude where it occurs. Voila! The regions between Cancer and Capricorn are called the tropics."

"Thank you, Jaz," said Dan. "There endeth the pre-quiz geography lesson. Give me your money."

Dan collected the entry cash and went to pick up a scoresheet and picture round. On his return, he was surprised to see a tall, slim man with long, straggly hair sitting in his chair talking to Jaz.

"Dan, would you believe it? Look who's here," said Jaz.

The straggly head turned towards Dan. *Jordan, the lad from Hendos petrol station.* Dan had to admit Jordan didn't appear as surly out of his supermarket uniform, but charm wasn't one of his assets. Nevertheless, the men nodded to one another.

"It's okay if he joins us, isn't it? The more, the merrier," Jaz said.

"Yeah, sure," Dan replied, adding a dash of enthusiasm to avert any awkwardness. He dragged a chair from the adjoining table and sat down.

"When's your birthday, Jordan?" said Jaz.

"Thirtieth of June." Jordan's tell-tale vocal tremble magnified in Jaz's presence.

"Perfect!" Jaz clapped her palms together then raised them to her lips in a praying position. "That means you're a Cancer. Our team name couldn't be better, Murph."

Jordan coughed up £2, Trish and Jaz pounced on the celebrity picture round.

"That's one of Madonna's husbands." Trish jabbed the first picture with her forefinger. "Guy somebody, oh, come on Jaz. He makes films, I think. Oh, yes. Guy Ritchie."

"Brilliant," said Jaz, writing the answer underneath the picture, "but the idea is to tell our team, not every team in the pub."

"Sorry. Was that too loud? I was glad I knew one." Trish pointed again, this time cupping her mouth with the palm of her hand and whispering towards Jaz.

Viewing Trish in a different light, Jaz wrote the answer. In turn, Trish was growing in confidence, like a football striker who's scored twice and is desperate to record a hat-trick.

Minutes later the hat-trick came, and with a little help from Murph and Dan, the team scored full marks.

"Ten out of ten. I'm enjoying this," beamed Trish.

"Told you it would be fun," said Jaz.

Trish pointed to the whiteboard by Jim's desk, showing the updated scores. "Look, we're in the lead."

"Just!" A woman's curt voice from neighbouring team, The Rage of Aquarius, squelched Trish's excitement.

Next, geography, which suited Dan, and a round on kings and queens, which drew groans from Trish, Dan and Murph. Jordan had barely said a word but suddenly piped up with unexpected knowledge of Alfred the Great to save the team from embarrassment. Jim announced a ten-minute break. People replenished drinks, and Murph excused himself and shuffled off to the toilet. Jaz tried to put Jordan at ease, asking how everyone was doing at work.

"All fine." It was the most she got before his knee began to shake.

Murph returned and picked up the Dingbats sheet, pictorial clues denoting well-known phrases. He rattled through the first five images then paused on the last one depicting three lions in front of a man tumbling off a ladder.

The biro went to the answer box: "Pride goes

before a fall."

"Fantastic, Murph," said Trish. "How do you do them so quickly?"

"Believe me, Trish, there isn't much to do all day in my place. Just read the paper, stare out the window and pore over the books of Dingbats my niece bought me for Christmas."

"Oh, Murph, I'll try to come to see you when we've got through this month."

"I'd like that, Trish. I know it sounds strange, but I've enjoyed the treatment so far. Some days I don't speak to anyone in the home. Most people keep themselves to themselves. Going to the Barrett Bailey is tiring, but it's like having an adventure every day."

The quiz reached its final round, and Dan's team answered every question, certain all were correct, except one. What was the second James Bond film? Dan thought Goldfinger. Jaz agreed. Trish admitted she didn't have a clue but was sure Bill would have known. Murph shook his head.

"From Russia with Love," Jordan said.

"Sure?" said Dan.

Jordan nodded.

"Does that nod mean for definite, as in absolutely because you have watched every Bond movie from Sean Connery to Daniel Craig, or does it mean you think so?"

"Stop intimidating him, Dan," said Jaz. "If Jordan says he's certain, I'm sure he means just that."

"If it's wrong we lose all the points for this round," warned Dan.

Jaz shrugged. "Come on. You only live once."

"Surely, you only live twice, said Dan, sliding into his best Connery impression and making everyone giggle. "I think that came after Goldfinger, didn't it Jordan?"

"No, after Thunderball," Jordan replied, reciting the first ten Bond films in a detached, robotic manner.

He would have continued if Dan, suspicious Jordan was on some medical spectrum, hadn't thrown up his hands. "Enough, Jordan, I'm convinced. Let's go for it."

With all regular rounds completed, Dan's team was joint top alongside Capricorn Six, and Dan glowed at the success of his little get-together. Murph was engaged, Trish excited, and Jaz adored the sense of fun and companionship. Cancer, apart from the star sign, had vanished from their thoughts, for two hours at least. Sod's law decrees such Zen moments can't last.

The team swapped its Dingbats answer paper with the Rage of Aquarius and Jaz marked as Jim read out the answers. Jaz studied the marked paper when it came back.

"Five out of six?" A puzzled frown scarred Jaz's face as she held up the sheet of paper to show Dan and Murph.

The Aquarius lady had drawn an ostentatious

cross next to the Dingbat with three lions.

"Excuse me," said Jaz, turning her head to face the woman, "we've scored six, this one's correct."

"No, it isn't." The lady's expression was stern, unyielding. "Jim distinctly said, 'Pride comes before a fall.' Comes, not goes."

"That's ridiculous. It means the same thing."

"But that's not what he said, and don't call me ridiculous, stupid woman. You're wrong."

Jaz's cheeks flushed. Her kind eyes smouldered, and she slid her chair back and stood up. The Aquarius woman responded by jumping to her feet. The women glared at each other – a pleasant afternoon was in danger of ending in a barroom catfight. Dan's money was on Jaz. Then an unexpected happening. Murph rose and confronted the lady with a commanding air, at odds with how he'd cowered in the presence of an emu earlier that week.

"Excuse me, madam. The phrase is from a verse in the Bible, the book of Proverbs. Pride goeth before destruction, and a haughty spirit before a fall. You'll note I said goeth, not cometh."

"I don't care what you said," hissed the woman, standing, hands on hips and ramping up the malice with a dismissive reworking of Murph's words. "You can goeth and fucketh yourself. The quizmaster said, 'Pride comes before a fall.' You got it wrong."

If Jim hadn't been an experienced landlord, the incident could have turned uglier. He strode from the whiteboard and positioned himself, metaphorically, between Cancer and Aquarius ruling that there were three essential aspects of the phrase: pride, fall and the timing. Before rather than after. He didn't care – comes or goes – they were both acceptable. Jim, the wise old White Horse saviour, had spoken.

The Aquarius lady sat down, grumbling and gesticulating.

Trish clapped her hands. "Does that mean we've won?"

The answer came via the microphone – a tie between The Topic of Cancer and Capricorn Six, both on 61 points. A tie-break question would settle the £60 first prize after Jim presented *We're All Virgos (Honest!)* with £10 for the best team name.

Once the squeals subsided, Jim explained the teams would have 20 seconds to write the answer to the tie-break question. Nearest would win. "Okay. Is everyone ready? How many baked beans are there in a standard four hundred and fifteen grams can?"

Eyebrows raised and eyes met, but not in a good way.

"No idea," said Murph.

Trish twitched her nose and shrugged.

"Maybe a thousand," Jaz offered.

As they deliberated, no-one noticed Jordan draw a circle and sketch 30 bean shapes inside. He stretched forefinger and thumb of one hand to gauge the height of an average can and computed it could house around 15 beans lying on top of each other. Thirty multiplied by 15.

"Four hundred and fifty," Jordan said.

"Surely more," said Dan.

"Four hundred and fifty," Jordan repeated in the robotic way he'd recited the Bond movies.

"Answers, please," said Jim.

The Capricorn Six captain handed in his team's answer and Jaz scribbled 450 and passed the paper to Jim.

Jim held the papers above his head. "One of the teams is incredibly close and the other as far away as the sun," he said. "One team says one thousand two hundred and fifty beans, the other, four hundred and fifty. The answer is … a pause for drum roll, please … four hundred and sixty-five. Put your hands together for The Topic of Cancer."

Jaz patted Jordan on the back, and the lad almost broke into his first smile of the afternoon. Dan accepted the £60 in £10 notes. He gave one each to Trish, Murph, and Jaz kept one for himself and handed two to Jordan.

"Fair play," said Dan. "He won it for us."

There were no objections.

On her way out, Trish passed acid-tongue from The Rage of Aquarius. Bending down, she whispered in the woman's ear. "See you next Tuesday."

11

The traffic was slow, like an old snake – the sort of snarl-up that doubtless slithers its way around downtown Los Angeles every Monday morning. It was the only thing Lexford had in common with LA.

While negotiating a tight corner on the High Street, a lorry had struck a traffic light. In an old market town with a wide river flowing through its middle, there were limited ways around the obstruction. That's the dichotomy of living amid English quaintness – narrow streets, picturesque houses, historical ambience. Wonderful for summer season tourist pictures, not ideal for the pragmatics of day-to-day living with an ever-increasing population. Calling for his passengers in the heat of the school run exceeded an hour. Dan could have walked quicker. Still, the many schools, impressive for a medium-sized town, were breaking up at the end of the week, which would make life easier.

A message pinged on Dan's phone. He'd usually ignore such activity while driving. As he was motionless, Dan checked the message from Cathy Wheeler: *An update! Give me a call when you can.*

Dan was intrigued, especially as he'd spoken

to Cathy only a few days earlier. He slipped the phone back into the console and made a mental note to ring that evening.

At last, Dan reached Bill's house, his final pick-up. Trish couldn't wait.

"We won, Bill, we won the quiz. I'm officially an egghead," she squealed.

Bill fumbled for the seat belt. "Can I get in first, Trish?"

"Oh, sorry, I should've asked how you're feeling."

Bill said he hadn't eaten for 24 hours, had drunk two bottles of an energy drink and gone through countless sachets of powdered medication, which had eventually worked. However, he wasn't confident about making any long journeys away from what he described as his 'comfort station'. He felt weak, looked drained – sallow features, parchment for skin, eyes missing their mischievous twinkle.

"Good job I picked you up last," said Dan. "The traffic's horrendous in town."

"Go on then, Trish, tell me about the quiz." Bill's voice was weary.

Trish explained each round, telling how the scores had ebbed and flowed in what amounted to a comprehensive match report. She was fulsome in her praise for Jaz and Jordan, then told the story of Jaz's altercation. Blow for blow.

"But Murph was the hero," said Trish, describing how Murph had stood up for the team and faced down the Rage of Aquarius.

Murph held up his hands in modest acknowledgement while shaking his head, attempting to play down the incident.

"Who would have thought? Murph, Lord of the Flies Down, a knight in shining armour," said Bill. "I did a good deed myself yesterday, you know."

"What?" asked Trish.

Bill said he'd been shopping in Hendos, feeling rotten, buying supplies, queuing at the check-out behind an old lady probably kicking ninety. "Her bill came to fifty-one sixty, but when she came to pay, she opened her purse and counted her change, fumbling with old, arthritic fingers and struggling to see through bottle-top glasses. When she emptied her purse, the money inside came to just short of fifty pounds."

Trish was looking at Bill with a sympathetic smile lighting her face.

"She didn't want my help, bless her. She wanted to be independent, but I insisted."

"Aww," Trish said, hugging Bill's arm.

"And, in no time at all, we had her shopping back on the shelves."

Dan and Jaz exploded, even Murph chuckled.

Trish gave a blank look. "Really?"

"No, Trish, he's pulling your leg," said Jaz. "Bill must be feeling better, after all."

Trish smacked Bill playfully on the knee. He reacted with a shrug and a non-committal roll of the eyes.

The traffic was beginning to thin out, and Dan picked up speed. Bursting onto the dual carriageway, he kept a careful eye on his rear-view mirror in case Tom Cruise or any of his colleagues were around. The passengers had known each other one week. Still, there was an ease, a warmth, a cosy familiarity that so far defied those philosophical assertions that say friendship is a slow ripening fruit. In seven days, they'd teased each other, supported each other and discussed some of their innermost hopes and fears.

There'd been much laughter, and Jaz had almost cried when Trish revealed her recent car-crash life. To her surprise, Trish's physical collapse and domestic chaos had affected Jaz. After such a brief time, she cared, and the feelings intrigued her. She'd read an American study on the subject of friendship. The report concluded it took 40-60 hours to form a casual friendship, 80-100 to transition to being a friend and more than 200 hours together to become good friends.

Not in Dan's car, it didn't, Jaz mused. Not when cancer was a common denominator. Maybe the shadow of mortality speeds up the senses. Perhaps the community of thought forges a powerful bond to fight adversity. Maybe the Beatles were onto something more magical than they could have imagined when writing *With a*

Little Help from My Friends.

"Now that you've been to your first quiz and won, what else is on the bucket list, Trish," said Bill.

"Are you suggesting I'd better crack on before I croak?"

"I think we're all sailing on that ship," Bill replied.

Trish pressed her little beaked nose with a finger and thought for a minute or two. There were many things she hadn't done. Places she hadn't visited. So much she'd missed. "Come back to me. Let me think of one I'm dying to do."

"Steady on," said Bill, pulling a face at the unfortunate phrase. Trish was oblivious.

"What about you, Jaz?"

Jaz didn't need time for reflection. The old *Star Trek* television series had fascinated her from being a young girl.

"Ever since I watched Captain Kirk and Mr Spock I wanted to go into space," Jaz said. "I imagined being Lieutenant Sulu. I know he's a boy, but his name sounded sweet. Can't see me travelling at warp speed anytime soon, even though there is talk of the possibility of space tourism for the masses in future. Instead, I'd like to visit Cape Canaveral to see a rocket launch. I know it isn't exactly going boldly where no man or woman has gone before, but that's my choice."

"An incredible one too," said Dan.

"What about you, Murph?" said Bill.

As usual, Murph began fiddling with his specs. "You might be surprised to learn that as well as music I've always had an interest in art. I've been to a few great museums and art galleries. In Paris, The Louvre and Musée d'Orsay, in London, the Tate Modern, but have never visited the Vatican to see the Sistine Chapel. I would like to do that, to see beautiful art in its own habitat rather than where it shouldn't be."

"Good effort, Murph. Your turn, Dan," said Bill.

During his career, Dan had travelled extensively and ticked off many of his bucket list locations. He didn't discuss them unless prompted but when Trish asked him about his favourite places they tumbled out.

Dan had listened to opera at La Scala, slept at Everest base camp, trekked to the Inca site of Machu Picchu and marvelled at the Taj Mahal. He'd attended World Cup finals in football and rugby and watched England's cricketers win the 2005 Ashes Test series. He'd even been in Barcelona in 1999 as a news reporter to see Manchester United clinch the Champions League with two goals in injury time.

"That was a night to play with the emotions," said Dan. "After the match, I interviewed Man United manager Alex Ferguson, or Fergie as he was known. He didn't always speak to the Press, but you couldn't shut him up that night.

"I don't have a bucket list destination, but I would like to sail the Atlantic. Not on a cruise ship. Not on one of those rowing boats either. I don't want to be one of those sailors who end up clinging to their upturned hull for days on end after capsizing. I'd die of shame. It must cost millions to find them and airlift them to safety, and as taxpayers, we pick up the bill. No, I'd like to sail on a replica of Drake's Golden Hind – as one of the crew so I could pay my way and step back in history at the same time."

Bill was next. His request was simple, if unrealistic. "Just five minutes on stage at the London Palladium. I could do a turn there in the footsteps of so many great comedians, raise a few laughs and die happy. I know it's not going to happen, but I can dream, can't I?"

Dan arrived at the Barrett Bailey and turned into the oncology entrance. "Okay, Trish, you can let us know what your choice is on the way home. Gives you plenty of time to think."

As they climbed out of the Ford, Dan noticed another Honeycomb vehicle at the far side of the drop-off bay. Alex, one of the drivers, stood behind an empty wheelchair waiting for a burly man in his late sixties to disembark.

The man, with a striking bald head and big Roman nose, flung the passenger door open, but it was the way he emerged that was unusual. Swinging a banana board onto the wheelchair, he formed a makeshift bridge and shuffled across after checking the board was secure. The man had no legs but completed the gymnastic manoeuvre with effortless elegance and efficiency belying his disability. He even refused Alex's offer of help and wheeled himself through the swing doors. A heart-warming, humbling sight.

"The next time I feel sorry for myself, I'll remember what I've just seen," said Jaz.

Trish nodded.

"Yep, doesn't matter what you've got, there's always someone worse off," said Bill, a heavy sigh accompanying the well-worn, if pertinent cliché. "It's how you deal with obstacles that counts."

As always, the hospital was busy, and Jaz and Trish hurried off to their waiting area. At the same time, Bill and Murph booked in at reception and began the routine of drinking a litre of water before treatment began. Bill had tried pretending it was beer. It hadn't worked.

Dan parked the car and headed for the drivers' bolthole, spotting Alex cradling a coffee in the corner of the room. The men had known of each other but hadn't yet met. Alex drove on Mondays only and had been on holiday the week before. However, it was easy to spot each other. They both wore the charity's navy blue polo shirt, Honeycomb emblem embossed on the left breast.

Dan introduced himself. They shook hands and Dan admitted he'd clocked Alex's passenger and the unusual alighting process in the drop-off bay. "That's independence. Did he come by himself?"

Alex's tone was full of admiration. "You bet he did. No escort or carer for Roy. Wants to do everything for himself, but he seems a great guy with a good sense of humour and thank goodness for that."

"What do you mean?"

Alex said he'd picked up two gentlemen that morning and asked them to sit in the back knowing Roy would need to sit in the front. He picked up Roy, and then a lady called Ruth.

Halfway to the Barrett Bailey, Ruth said, "I'm trying to work out who you remind me of, Roy."

Roy half turned his head, and a flicker of recognition crossed her face. "I know – my brothers. They were all big, impressive men, all farmers, handsome, with noble features. Not one of them stood less than six feet four. How tall are you, Roy?"

The men in the back cringed. Alex thought how best to alleviate the embarrassment. Ruth was a tad bewildered that her compliment sparked an awkward silence.

Eventually, Roy spoke. "Three feet, nine inches."

"Pardon?"

"Three feet, nine inches, but it's good to know I'm still impressive and handsome."

Alex intervened. He said Roy had lost one leg during the Falklands War, the other years later when chronic diabetes and the onset of gangrene resulted in a second amputation at the upper thigh. Ruth covered her open mouth, her face turning a fierce hue of crimson. If there had been a pothole big enough in the road she would have jumped into it. Roy sensed the discomfort and, like the impressive, handsome man he was, set about putting her at ease.

"Don't worry, love. I've heard a lot worse out of the mouths of children. Kids are always coming up to me in the street and asking, 'Mr, do you know you've lost your legs?' or 'Where have they put your legs?' or 'Are your legs under the blanket?'"

Dan chuckled at the story, but the image of Roy manoeuvring himself from the car and the over-developed muscles of his upper body taking the strain triggered flashback memories of Afghanistan, Iraq, and Syria. The sight of mutilated bodies had been a daily occurrence. In those places, legless men didn't warrant questions or interest from children.

The men chatted for half an hour. Alex said his wife, Sarah, had breast cancer five years before. She'd used the Honeycomb service then and was impressed by the professionalism and caring attitude of its staff, especially the drivers. When Alex took voluntary redundancy from his job in insurance, he'd contacted the organisers and waded through the rigorous application procedure and interview. He negotiated a driving test refresher and Highway Code exam, albeit with the odd flutter of apprehension, before completing a police crime check. Finally, he joined.

For the last two years, Monday was 'Honeycomb day', and Alex had to admit it was the best job he'd ever had. "I don't get paid a penny, but I've met many characters, lots of friendly, interesting people all with a fascinating tale to tell."

So far, Dan had met only Jaz, Trish, Bill, and Murph. *Interesting?* Yes, that was one word to describe them.

As usual, Jaz and Trish were first to finish their treatment. As they walked down the corridor, they heard the prolonged sound of a bell ringing and a spontaneous burst of applause from one of the waiting areas. They turned the corner and spotted a nurse hugging Andrew, white carrier bag in one hand, an unlit cigarette in the other. The Barrett Bailey prided itself on a charming custom that involved ringing out any patient on their last day who'd undergone 20 sessions or more. Andrew had completed treatment 25. He'd become something of a personality, mostly for his run-ins with security and the clanking of his cans.

The nurses queued to proffer their well-wishes.

"Look after yourself, Andrew."

"Make sure you don't forget to eat and keep drinking those protein shakes. You need to build yourself up."

"It's been lovely meeting you. Take care and try to cut down the cigs."

Andrew nodded shyly. His mouth broke into a wide, toothless grin as he shuffled along the corridor, applause sweeping after him. As he reached Trish, she stepped in front of him, stood on the tiptoes of her high heels and threw her arms around his neck. She could smell stale tobacco on his clothes and the alcohol vapour from his breath overpowered. Still, she pulled his emaciated body tight to hers.

"Fuck 'em all, Andrew," she whispered in his ear. "Don't listen. Have a fag whenever you want. Take a drink whenever you like. If you want some crack, then smoke some crack. It's your life, no one else's. Have a good one."

Trish released Andrew from her embrace. He gazed mischievously into her eyes and chuckled. An earthy, rib-shaking chuckle disturbed something deep, dark and tarry inside his lungs, sending him into a deep-seated paroxysm of coughing and drooling. Two concerned nurses strode towards him. He waved them away.

"I wish I'd met you before," he wheezed at Trish, wiping his mouth and nose on the sleeve of his jumper before shuffling to his waiting taxi.

"What on earth did you say to him?" asked Jaz.

"Oh, I told him to concentrate on the important things in life," said Trish, with a coy smile.

Fifteen minutes later, Bill and Murph were ready, and the foursome headed off to meet Dan, who'd brought the MPV round to the pick-up spot and sat waiting with the engine running.

They were leaving the hospital grounds when Trish announced, "I've decided."

"What, exactly?" said Dan.

"My bucket list."

"And? Don't keep us in suspense, Trish," Dan pressed.

"It involves everyone. I want us to climb a mountain."

"What?" said Dan.

"Are you joking?" said Jaz.

"You must have been drinking something stronger than Murph and me," added Bill, who looked much perkier.

Murph shook his head, crossed his arms, and shut his eyes.

"No, listen, hear me out," said Trish. "When the surgeon explained how I needed an operation and radiotherapy and chemo tablets, I distinctly remember him saying, 'It's going to be tough, Trish, you've got a mountain to climb.'"

"He didn't mean a *real* mountain," said Dan, emphasising real with a sarcastic lilt.

"I know he didn't, I'm not stupid, Dan, but that phrase stuck in my mind, and I thought, do you know what, if I get through this, that's what I'm going to do. Climb a mountain."

"In those heels?" said Bill. "Good luck. I'd pay

to watch."

"Of course not. I'll buy some boots and climb a mountain where I don't need ropes, irons and all that malarkey. I've decided on Mount Snowdon in Wales. I didn't think of it being on a bucket list earlier, but now it's perfect."

"When's all this going to happen?" said Jaz.

"That's where you lot come in. I want to do it a year today on July twentieth, and I want us all to meet at the summit at two in the afternoon."

"What? Plant a flag and say we've all beaten cancer?" said Bill.

"Something like that."

Trish said she'd been researching Snowdon on her phone in the waiting room, and the easy route up and down meant walking around seven miles. Anyone who felt they couldn't manage physically could take the train instead, which went all the way to the summit and dropped passengers off outside the café.

"Does it have any toilets?" said Murph.

Dan, Jaz, and Bill took Murph's question as a joke.

"The café does, Murph, I'm not sure about the train," said Trish. "What do you reckon? I think it's a great idea. I mean, we can't all sail the Atlantic or just rock up at Cape Canaveral or even get to the Sistine Chapel, but Snowdon is only a few hours away."

There was an awkward silence, and Trish's balloon-ride of excitement appeared in danger of deflating as her gaze flitted from face to face and struggled to find support.

Jaz, recognising that this bucket list plan, however madcap, meant the world to Trish, was first to man the pump. "Count me in. It'll give me a target to aim for and an incentive to get out, do some proper exercise and a reason to catch up with you lot. We've known each other a week, but I'm going to miss you when this is over."

"Okay, count me in too." Dan's tone suggested he wasn't convinced.

Bill reluctantly agreed to be there 'if he was still breathing,' but only if Trish promised to see him at the London Palladium. She agreed. He also insisted he would be taking the train. In that case, Murph said he'd do the same.

"Brilliant. That's it then," said Trish. "July twentieth. Two pm. A year today. Don't tell anyone else and we won't speak of it again. It will be our secret pact. It's exciting. Touch on it."

Trish extended her right hand to the back of the driver's seat, alongside the headrest. Jaz reached over and clasped. Reluctantly, Murph and Bill laid their hands to the pile.

"Come on, Dan, you too. It's not a pact if we don't all clasp," said Trish.

Dan rolled his eyes but took the wheel with his left hand and joined the rest of the hands with his right. He thought Trish's idea was cheesy, wishful thinking, a terrible cliché as well as a bit bonkers. He was almost certain the ascent of

FRANK MALLEY

Snowdon would never happen but was he going to tell Trish? Not bloody likely.

12

On his way home, Dan called at Ernie's. The car wash was relatively quiet – no sign of Barcelona Boy. Two or three young lads were cleaning hoses and washing down the Perspex cover over the large revolving brushes. A lady customer battled with the suction pipe on the industrial vacuum trying to suck up months of debris in the allotted four minutes before the coin slot gobbled another pound.

Dan could see Gheorghe sitting in the back of the little office smoking a cigarette and talking on a landline phone. As he waited for the lads to clear their gear, Dan studied the site and was surprised at how far the steel perimeter fence extended. As well as the car wash area, there was a concrete and corrugated warehouse with big steel-shuttered doors. At its side, a collection of steel shipping containers. Dan counted eight in all, arranged in double-decker groups of two. Like four oversized bunk beds, the bottom containers lay on cement blocks at each end, suspended about three feet off the ground. *Excessive storage space for a cut-price car wash.*

One of the lads waved Dan forward and soaped the MPV's alloy wheels. As the lad passed the driver's side, Dan recognised him as the older boy who had washed his car following the altercation the week before. He wound his window down.

"Hi," Dan grinned, putting his hand to his head to simulate pulling on a peaked cap. "Where's your friend? The one with the Barcelona cap?"

The lad lowered his head and averted his eyes. Dan couldn't be sure, but he sensed the lad glancing sideways to check whether Gheorghe was around.

"Not here. Nico go home." The lad spoke with a heavy accent.

"To Romania?" said Dan.

The lad nodded and moved on, clearly recognising Dan but not wanting to prolong the conversation. Another teenage attendant motioned Dan forward onto the belt that propelled vehicles through the wash cycle. The MPV moved through the rolling brushes and into the turbo air dryer, its fabric strips dancing across the windows like two feuding octopuses. When the car emerged, Dan saw Gheorghe only metres away, clutching the hair of one of the lads with his right hand and frogmarching him behind the shipping containers.

It was no more than a glimpse, and with water and the Perspex cover skewing his view Dan couldn't be sure, but it looked as though another beating was imminent. He strained his eyes. When visibility cleared the pair had disappeared, but Dan noticed something unusual. On the lower level in the back of the two central containers, someone had made a rough job of cutting two jagged holes and fitting doors into the metal. The same workman was responsible for the two closed window flaps, around two feet square.

By now, the car was alongside the exit board. Dan started the engine and within half an hour was back home sipping a refreshing iced lime juice cordial. He dialled Cathy Wheeler's number.

The call connected, and Cathy's name illuminated the screen. "Cathy, hi, what have you got for me?"

"Hello, how are you, too?" The tone was sarcastic. "I'm not your wingman here, Dan. I don't work for you. I said I'd keep you in the loop, that's all."

"Sorry, it's been a long day, and I'm anxious to hear your update. Honest. I appreciate you staying in touch."

"Okay." Cathy accepted the apology but still felt taken for granted. The remnants of her disappointment would take longer to fade.

"I can't tell you too much, except that the police believe the network is huge and the UK arm probably controlled by a man named Jimmy Collins. He's a dangerous guy, Dan. Works out of Belfast but maintains headquarters and safe houses all over. He's into running drugs, prostitution, bank jobs, human trafficking, you name it. Word is he's behind some of the big cybercrime hits over the past few years."

"Nice man."

"In a table of underworld badasses, he's Premier League. He hasn't done time, but police arrested him a few years back after the shooting of an undercover copper in the East End. Collins wriggled out of it because of mistaken identity. I understand his boys got to the only credible witness."

"Don't the cops have enough on him?"

"That's the problem. Collins keeps everything at arms' length. Any time the police, Customs and Excise or the taxman get too close, he sends in his *cleaners* to shut down the operation then concentrates elsewhere. His cleaners are some of the most ruthless villains you could run into. Most of them pack the latest weapons and aren't afraid to use them. Think the Kray twins, and you're close to the picture. My contact at the National Crime Agency told me there isn't a town in the UK Collins hasn't infiltrated."

Cathy adopted her concerned voice. *Soft. Low. Serious.* "And Dan, I'm told most of the fronts for his operation are nail bars, tattoo parlours, dirty coffee shops, and car washes."

"Don't worry, Cathy, if I see Jimmy Collins, I'll phone the cops and run in the opposite direction. I think my man's a bully who likes to slap around kids smaller than himself. In his case, all kids."

"Okay, Dan. Stay safe."

"You too, Cathy."

Dan ended the call. As he did, the ring tone trilled. It was Jaz, slight panic in her voice.

"Sorry to bother you, Dan, but I can't find my phone. Is it in the car by any chance? I remember rummaging in my handbag for a tissue and maybe put it down somewhere. I feel lost without my phone."

"You're in luck, Jaz, I haven't taken the car back to its parking spot yet. I'll pop down and have a look. Will call you back in five."

Dan picked up his keys, bounded two-at-a-time down the stairs of his apartment block and zapped the central locking. As he leant across to the passenger side where Jaz sat, he glimpsed a familiar face through the window on the other side of the road. *Jordan.* Dan knocked on the window. When Jordan didn't respond, Dan backpedalled out of the car and shouted across the street.

"Hey, Jordan, what are you doing around here?"

Jordan turned his head. He didn't show surprise at Dan's greeting but did raise a half-smile. "Just visiting a friend," he said, walking on and pointing to a row of Victorian terraced houses in front.

"Okay, see you," said Dan, perplexed at the antics of the petrol station worker-cum quiz champion-cum-all-round-awkward young man. *Wouldn't be the first time.*

Dan clambered back inside the car, checked the central console between the seats and searched underneath where a black phone could easily hide on the black upholstery. No luck. Fumbling in the side pocket of the passenger door, he found the phone – one of the slimmer, smaller models – amid a couple of pens, a discarded tissue, and a few petrol receipts.

He called Jaz's landline. "Panic over. I'm holding the phone in my hand," said Dan.

"Where was it?"

"In the side pocket of the passenger door. You would not believe who just walked past my flat. Only your mate Jordan."

"I hope you were nice to him."

13

A fragile Bill creaked and groaned as he slid into the MPV. "There are three bad things about growing old. Despite medication controlling the worst of Bill's symptoms, there was an increasing soreness to go with general tiredness, and it was only Thursday in the second week of treatment. He was sore when he walked, sore when lying down, sore when sitting. He was even sore when asleep because he kept waking up.

"Go on then, Bill, what are they?" said Trish. "This isn't a joke, is it?"

"I'm past joking, love. Number one is losing your memory."

Dan tapped Jaz on the arm, she looked at him, and he winked and moved his head to indicate Bill was reeling Trish in again. Bill paused and wriggled in his seat, trying to ease into a comfortable position. Trish moved sideways to give him more room.

"What are the other two bad things? Trish asked.

"I can't remember. "Didn't I tell you about number one?"

"Bill, you are a pain," said Trish.

"I know, a pain in the … oh, well, at last, we can laugh about it."

Thursday was review day, which meant seeing consultants who monitored progress. It was always a smart move to take someone else with you at such times if only to lend a second pair of ears. Most patients exit the consultant's room without asking the question they wanted to ask. The rest leave and can't remember what the consultant said. Bill was determined not to belong to either camp. He fished inside his jacket pocket then waved a piece of paper in the air.

"I have my crib sheet here. Last night, I wrote down ten questions, and I'm not leaving the consultant's office until I have answers to each one."

"Good for you," said Murph. "I should do something similar. I'm hopeless at remembering. There's so much going through your mind when seeing the consultant. I find myself thinking of my next question instead of listening to the answer to the question before. I used to be good at concentrating in such situations, but not now. It can be awfully confusing."

Dan slipped down the gears as the car approached the roundabout before the dual carriageway. He didn't realise there was a little test of his own around the corner. A Ford Fiesta had stopped on one of the roundabout's exit roads, half on the grass verge, half on the tarmac, hazard lights flashing. As Dan neared, he saw a woman at the wheel on her mobile phone.

An overtaking car squeezed past the MPV on the outside, and Dan braked and weaved around the Fiesta, studying the car's interior and the woman's demeanour before accelerating away.

"Why didn't you stop, Dan, you might have been able to help?" Jaz was concerned.

"And I might have added to the problem, Jaz. Look at the facts. She's in an awkward position, not the best place to break down, but she was probably on her phone calling for help. There were no kids or anyone else in the car that I could see, and she's not isolated. It's a busy roundabout, someone will be along, probably in the next minute or so to offer a hand. By the way, did I mention I have four cancer patients in my car?"

"I think I would have stopped," said Murph. "Poor woman might be sitting there hours."

"Me too," said Trish.

"I wouldn't," said Bill. "Dan's right – he summed it up nicely. What could a set of crocks like us have brought to the party? It's a job for the RAC. Good decision, Dan."

Decisions. Decisions. Cruising down the carriageway, Dan told his passengers about a work course he'd attended a few years earlier. Called Decisions, Decisions, it was designed to teach better decision-making under pressure. The course proved valuable in places such as Afghanistan and Iraq when life and death could depend on something as simple as whether you turned right or left. He'd learned that sometimes good decisions require a person to think outside the box.

"I've never understood that phrase," said Trish. "What is the box? Where is the box? What's inside the box? You need to know that, don't you before you can think outside the box?"

"Good point, Trish," said Jaz.

"Okay, let's try you with the bus stop test," Dan said.

"I'm not good at tests, Dan." Trish was immediately wary, but the test idea intrigued the others.

"Don't worry Trish, this is right up your street," said Dan. "Three people are standing at a bus stop in the pouring rain when you drive past in your car. None have umbrellas, all soaked to the skin. The first person is on his way to work – a dear, trusted friend who once saved your life. The second is the woman, or man, of your dreams. The third, an old lady, who you know has a terminal disease and needs to get to hospital fast. You have one spare seat. Who do you pick up?"

"Judging by what just happened, you wouldn't pick up anyone," said Trish, only half-joking. "You would have said, 'Don't worry, someone else will be along in a minute.'"

"Come on, Trish, that's not fair," said Dan.

"I would pick up the woman of my dreams," admitted Bill. "The other two would get sorted out eventually. It's only water, after all. If I missed meeting the woman of my dreams, I would regret that for a lifetime."

Murph expelled a heavy sigh. He was giving this conundrum serious thought. Among other things, Murph had been a psychiatrist and, as such, a man accustomed to a considered analysis of the human mind. In his working life, he prided himself on being able to distinguish the merely eccentric from those likely to walk into the nearest police station and claim they were Napoleon. His decisions were usually spot-on, although, on life issues, he invariably trod the middle path.

"Hmm, I think I would pick up the man who saved my life," Murph said. "I would feel bad about the old lady but have always thought loyalty is one of life's most heart-warming qualities. If someone saves your life, then you're in his or her debt forever, don't you think?"

There were no surprises with Trish and Jaz. Trish went for the man of her dreams. "I've been searching for him all my life. No chance he's slipping away this time."

Jaz went for the old lady. She reasoned the other two would understand and said she wouldn't have been able to sleep at night if she'd left the oldest and most vulnerable to fend for herself.

"Two going for love, one for loyalty and another opting for compassion," said Dan.

"What if we could combine all those? You might have the man of your dreams then, Trish."

"What about you, Dan. Who did you go for?" said Trish.

"I thought you'd decided I was speeding past the bus stop with two fingers in the air."

"No. Come on, you know I didn't mean that."

"Well, if you must know, the first time I heard the bus stop test, I chose the woman of my dreams."

Jaz narrowed her eyes and knitted her brow. "Oh, did you?" she said. Dan couldn't determine whether she was impressed or disappointed. On balance he opted for the latter. "And who would that be?"

Dan smiled, letting Jaz's question hang in the air.

"We had to find a scenario that pleased everyone," Dan continued. "Think outside the box the tutor kept saying."

"What, like stick one of them in the boot?" said Trish. "I don't think it should be the old lady. Better still, stick two in the boot."

"That's a suggestion, Trish, and don't think people didn't think of that but there's no room in the boot. It's probably full of your shoes."

"What's the answer, Dan?" said Bill.

Dan modestly admitted he wrestled with the problem for some hours before finally cracking the problem.

"Stop at the bus stop."

That's a good start," interjected Trish.

Dan ignored her. "Hand the car keys to the trusted friend who'd saved my life and ask him to take the sick old lady to hospital on his way to work. I stay at the bus stop to catch the bus with the woman of my dreams. Oh, yes, I also remember to take an umbrella out of the car boot. That way, we don't get wetter."

"Brilliant," said Trish.

"*That is lateral thinking,*" Jaz declared.

"Come on, who is this woman of your dreams?" Bill asked, picking up Jaz's theme.

Jaz turned sideways to observe Dan's reaction.

"Never you mind," said Dan, with a teasing smile.

Apart from usual Highway Code protocol, no more decisions presented themselves before Dan turned into the Barrett Bailey. He took his time parking the car, even went to the ambulance bay at the back of the hospital to use the hose and attachments. The vehicle wasn't dirty, after all, he'd been to Ernie's on Monday, but somewhere along the way, a pair of doves had left their mark on the bonnet and headlights.

Dan headed to the hospital's central concourse and browsed the varied line of shops, including a travel agent. *Who on Earth went to hospital, either as patient or visitor, and booked a holiday?* He popped into Pret a Manger, bought a meal deal – sandwich, drink, and carrot cake – and headed back to the drivers' room. On the way,

Dan passed the ice-blue waiting room wall, its eclectic artwork quite famous among frequent flyers at the Barrett Bailey. He admired the cartoon of American biologist James Watson and English physicist Francis Crick, entwined together in the artist's impression of the double helix structure representing the defining image of their pioneering work on DNA.

He studied the portraits of medical men, Alexander Fleming, Joseph Lister, and Louis Pasteur, while a more recent but rather less iconic crooked sign proclaimed:

STATISTICALLY ... 9 OUT OF 10 INJECTIONS ARE IN VEIN

Evidently, the wall's decorator possessed a sense of humour. The centrepiece print intrigued Dan – *No. 5 by Jackson Pollock*. He sat down, unwrapped his sandwich, and consulted Google on his phone.

"Holy Moses," Dan muttered. The article revealed the original senseless splatter of brown and yellow paint was once the world's most expensive painting. Pollock's unique mode of abstract expressionism involved pacing around his canvas laid out on the ground. He would drip or fling paint from brushes, sticks, and basting syringes. This signature technique dubbed him 'Jack the Dripper'. Dan vaguely remembered learning about the abstract expressionist movement during his art course in the 1980s.

Slipping his phone back in his pocket and taking a bite of sandwich, Dan smiled at the memory the painting triggered. *The last time he'd seen paint dripping down a wall and how his wife, sweet and beautiful Annie, had laughed when he told her.* The couple hadn't been married long and were still in the process of redecorating their new house. Arriving home in the early hours from a late reporting shift, Dan slid his key into the front door so as not to wake Annie. Illuminated by a shaft of moonlight streaming through the glass panel, he spotted a glint of red paint on the wall to his right.

DIE it said in foot-high letters. Terror raced through his mind. He threw the door wide, stumbling across the front step, imagination jump-starting into serial-killer mode. As he screamed Annie's name, moonlight flooded into the rest of the shadowy hallway to reveal a final blood-red T transforming the word into DIET. Nothing more sinister than Annie's aide-memoire to lose a few pounds after the festive excesses. Still smiling, Dan sauntered back to the drivers' room to find Jaz and Trish. They'd completed their treatment and seen their consultant in 40 minutes.

"How did it go?" said Dan.

"Fine," said Jaz. "No problems. He's pleased with how everything looks."

"Me too," said Trish.

The trio sat at a table in the corner where a

half-completed communal jigsaw puzzle of John Constable's *The Hay Wain* sat. Jaz concentrated on trying to find the missing piece for one of the cart's wheels, Trish was intent on completing the canopy of a large tree.

"Isn't it a beautiful painting?" said Jaz. "Calm, natural, real. I remember studying the piece in art class at school. Can't say I remember much about the work. All I remember is Constable had seven children and raised them himself after his wife died of tuberculosis aged forty-one. That can't have been easy at the turn of the nineteenth century."

"How sad," said Trish. "What do you think he would say if he could see us now, pushing around pieces of wood and putting together a copy of the picture he painted all those years ago?"

"The world's gone mad, probably," said Jaz. "No, I think he would be quite proud. Most things in life fade in value and popularity as they age. But inspired works of art do the opposite. They gain in reputation. Two centuries on, people all over the world recognise this painting as a masterpiece. It's a pity dear old John isn't around to see us deriving pleasure from his talent."

Murph shuffled down the corridor reporting that his progress update was satisfactory although he'd suffered a bit of a shock.

"What do you mean?" said Dan.

"I saw Professor Carling – first time I've met the man."

Murph had heard from a few patients that the internet described the professor as a brilliant, world-renowned expert in his field. Murph also learned that Carling was a mite eccentric. He wore a pair of spectacles pushed high above his hairline but never seemed to use them and was also a practical joker as well as being somewhat brusque. Still, Murph concluded brusque and brilliant were infinitely preferable to user-friendly and useless. As his story developed, Murph polished his spectacles with his tie.

"When he walked into the cubicle, he was cradling a blue folder in his arms," Murph said. "He seemed preoccupied, looked at his notes then at me then back at his notes and back at me again. He reminded me of a vicar narrating a church reading. Then he glared at me and just came out with it."

Jaz and Trish had broken off from the jigsaw to listen.

"What did he say?" said Jaz.

"There's no point beating about the bush, Mr Murphy, you *are* going to die."

"Oh, Murph, how horrible."

"I have to say, my heart missed a beat, but then he said, "We all are. We're all going to slip off this mortal coil one day but not today, nor this week, this month, or this year. God willing, not for many years to come."

Professor Carling then informed Murph that his scans were sound, and his prostate problem appeared under control.

"What did you say to him?" said Jaz.

"Nothing at first. I saw the silly grin on his face and thought of all the people I'd met who are committed to helping the sick and disabled. All the people who've helped me or patients like me, who are saving the world in their own way and been wonderful. Then I thought of a phrase I'd never uttered before."

Trish's mouth was open, eyes wide anticipating what might have passed Murph's lips for the first time. "I would have called him a complete bastard."

Murph fiddled with his glasses and to Trish's disappointment, said, "But I didn't say what I was thinking. It wouldn't have been kind. I said, 'You don't know what that means to me. Thank you, doctor.'"

By the time Bill showed his face an hour later, *The Hay Wain's* cart was fully operational, and the trees had grown. Bill's report wasn't so positive. The consultant was concerned about the soreness and symptoms he was experiencing. His choices were, plough on with treatment and manage the symptoms or take a break followed by a lower dose of radiation over a longer period.

"What did you decide?" said Jaz.

"I thought outside the box. I said I'd skip tomorrow, take a long weekend break before starting again on a lower dose. I might have to do an extra week, but that's better than how I'm feeling now."

It sounded to Jaz as if that thinking came from deep inside the box, the consultant's box, but she let it pass and said, "Good for you."

The journey home was unremarkable and quiet, apart from Murph's snoring. They passed the Ford Fiesta at the roundabout, no longer on the road but lying at an awkward angle on the grass verge awaiting recovery. There was no sign of the driver. She was probably at work, cursing her luck, wondering how she was going to pay for the repairs.

Dan dropped off Bill, Trish and Murph and made for Meadow Drive when Jaz asked if he would mind dropping her off at her parents' house instead.

"No problem. Give me directions."

"Thanks, Dan. Left here. Left again, then right. Straight on, just past that row of shops, there's a lay-by. You can pull in there."

Dan brought the car to a halt in the tree-lined road outside a semi-detached house, with a small wall and tiny garden behind a metal swing gate. On one side of the driveway, a tidy row of marigolds stood to attention, on the other, vibrant geraniums in white and purple provided colour and life to the entrance. A slate nameplate by the door read Three Jays. Built in the 1930s, the building was a typical Lexford house. Sturdy, well maintained, and unpretentious, lace curtains hanging at the attractive bay windows. A shade old-fashioned perhaps, yet oozing pride and wholehearted values.

"Thanks, Dan," Jaz said, opening the passenger door. "Hey, come in and have a cup of tea. Mum would love to meet you."

Dan couldn't think of a good reason to turn down the invitation. Jaz led him up the short driveway and turned a key in the lock of the heavy white door. Although she looked barely 60, a petite lady in her early seventies greeted them. She had grey hair brushed back in a neat bun and wore an apron tied in a butterfly bow around her waist. The aroma of freshly baked scones chased her down the hallway as she emerged from the kitchen.

Her face lit up when she saw Jaz. "Jasmine! How lovely to see you."

"Mum, this is Dan. He's the gentleman I told you about. The one who takes me to hospital."

"Come and sit down, Dan. You must have a cup of tea and a scone. You like scones, don't you?"

Dan grinned and nodded.

"Is the Pope Catholic?" he said, immediately wishing he'd thought of a response that didn't sound so tired and predictable.

He wandered over to a solid mahogany cabinet and eyed a collection of photographs in silver frames. One of Jaz with a toothy grin in her school uniform. Another of Jaz surrounded by emus, which Dan took to be part of her Australian adventure. The biggest photo pictured Jaz on a cruise liner with her parents and there was another of Jaz with a young man acting out the famous scene from *Titanic* on the prow of the ship – arms wide, hair blowing in the wind. Happy photographs. Fun times.

The back door swung open. A tall, broad man with a shuffling, stooped gait, grabbed the door frame and struggled up the step from the garden. Jaz's dad, looking nearer 80 than 70. His head was bald, but grey hair at the sides had grown long and wispy, giving an unkempt, slightly feral appearance.

He studied Dan. "Who the fuck are you?"

"Pardon?" said Dan.

"Another one of her fucking boyfriends, I suppose. Not much of a looker, are you? Ugly bastard."

The hairs on Dan's neck bristled. Gritting his teeth, he glanced at Jaz. Her lips were tight, eyes sheepish. She looked at her mum, who took her husband's arm and coaxed him into a conservatory at the back of the house.

"Come on, Jack, I'll bring you a scone and a cup of tea, and you can watch the birds playing in the birdbath."

"Fucking birds. Been shitting all down these windows, Joyce. Do you never clean up around here? Lazy bitch. Looks like a fucking shithouse."

Joyce closed the conservatory door.

"Sorry, Dan, I should have warned you. Dad

usually goes to the respite centre on Thursdays. I didn't think he'd be here."

Dan learned Jack suffered from a rare form of dementia. Pick's disease, caused by atrophy to the frontal lobe of the brain, created symptoms including incessant swearing, extreme rudeness, and disinhibition. Joyce first noticed a problem when Jack demonstrated memory lapse and slurred speech. He had moments of indecision too, becoming irritated when he couldn't find a pen, even though one was under his nose. At other times, he would switch off in mid-conversation and be insensitive to the nuances of people's body language. He would laugh inappropriately on occasion or call out in the middle of Sunday's church service they used to attend. Children would turn, giggle and point Jack out to their parents. Embarrassing, although Joyce never let it show.

When driving, Joyce noticed Jack would become agitated over trivial issues. He would blast the horn for no reason, and even simple parking manoeuvres assumed a complexity neither of them relished. Also, he failed to see other motorists to the side of him. That was worrying, although by far the worst aspect of Jack's condition was his temper. His conversation used to be forceful. Now, there was the risk he might turn violent if contradicted.

"Your poor mum," said Dan. "That must be tough to live with."

Jaz nodded. "She's brilliant with him, though – the only one who can distract him or calm him down. If it weren't for her, he would have been in a care home long ago. To be honest, he could be irritable before the disease took hold. I remember him swearing when football was on or if he banged his knee or stubbed a toe, but it was never personal or rude. I always remember him being smart and funny when I was a child. He would make me laugh."

"Is he always like that now? You know, rude?"

"Sometimes there are glimpses of the dad I remember, and I pretend that he's back to normal, but not as often anymore. You hear of some forms of dementia erasing the whole person. Not Dad. He's still recognisable at times as the clever, considered man Mum married, but most of the time he's a cruel caricature of irritability with uncontrolled mood swings no one can predict."

"Poor mum," repeated Dan.

Joyce bustled back into the room, wiping her hands on her apron. No mention of Jack. "Time for scones and that cup of tea." She headed into the kitchen.

The scones were heavenly. Still warm, so the butter melted, fluffy and full of juicy sultanas. They reminded Dan of those his mum used to bake when he was a boy when he'd beg to lick the bowl and end up with a face full of gooey mess.

"Magnificent scones, Mrs Sharkey." Dan raised

the remnants of one to his lips before licking his fingers.

"Glad you approve. You've been so kind. I don't know what Jasmine would have done without you looking after her. It's a wonderful service you work for. More tea?"

"No, thanks, I should be on my way. I have some paperwork to catch up on, and I need to give my bike an overhaul." Dan motioned to Jaz. "I can drop you off at your place on the way if you like."

Jaz nodded and picked up her handbag. She gave Joyce a hug and a kiss and said she'd see her again on Sunday to help look after Dad.

Dan and Jaz walked to the front door as a muted bellow emanated from the back of the house.

"Little fucking shits!"

14

The journey to Meadow Drive took five minutes, the incident with Jaz's dad stuck in Dan's mind throughout. *How depressing.* Losing someone to dementia was bad enough, but when that person's personality changed through no fault of their own, that was cruel. Cruel to everyone. Victim, family, and carers alike.

Dan pulled up outside Jaz's house and killed the engine.

"Can I ask you something, Jaz? You don't have to answer."

"Of course."

"Actually, there are two things."

"Okay."

"Why have you never married? You're a good-looking woman. Vivacious, funny, smart. You must have had loads of boyfriends. All the guys that go through the petrol station, you must be fighting them off."

Jaz accepted the compliments with a coy glance and demure smile, which Dan took to mean she was flattered.

"I don't know about loads, but you're right, a few customers have asked me out. There was one chap only a couple of months ago. He kept coming in and talking to me. I didn't fancy him and didn't know what to say. He was insistent. 'Why won't you go out with me? I've got money, a nice car and a good job,' he'd say. He wouldn't take no for an answer, and I didn't want to tell him about this." She pointed to her breasts. "Cancer, I mean."

"How did you get rid of him?" said Dan.

"No. I can't tell you."

"Go on."

"No, honestly. It's awful. I'm ashamed." Jaz shook her head, half chuckling as she recalled the incident. "I can't believe I did what I did. You wouldn't like me if I told you."

"Come on. Can't be that bad."

Jaz held her breath as if teetering on the edge of a high board, ready to dive into the deep end. She jumped. "He'd been in about five times that week. No one needs that much petrol. Each time, he asked me to go out with him or explain why not. 'Give me a reason,' he'd say. 'Just give me a reason.' I snapped and screamed, 'Are there no mirrors in your house?' The other customers were staring at him, and he looked stunned. He turned and strode out without saying anything, and I've never seen him since. I feel bad about it. I'm ashamed."

"Jasmine Sharkey," said Dan, feigning a shocked tone, "you've probably scarred him for life. There's a decent guy out there with a good job, nice car and lots of love to give and now, he thinks he's the Elephant Man."

"I know," said Jaz, collapsing into infectious giggles. "I told you it was bad."

Jaz's mock attempts at remorse triggered another convulsion. Before they knew it, the couple were laughing like drains, Dan wheezing, tears springing from Jaz's eyes, falling off her cheeks and soaking her thin blouse as she rocked back and forth. She dug inside her handbag, pulled out a wad of tissues and passed half to Dan. He blew his nose and wiped blurry eyes. When his vision cleared, he looked at Jaz and exploded into another wave of giggles.

"What?" said Jaz.

"Look at you," gasped Dan, pulling down the passenger sunshade to point out the vanity mirror.

Jaz glanced up and squinted through watery eyes. *A sight straight from a horror movie.* Smudged mascara revealed big panda eyes and two black-purple rivers of tears cascaded down her face. "What do I look like?" She sucked in a deep breath to calm herself, grabbed a make-up remover pad from her bag and dabbed away the smudges.

"You haven't answered the question, though, Jaz. Why did you never marry?"

"It's a long story, Dan. I suppose in a way part of it is also the reason why I am working in a dead-end job in a supermarket petrol station."

"That was my second question," said Dan.

Jaz took another deep breath. If this had

been one of her workmates, she would have cut and run for the hills long ago. Jasmine Sharkey resembled Dan in that respect – she did not share her problems. She dealt with her feelings and emotions, her business, no one else's. Heaven knows, there'd been times when all she wanted to do was scream her frustrations from the rooftops. She never did, always charting the middle course. Settled for the safe option, took the considered view.

"Isn't Jaz always bright and happy," everyone always said, and she went along with the stereotype. Full of fun, always smiling, asking questions and interested in other people's lives. Never pushing herself forward, the one whom people confessed their innermost thoughts and anxieties to. Yet here she stood in the middle of a battle for her health, maybe even her life. These past few months, she had never felt more alone or more vulnerable. Perhaps the time was ripe to let someone in. Maybe that person was Dan.

"Straight after university, I wanted a year out. I needed one," said Jaz. "I'd graduated from Durham with a first-class degree in English and history, and I'd worked hard. I loved the course. Adored reading Jane Austen, the Brontës and the wonderful, romantic poets. I used to revise for exams listening to Oasis. I still remember the words to all their hits.

"It was a wonderful time, but after all that mental work I yearned for adventure. I was twenty-one. I wanted to see the world, do something different. When I saw an advert on the Uni's notice board offering twelve months' work on a farm in Australia, I jumped at the chance. I knew next to nothing about animals, but within weeks of landing in Sydney I was tanned, fit, my hair bleached, hands calloused, and I'd learned more about life than I had in three years at Durham. It was invigorating."

Twelve months later, Jaz knew the subtle differences between Australian beef breeds as well as most nuances of the emu. What's more, she'd won respect and admiration of experienced farmers. Her boss offered an apprenticeship. She turned it down.

"Why?" said Dan.

Jaz paused, lips tightening. "Not sure. Not even now. Probably because Australia's so far from home and I missed Mum. And also because of David."

"Is he the guy in the picture?" said Dan, backing a hunch. "The guy in the *Titanic* pose?"

Jaz nodded. She had met David on Manly Beach on a glorious summer day when the Pacific Ocean breakers thundered in. He'd taught her to bodyboard in perfect surf then introduced her to the laid-back bars and nightlife, a thousand miles from the hustle and bustle of Sydney. Jaz chuckled as the memories began to rush to the surface. Fresh and vibrant.

"He wasn't Australian. He was from Stoke-on-

Trent, a place called Burslem. He had a drawly, Midlands accent and worked as a waiter to fund a gap year, doing nothing other than indulging his yearning for the surf. He was passionate about surfing. He'd learned as a teenager on family holidays in Cornwall."

Jaz shook her head and giggled as another memory sliced through the fog of time. "He could lie on Manly or Bondi beach for hours at a time. Sand in his hair, cigarette dangling from his lips, a can of lager cradled in his hand. Under the blue sky with the sun burning down, I would hear him chuckling and knew what was coming next."

"What?"

"Without fail he would say, 'People say nothing is impossible, Jaz, but I do nothing every day.'"

Dan smiled.

"I thought he was clever," said Jaz. "I never realised until years later that he'd borrowed that phrase from AA Milne. But that was David. Confident. Charming. Irresistible. Well-read, too, but so lazy. Always took the easy route from A to B."

"But you fell for him big time by the sound of it," said Dan.

Jaz nodded and described David's striking looks. Chips of blue ice for eyes, blond hair bleached by a combination of the summer sun and lemon juice applied each evening. She worked on the farm all week and once a month came down to enjoy idyllic weekends with him in Manly. "It was little short of a year in paradise. I would have stayed, but David wanted to go home. He felt obliged to offer support to his parents embroiled in a messy divorce."

Jaz's misty eyes looked across at Dan. "I thought we would get married, have two children, a boy and a girl and live in a thatched cottage in Devon or Dorset, with a dog, probably a golden retriever. Roses around the door. It didn't happen. Instead, David became a fireman in London, and I went to work for the Foreign and Commonwealth Office in Whitehall. At first, the work was routine but after promotion, I gave practical and emotional help to British families affected by murder and manslaughter overseas. It was stimulating and fulfilling, and I was good at my job, Dan."

Jaz's tone was earnest, and Dan nodded in agreement. He could imagine Jaz empathising with victims.

"I loved my job, I loved David. We lived in a neat little rented flat in Battersea. The only problem was London's silly property prices. The flat cost the same per month as what I had earned in a year in New South Wales."

"What happened?" said Dan. "What went wrong?"

"Good question. I still don't know. We didn't fall out. I realised we wanted different things.

He was happy to come home and drink beer and play his guitar and watch another video night after night, not that there's anything wrong in that. After nearly nine years, it seemed that I was redundant in my own house. I felt superfluous. Matters got to a stage where all I longed for was work because that's where I felt valued. Where I felt most loved."

Jaz's bottom lip trembled, wondering whether picking at old sores was a good idea. She bit back the emotion and continued. "Things came to a head when I asked David how committed he was to our relationship. Do you know what he said?"

"What?"

"About seventy-five per cent," said Jaz, a tremor in her tone. "That's seventy-five fucking per cent," she repeated, using the F-word for the first time since Dan had met her. Somehow, the word didn't suit, unlike Trish. The F-word fitted Trish as snugly as designer heels but stumbled from Jaz's lips as if wearing hiking boots.

"Seventy-five per cent is what you're pleased to score in a maths test. It's how many young people voted to remain in the EU in the referendum. Three-quarters when expressed as a fucking fraction. Seventy-five per cent is not a commitment. It might as well be zero."

Jaz's voice had risen an octave, fire and a haunting melancholy in her eyes.

"I never came close to seventy-five per cent in a maths test. Most I ever got was fifty per cent. I was useless at maths," was all Dan could say.

Jaz looked at Dan and chuckled, appreciating his attempt to lighten the mood. The pain drained from her face, and she continued her story. "We split up not long afterwards."

"Sorry," said Dan.

"Don't be. It was for the best. I took on a new flatmate, a woman I worked with at the FCO. She spent an absurdly long time in the shower and even longer applying hideous crimson nail varnish to fingers and toes. Then she'd totter half-dressed into the lounge and without fail, announce, 'Nailed it.' She could be annoying but made me laugh. At last, I no longer felt trapped in my own home. I knew then I'd made the right decision."

Dan learned that a couple of years later, Jaz's father showed the early signs of dementia. At first, she took the 50-mile train journey home as often as she could to lend a hand with his care. Often four times a week.

When doctors diagnosed Pick's disease with more attentive care required, Jaz decided to leave the Foreign Office and return home to Lexford.

"That's how I ended up at the petrol station. It doesn't tax the grey cells like Whitehall, and I no longer enjoy the odd trip to places such as Yangon and Islamabad, but I work fixed hours and meet lots of people. What about you, Dan? What's your story?"

Dan looked at his watch. "Crikey, is that the

time? We've been chattering for more than an hour. I should be going. I have a bike to service."

"Oh, no, you don't. At least give me the bullet points to Dan Armitage's life in five minutes. You can fill in the details another time."

And that's what Dan did, firing off the milestones of his life in machine-gun fashion. "Studied politics and sociology at Manchester University. Started work at the *Lexford Journal*, went to *the Guardian* and *the Daily Mirror* before joining *the Daily News* and becoming the chief foreign correspondent.

"Married Annie when I was twenty-four. She was beautiful, clever, kind, generous and died at twenty-eight when struck on her way home from work by a high-powered sportscar stolen by a drugged-up loser. She was six weeks' pregnant at the time. She never got the chance to tell anyone. The killer got six years. I spent the last twenty years covering wars in Iraq, Afghanistan, and Syria and still blame myself for the death of my best friend."

Dan surprised himself, especially with the last bullet point, which slithered out on the back of the rest. Jaz reached over, slipped her hand into his and squeezed. *Soft. Gentle. Compassionate.*

"Oh, Dan, I'm sorry. I didn't realise. I shouldn't have … I wish I'd never …"

"No worries, Jaz. It's okay. Better out than in. I should be going. See you tomorrow morning."

Jaz climbed out of the car and waved.

Dan gunned the accelerator to the floor, the tyres spinning violently, searching for grip. Much like his mind.

15

The sound resembled a swarm of angry bees – bzzz, bzzz, pop, pop, bzzz, bzzz.

"Heads down!" Farez Osman yanked on the steering wheel. The jeep swerved off the road and careered down a dip, fishtailing from side to side, heading for lower ground to escape the hail of bullets.

Dan's left shoulder rammed into a metal stay with such force his upper left side went numb. His head smashed against the roll bar and a canine tooth sliced through his lip. The jeep halted, and the coppery taste of blood hit the back of Dan's throat and streamed down his chin. Instinctively, his right hand ran down his left side to check for wounds. None.

"Are you okay, Faz?" Dan asked.

Dan's driver, interpreter and loyal, trusted friend threw a wide grin and saluted. "All good, boss."

"How about you, Lance?" Dan said.

"I think we can safely say it's started." Riding with the bags in the back, Lance James growled. "Some birthday this is."

Three days before, a United States airstrike had destroyed parts of the Presidential Palace in Baghdad. The day after, coalition forces from the United States and Britain had launched an incursion into Basra Province from their holding area on the Iraq-Kuwait border. Today was 23rd March 2003, Lance's 36th birthday and the US 2nd Marine Expeditionary Brigade had chosen to celebrate by launching the Battle of Nasiriyah in the first brutal days of the invasion of Iraq.

Unknown to Dan and his jeep, that morning a US Army supply convoy from the 507th Maintenance Company veered off Highway 8, turning onto Highway 7 towards the city and into enemy territory. Lost and disorientated 18 US vehicles drove into an ambush, attracting enemy fire from all directions. Pinned down, the American troops took casualties from small arms, rocket-propelled grenades (RPGs), mortars, and tanks.

Trundling down Highway 16, Dan's jeep, bearing PRESS logos on every visible surface, drove straight into the eye of the firestorm at the intersection with Highway 7. Rather than coordinated shots, the missiles were stray bullets, but there was no way of knowing. Faz jumped out of the jeep, scrambled up the bank and lay down at the side of the highway, fumbling for his binoculars. It was mid-afternoon, 27 degrees Celsius and a red dust haze settled on the horizon.

"What's the score?" said Dan, dabbing his mouth with a tissue as he crawled alongside Faz.

"Looks like we're in the middle of a holy shit

storm," said Faz, who hailed from Lebanon and was fluent in six languages, including Arabic and Kurdish.

Dan met Faz as an undergraduate at Manchester University. As students, they played football for the same team, drank beer together and regularly solved world problems into the early hours. They became good friends, so close that when Dan married Annie, he chose Faz as his best man. They'd teamed up together in Afghanistan as Farsi was another of Faz's linguistic talents then Iraq as the search for Saddam Hussein's elusive weapons of mass destruction began. Faz, a freelance, had secured interviews for Dan with Hans Blix, head of the United Nations Monitoring, Verification and Inspection Commission – on-the-record briefings, keeping Dan ahead of the news.

In the past few weeks, Faz was back on *the Daily News* payroll as Dan traversed parts of the country still routinely passable. Filing features on the growing refugee crisis and the increasing sabre-rattling by Saddam's generals. Faz, who delighted in telling everyone that his first name in Arabic meant 'An eloquent person' allowed Dan to probe the heart of the stories. Faz's permanent grin always lifted Dan's spirits. His sharp instincts and knowledge, as well as his linguistic skills, also kept Dan safe or as safe as possible in a war zone raked with confusion and misunderstandings.

Faz passed the binoculars to Dan as the crackle of gunfire and whine of artillery shells intensified.

"I wouldn't like to be down there," said Dan, who could see the flash of gunshots and shell smoke exploding in a valley about a mile away. "Whoever's on the receiving end of that shower of metal is taking a pasting."

"I'm not sure I want to be here watching," said Lance. "This feels too close for comfort."

"What do you reckon, Faz?" Dan asked.

Faz took the binoculars and scanned the field of fire, spotting a couple of abandoned Humvees and a heavy tactical truck smouldering in the distance. "Best guess is an American convoy has been ambushed. It looks like they're pinned down. Not much hope for them if help doesn't arrive soon."

"What about us?" said Dan.

Faz took a packet of sweets from his pocket, slipped one into his mouth and offered the pack to Dan and Lance. Both men declined.

Faz pointed at a mound of earth and rock. "We have two options. Either sit it out here and park the jeep out of sight behind those rocks, but that might mean staying here all night, not knowing who we might run into."

"Or?" said Dan.

"Make a dash for it – we're around four-hundred metres from the junction with Highway Sixteen. From there, we could retrace our tracks and take a detour around this little party. I think we could make it. That's the smart move."

Dan was torn. This was his first sight of action since the invasion began. He'd never felt happy as a war correspondent embedded with friendly forces, following orders, escorted everywhere, reporting third-hand news rather than what he'd seen. He hated the thought of becoming a mouthpiece for either side, peddling propaganda instead of rooting out the truth. Dan made decisions on his terms, not recklessly, always with due consideration for safety, always weighing risk and reward in the pursuit of the real story. That was why he was out here with free rein, following his nose for news. *The Daily News* had dubbed his dispatches, 'The Reports You Can Trust', an ideal Dan was determined to live up to.

Half a mile away, a brigade of soldiers from the most powerful military nation was taking a fearful beating in one of the first significant firefights of a war that many in Europe and the United States regarded as dubious, if not downright illegal. *That was a story.*

"I think we'll hang around and see what happens," said Dan, glancing across at Lance to gauge his reaction.

Lance nodded. "Okay, mate. We could fashion a front-page lead and an inside spread out of this."

"Or we could get ourselves killed," said Faz,

with a laconic grin meaning he was behind Dan whatever the decision.

Faz scrambled down the embankment and drove the jeep into the shadow of the rocks. Dan and Lance tightened straps on bulletproof vests, adjusted helmets and made sure PRESS bibs were visible. No side in war guaranteed safe passage for reporters and they were occasionally targeted. Still, press was an internationally-recognised word affording a measure of protection. For the next hour or so they waited and watched. Dan took photos with the zoom lens of his digital camera as the firefight intensified before them. A sandstorm blew, the sort that rolls in without warning in the Iraqi desert. Dan pulled his jacket around his neck and angled his head to avoid stinging sand grains. Visibility worsened. Dan and Lance squinted into the gloom as the battle wore on.

The rumble was sudden, disorientating. Faz felt the vibration first. The ground around shook and the view menacing when he glanced over his right shoulder. Four Iraqi tanks cut through the sand cloud and headed towards them, each with gun barrels trained in their direction. A brigade of infantrymen marched behind. It seemed as if the entire Iraqi Army was advancing and the three men were no more than 250 yards away.

Dan and Lance had the same thought. *Get the hell out.* Run for the jeep parked by the rocks 40 metres away.

Sensing his urge to flee, Faz put his arm across Dan's chest. "Too late. Run now, and they'll shoot as sure as eggs is eggs."

Faz's dubious grammar and use of English clichés in a Lebanese accent was one of his many engaging qualities, always making Dan smile.

"Eggs *are* eggs," scolded Dan.

"Are you sure?" said Faz.

"Who gives a flying shit?" said Lance. "We're done for, eggs or no eggs."

Faz slid down the bank, put both hands in the air and ambled towards the leading tank. Dan and Lance followed. The tank commander's head and torso appeared from the hatch, and he shouted in Arabic. At the same time, several Iraqi soldiers surrounded the three men, guns raised.

"Tell him we're press, neutral and have a right to report both sides of the conflict," said Dan.

"Funny. I was just about to tell him to get out of his tank, or we would shoot. What do you think I'm going to say?"

A short exchange in Arabic followed then, using rifles, six soldiers prodded Dan and Lance in the back ushering them towards the rear of the tank.

"What's going on?" said Dan, his tone more affronted than frightened.

"They want us out of here and into one of their armoured vehicles," said Faz. "I said we had our own jeep, thank you, we didn't need a lift, but we don't have a choice."

The tanks rumbled past followed by six trucks and around 150 troops. A soldier directed Dan and Lance to one of the armoured vehicles and bundled Faz into another. The tanks continued towards the firefight, the sandstorm lifted as quickly as it had begun and the three armoured vehicles turned right onto Highway 7 towards Nasiriyah. Minutes later, the leading armoured vehicle exploded in a cloud of flames and smoke.

Faz's vehicle swung to the left to avoid shrapnel. Dan and Lance's driver followed, and as they lurched sideways down the embankment, Dan caught sight of the A-10 Tankbuster silhouetted against the blue sky in a gap of the weakening sandstorm. The sight was familiar to Dan and Lance. The A-10 had forged a reputation in Afghanistan for its ability to attack tanks, armoured vehicles, and buildings as well as giving close air support to ground forces. A pugnacious aircraft – nicknamed the Warthog or Flying Gun. Ugly on the eye, packing a deadly punch.

"Tankbuster!" Dan yelled.

"Oh, fuck. The cavalry's arrived at last. Trust us to be on the wrong side when it does," Lance said.

The Iraqi drivers clicked into panic mode. They could take refuge behind a mound of earth and rock to their left but instead, headed for the cover of the sandstorm rolling 500 metres ahead. The pilot in the A-10 banked to his right and turned to make another pass. Soldiers in the armoured vehicles, many of them teenagers, screamed orders, others wailed prayers in Arabic, and the drivers accelerated. The scene turned into a race against time and plane. Land versus air. Two hundred metres to go – 100, 50, 25 metres.

Lance was thrown to the floor of the vehicle as it careered on its frantic path. Dan clung to the ledge of one of the slit windows and saw the vapour trail of the Maverick air-to-surface missiles exiting their pods on the Tankbuster.

"Incoming!" screamed Dan, though Lance was the only one who understood what he said.

With a thunderous explosion, accompanied by a fearsome tearing of metal and a stench of petrol fumes, the missiles hit. The armoured vehicle ahead of Dan lifted clean into the air. Dan saw six spinning wheels, watched the frame disintegrate in mid-air as shrapnel, weapons, and body parts flew in every direction. Seconds before black smoke and a raging inferno consumed the vehicle Dan saw a face at the rear slit window. A surreal image. Faz, eyes wide open in horror, mouth fixed in that stupid grin.

Dan screamed. A visceral, prolonged howl of agony and despair. "Faz. Faz. Faaz!"

Dan's lungs began to burst and burn as they filled with toxic pollutants. There was blackness. Stillness. Warmth. Then came the bangs. Deep in the limbic system of his brain, something told Dan the sound was the guns of a Cobra helicopter. *Pop ... pop ... pop.* They were coming to finish the job. He tried to lever his body on one of his elbows, needed to keep moving. The first law of the battlefield – escape the line of fire. He had to live. Then Dan heard a familiar voice, muffled, distant, but increasingly anxious.

"Dan. Dan. Are you all right, Dan?"

Bang! Pop ... pop. *Oh, God, no!* Dan's heart hammered to the beat of the bangs. Blood pounded in his ears, and the voice drifted away. His feet tingled – every breath hurt as if he'd run a marathon. He could smell sweat, taste salt. His mind fizzed. Move, and he might die. Don't move, and he would die for sure. *Help!* He screamed, but no sound came.

He heard the voice again, "Dan, Dan."

Then his eyes opened, expecting to see acrid smoke and whirring Cobras against the blue sky of Nasiriyah. Instead, he saw the ceiling of his Lexford flat, its four downlights, smoke alarm and a couple of luminous stars he'd thought were a good idea to catch the moonlight streaming through half-closed blinds. Dan's body shook, and his nightshirt clung to his back, but he swung heavy legs out of bed and staggered from the bedroom, across the narrow hallway towards the banging on his front door. He fumbled with the safety chain.

"Dan, are you all right, mate?" Mike from the flat next door stood outside. He was one of the neighbours Dan supplied with a free copy of *the Daily News*. "I heard screams and shouting, and it sounded like you were in trouble. I couldn't get an answer."

"No problem, just a nightmare, Mike. I must have got a bit excited. Sorry to trouble you."

"Okay, Dan, if you're sure you're okay."

Dan nodded, shut the door, and walked back to bed. His legs and hands shook and sweat stung his eyes. The Billy Bass alarm clock read 3:35 am. He breathed deep, reaching into the bedside drawer, fiddling around until he located a small package taped to the underside of the drawer. He took one of three small cannabis spliffs wrapped in cling film, lit up and lay back, head and shoulders resting on the bedhead. He sucked two long draughts into his lungs, exhaling slowly to savour the uplifting, relaxing effect. He hoped it would counteract the painful memories and anxiety unleashed by his conversation with Jaz the afternoon before. The same anxiety that overcame him during the award ceremony for Journalist of the Year when he'd seen the photograph on the big screen. *Faz, wearing a bandana, driving his jeep.*

It was only the second time Dan had resorted to an artificial high since his days as an undergraduate. Within seconds he felt calmer as the lopsided combined chemical ratios of tetrahydrocannabinol and cannabidiol reduced the panic. Lance had supplied the spliffs when

Dan had refused to join a counselling group for post-traumatic stress disorder.

Lance had joined, informing Dan he'd told the group everything. His night terrors. How every day, he woke up screaming, reliving the events of that afternoon in Iraq when he and Dan scrambled clear of the armoured vehicle. Lance had described how they only escaped because their vehicle overturned after the blast from the direct hit on Faz's enveloped them. Dan had suffered superficial cuts and bruises, while one of Lance's legs became snagged in the metal stanchion of a steel seat. When the vehicle flipped over, his left ankle had snapped.

The A-10 pilot must have believed he'd wiped out both vehicles and had turned his concentration to the tanks rolling towards the ambushed American brigade. With tanks firing, bombs falling and Iraqi soldiers running for cover, Dan and Lance exploited the confusion to drag themselves back to their jeep. They escaped on Highway 16 away from Nasiriyah. Using a strap from a rucksack and a couple of sticks, Dan fashioned a makeshift splint for Lance's ankle and made him munch half a dozen painkillers washed down with a can of cola. On reaching an American field hospital 40 miles away, staff set Lance's ankle in plaster, but not before both men filed their stories. Their editors also requested each of them to send personal dispatches.

Dan's main story headlined:

MY TERROR IN AMBUSH ALLEY

Alongside, a tribute to Faz:

NEWSMAN DIES A HERO

There was no trace of Faz's body. Months later, a memorial service took place at St Bride's in Fleet Street, the journalists' church. Lance limped in carrying Faz's favourite book, J D Salinger's *The Catcher in the Rye* and Dan delivered a touching, fulsome eulogy. That evening, Dan smoked a spliff for the first time since university days.

A year later, Dan returned to the scene of the skirmish to collect a sample of desert sand in an ornate urn. To this day, the urn resides in a special place in the peace corner of London's Highgate cemetery under a plaque:

FAREZ 'FAZ' OSMAN: AN ELOQUENT HERO

Dan took another drag. The euphoria generated by the spliff deadened pain within, but still, the thought that had troubled him every day for more than 15 years smouldered in his brain.

It was my fault. If only I'd listened to Faz.

16

The wail was tuneless, drawing sniggers around the waiting room. "Ohh ... ohh ... ahh ... umm ... ohh ... ahh ..."

Jaz tapped Trish on the shoulder. "What on earth are you doing?"

Trish unhooked a pair of headphones connected to her mobile phone.

"Hi, Jaz, are you all done?"

It was Monday, the third week of treatment at the Barrett Bailey. As usual, Jaz and Trish were first out, although problems with two machines meant a 45-minute delay. Murph was still drinking water and waiting. Bill hadn't made the trip – he was feeling too fragile to travel.

"I'm learning Persian music," said Trish.

"What? And why?"

Trish said she'd been chatting to a 'nice lady from Iran' in the waiting room. Turned out she was an exponent of traditional Persian music, with its use of the sitar and repetitive and ululating phrases emanating high up in the larynx.

"It's complicated music to master," the nice lady warned. She gave Trish an impromptu 30-second rendition and said if Trish was interested in the mystical qualities the music afforded, she should download a tutorial from YouTube.

Trish followed the advice, stuck in her headphones and part hummed, part ululated, unaware the entire waiting room could hear her wailings, but not the music. The only mystery to Jaz was why a nurse had not investigated the peculiar sound.

"You never cease to amaze me," said Jaz with a puzzled frown.

"Oh, thanks, Jaz."

"Anyone else you've been talking to who I should know about?"

"There was this Polish chap."

Trish had sat next to Tomasz a couple of times during the past fortnight. That morning, in fractured English, he'd told her he'd arrived in the UK from Poznan 13 years ago. His wife returned to Poland, but his daughter lived around the corner in a terraced house with his three grandchildren.

"Oh, that's nice," said Trish. "You must like England then."

"No."

"Why not?"

"Too dirty." Tomasz pointed at the floor. "Always rubbish everywhere. Not like Poland. Poland clean."

Trish looked down at the polished surface – she could use the gleaming floor tiles as a mirror. "Looks clean to me," she scrunched her nose and marvelled at a language including words such as polish with a short 'o' and Polish with a long 'o' meaning different things in the same sentence. She surprised herself with her thoughts.

"Not here," said Tomasz. "On roads and motorways. By the side. On the grass. Always litter. No one cleans. No one takes away. In Poland not like this."

"You mean on Polish roads there is more polish," said Trish mischievously.

"Eh," said Tomasz. "No understand."

"Never mind."

Tomasz went on to tell how doctors had diagnosed liver cancer three months before, and he'd been off work – ironically as a waste disposal operative – for two.

"But they pay me every month. Still get big cheque." The smile was wide.

His treatment had been fast-tracked because of the aggressive nature of his condition. For the past five weeks, Honeycomb cars had transported him daily on the 60-mile round trip.

"Let me get this straight," said Trish. "You're paid full whack even though you aren't working, you've had fantastic treatment and a charity brings you here every day, free of charge. Would that have happened in Poland?"

"No."

But you don't like England because of paper blowing in the wind?"

"That's right," said Tomasz.

"And you work as a bin man?"

"That's right."

Trish bit her lip.

"Oh, please, tell me you didn't say anything nasty to him," said Jaz.

"Of course, I didn't, but I thought it. I'm sure there are lots of people from Poland and Latvia and Lithuania and many other places who love living here. It's great to meet them. My nurse this morning was from Valencia. She was lovely, and that lady from Iran was delightful. I just don't like listening to people whining about litter when they take important things in life for granted."

"You're right, Trish. Mind you there are so many discarded coffee cups at the roundabout by that café we pass it should be called Cappuccino Crossroads."

Trish laughed. "Or Latte Lane."

"Or Espresso Expressway," said Jaz, milking the play on words.

Giggling, the women linked arms and set off down the corridor to meet Dan in the drivers' room. Ever since their chat, Jaz thought Dan had seemed a little distant. There was still the same cheery smile when he called to collect her, but he didn't drive the conversation as he had the past fortnight. Had their intimate chat, in which she'd revealed more than intended, and he'd felt compelled to do likewise driven an emotional, accidental wedge between them? Jaz felt better for unloading her baggage about David and her

Dad. Perhaps revealing secrets had the opposite effect on Dan. Maybe Dan saw such emotional revelation as a sign of weakness requiring consignment to a box and sealing with super strength duct tape.

The situation played on Jaz's mind as she spotted Dan in the far corner sipping a cup of coffee, reading a copy of *the Daily News*. She sat down beside him. Trish sat too. Jaz glanced at the feature Dan was reading:

SHAME OF THE SCHOOL BULLIES

The report revealed how 50 per cent of children worried about returning from school holidays because of bullying. The article highlighted extreme cases. In particular, one story told how an 11-year-old girl was disfigured when bullies slashed her with a pencil sharpener blade for defending a shy boy who'd suffered relentless taunts for being overweight. The report said children were afraid to raise their hands in class in case their peers perceived them to be showing off. Others failed to do homework, scared that bullies would brand them a geek, a nerd, or worse.

"I can't imagine you being bullied at school, Dan," said Jaz.

Dan looked up from his paper. Jaz was glad to see his cheery smile.

"No, I was lucky. I played rugby and cricket. The lads who excelled at sport tended to be immune from bullying. Bullies only pick on the weak, don't they? Most of the bullying at my school came from the teachers."

"Really," said Jaz, mindful that she might be drawing out some more secrets, but too intrigued to stop there.

Dan revealed he attended a school run by Irish Christian Brothers with a fearsome reputation for physical abuse. Almost every schoolboy who came into contact with them bore marks and weals on hands, buttocks, and minds, some of which lasted a lifetime. It became a stain on their order.

"I can't hear Prokofiev's *Peter and the Wolf* without wincing," said Dan, explaining that any boy who played a wrong note in the school orchestra would be reprimanded by the music teacher. A smack over the head or occasionally a fist by the Brother with a middleweight boxer's physique.

In Prokofiev's piece, Dan had the task of playing the kettledrums representing the shooting of the hunters tracking the wolf.

"I don't think you can play a wrong note with a drum, but I still got whacked," said Dan. "If that's not bullying, I don't know what is."

"School kids are cruel, aren't they?" said Jaz. "They'll pounce on anything for a laugh at someone's expense."

The topic triggered a schoolgirl memory when she was around 11. Some friends nicknamed her 'The Shark' because of her surname but also because *Jaws* was showing at the cinema. At first, she rather enjoyed the attention.

"But then *Jaws 2* hit town, and whenever they saw me, kids would start singing the theme music. Louder and louder, 'dumdum ... dumdum ... dumdum – I felt as though the entire school was looking at me. It wasn't bullying exactly and probably only lasted a week or two, but I was young and self-conscious. I would go hot, and my cheeks would burn, and I still get a shiver when I remember the experience. No, not conducive to enjoying school. You're lucky, Dan, you can't go far wrong with a name like Armitage."

"Mmm, you would think so, wouldn't you?" Dan said, remembering an incident of his own.

"Oh, go on, tell us," said Trish.

"It's pretty juvenile, Trish."

"Juvenile's good. All the better."

Dan described how one 15-year-old wag had decided to deface the school toilets in Dan's honour. Armed with a Stanley knife, the lad made his way along all 12 urinals, scraping S and H from Armitage Shanks, the manufacturer's name.

"He replaced the letters with a W, written in permanent ink. Very clever. So clever that the headmaster suspended him for a week and ordered him to write, Armitage Shanks does not have a W in its name 10,000 times. He must have filled ten exercise books."

Both Jaz and Trish sniggered.

"What about you, Trish?" Dan asked.

"What do you think, with a name like Parker? It is my maiden name by the way."

"Nosy maybe?"

"Got it in one, which is what happened to the girl who couldn't take the hint that by age fourteen, I was fed up with the name."

"What happened?" said Jaz.

"Her name was Donna Allen, and I warned her Jaz. Honest, I did, loads of times, but she refused to listen. Day after day, she stood in front of me during mid-morning break, chanting her Hare Krishna mantra, 'nosy Parker, nosy Parker.'"

"One day, I snapped. I popped her one – bang on the nose. She looked at me all puzzled-like, with blood running down into her mouth. 'Who's nosy now then?' I said, and she ran away crying. But guess what? She never called me nosy Parker again."

Jaz and Dan exchanged a knowing glance. Yet another mental note. *Cross Trish at your peril.* Murph shuffled into the drivers' room. He looked paler than usual, although that wasn't easy to determine in a man with white hair, white beard and whose wide-brimmed hat cast his face in shadow.

"Everything all right, Murph?" said Dan.

"I'm a bit slow today. Sorry."

"You take your time, Murph," said Trish.

"We're in no rush."

Dan brought the car to the entrance, and they set off for Lexford. Within minutes, Jaz and Trish were deep in conversation reminiscing about their schooldays. Dan searched for Classic FM on the radio – talking of Prokofiev had stirred a passion he hadn't indulged for years. They passed the Lord of the Fries café, and Jaz pointed out the trail of coffee cups on the grass verge playing blow football in the breeze.

"I must admit it doesn't look pretty. Maybe Tomasz had a point, after all," said Trish.

"It's all to do with recycling," said Jaz. "We're just not good at it."

"Surely, that's not about recycling but more to do with people dropping coffee cups on the ground rather than putting them in the correct bin," said Dan.

There followed a technical discussion on what was and wasn't suitable for recycling. Jaz and Trish were sure coffee cups qualified as paper or cardboard and therefore recyclable. Dan thought most coffee cups contained impregnated plastic and only a handful of recycling plants in the UK possessed the technology to separate plastic from paper.

"Why don't they make paper cups then?" said Trish.

"Paper and water, especially hot water, don't mix well," said Dan. "You'd be leaking hot coffee all down your white top, Trish."

"What do you think, Murph?" said Trish.

No answer.

"Murph?"

Nothing.

"Leave him be, Trish. Let him sleep. He looked tired," said Jaz.

Murph was slumped in his usual position in the back seat, head resting against the window, hat covering half of his face.

"But he's not snoring," said Trish. "Murph always snores, and if he doesn't, he always lets out that piff piff sound through his lips. I've sat next to him for more than two weeks. He does it every time."

Dan glanced in the rear window and agreed that Murph didn't look well.

"He's cold, Dan, he's cold," said Trish, agitation in her voice.

Dan put his foot down, promising to stop at the next lay-by on the dual carriageway. Jaz looked concerned. Trish told Dan to hurry up and said it was like a play she'd seen where a man died in the back of a taxi, and two female friends didn't know what to do. In the end, they told the taxi driver to take them to hospital, dragged the man into A&E, sat him up in a chair and left.

"Don't most people die in hospital?" said Jaz.

"No. Statistics prove most people die in bed," said Dan.

"I think it's hospital."

"Bed. Hospital. Hospital bed. Who cares?" said

Trish, putting her hand over Murph's face. "I don't think he's breathing."

"Pinch his ear, Trish," said Jaz.

"Why?"

"Just pinch his ear. I read in a magazine that's the best way to see if a person is unconscious. They teach you that on all those first aid courses, I believe."

Trish took hold of Murph's right ear lobe and pressed. No response. She pressed again. Nothing.

"Oh, Jaz, I'm scared. I think he's gone. What's that tune you have to hum when someone is dying? You know, to get the rhythm, pressing his chest. *Nellie the Elephant*. No. *Staying Alive*. No. What is it?"

"Calm down, Trish, you can do either of those, but first nip his ear with your nails, not the fleshy part of your finger and thumb."

Trish's nails were not dissimilar to her heels. Long, sharp, painted white.

Dan watched in the rear-view mirror and grimaced as Trish grabbed Murph's ear lobe with a pair of eagle's talons and squeezed.

Oh, dear God, thought Dan, seeing Murph's head jerk backwards and upwards before crashing into the roof of the MPV, crumpling his hat and sending it spinning into the footwell. Murph's eyes shot open, his mouth gaped wide, and he let out a high-pitched scream. A combination of excruciating pain and sheer incredulity.

"What the f...!"

Murph – affable, amiable, serene, almost said the F-word. Only a lifetime of reserve, decorum and old-fashioned deference in mixed company prevented him from doing so.

Trish was fussing all over him, squealing, gabbling, apologising, straightening his jacket, reaching for his hat, trying to rub his face.

"Oh, Murph, thank God, you're alive. We thought you'd gone. You were cold. So quiet. I didn't think you were breathing. You gave us such a fright. Don't ever do that again."

Murph put the palm of his hand over his throbbing ear and fixed Trish with a perplexed *I don't understand this woman* glare before delivering his considered riposte. "Remind me never to sleep with you again, Trish."

17

After dropping his passengers off, Dan drove to Ernie's even though the car didn't need cleaning. Something in the back of his mind pulled him there.

Instead of turning left and through the gates leading to the wash facility, Dan turned right up a sloping driveway into the car park of Carlo's furniture shop directly opposite. He positioned the MPV, so the car was pointing towards Ernie's and killed the engine. The view was perfect, as if he were sitting on the elevated tee on a golf course, everything he needed to see set out before him. If only he knew what he needed to see.

Dan checked his mirrors. He saw the vast furniture showroom, busy for a Monday afternoon. He counted at least three customers browsing their way along the line of settees and chairs, occasionally sitting down, assessing the merchandise. A couple of salesmen in cheap suits sat at a desk inside the main doors. Both looked bored. One flicked through a magazine, leaning back on his chair at an angle challenging the laws of physics, the other tapped away at a computer, partially obscured by a sign:

SUMMER SALE. HUGE REDUCTIONS!

Dan tuned the car radio to Classic FM. Perfect. The strains of *Air on a G String* by Antoine Coercy. *Nothing better than a piece of relaxing music to stake out a car wash.* That wasn't his only thought.

What am I doing here? This isn't Iraq or Afghanistan. It's not even London. This is sleepy little Lexford, where nothing of note ever happens. Christ! When Benedict XVI visited the UK, the front-page headline of the local rag screamed, 'Pope Flies over Lexford.' That's how hard up the place was for a story.

Dan stuck with it for an hour watching a trickle of customers pitch up for their 99p basic wash. He reckoned it took three minutes from handing over money to completing the cycle, which meant even queuing at full capacity would bring in less than £20 an hour. He counted six cars in the hour, fussed over by five attendants – an income of £5.94. Under the general law of economics, any mathematician would conclude this was not a viable business. Schoolkids delivering the local paper earned more.

Dan was about to leave when his attention focused on the warehouse to the left of the car wash. There was a door to the side of the building, but it was shut. Big metal shutters opened, and a silver mini-bus with black-tinted windows emerged. Although he couldn't make out his features, Dan estimated the driver was mid-thirties. Stocky, broad shoulders, a mass of curly black hair protruding beneath his baseball cap. Dan made out silhouettes in the bus but couldn't determine characteristics, nor give an accurate headcount but guessed the vehicle could seat a dozen people.

Who were they and what were they doing? What was the warehouse's purpose?

A figure stepped from a prefabricated, single-storey building between the car wash and the warehouse. The gut gave him away. As did the attitude. *Gheorghe.* He threw up his right hand to stop the bus and went to talk to the driver, handing him a piece of paper. The conversation lasted seconds. Dan heard Gheorghe's gruff tones, saw his finger jabbing as he barked orders before the bus driver swung out of the site and accelerated away.

Gheorghe strolled over to the car wash, grabbed the broom handle and slapped the smooth, rounded wood into his palm. Dan expected him to lay into one of the boys. Instead, he used the broom as a pointer, ordering one lad to clear a patch of oil on the forecourt and dispatching another to clean the office windows. Then he disappeared around the back of the shipping containers. Twenty minutes later, he hadn't returned. Gheorghe may have resembled a weightlifter, but from Dan's observations, he wasn't someone who did much heavy lifting around the car wash. *What was he doing?*

While musing on that point, Dan heard a knock on his car window. Looking up, he saw a man with a closely shaved bullet-shaped head. He wore a bulky black jacket, the words A1 SECURITY in white letters on the left breast. The man motioned Dan to wind down the window.

"What can I do for you?" Dan kept his tone polite.

"Can I ask what you're doing here, sir?" Dan detected a patronising tone.

Nettled at the guard's officious manner, Dan was spoiling for a bit of fun. "Deciding whether I want the blue-based purple settee or the buttery tan option. Then again, I might go for the oyster grey corner sofa. I never knew there was so much choice. Cotton, velvet, leather. It's a big deal buying a new three-piece at Carlo's prices, don't you think? What about yolk yellow, or is that too bold?"

The guard gritted his teeth, rolled his eyes, and drew a deep breath. "I've been watching you on closed-circuit TV for the past hour and a half, and you haven't moved, sir."

"I'm waiting."

"Waiting for what?"

"Waiting until I see a member of staff I recognise."

"Why?"

"My mum always told me never to take suites off strange men." The serendipitous wisecrack was a gift from Bill a few days before and a first-time opportunity Dan couldn't miss.

The guard wasn't amused. "Don't be facetious, sir."

"I'm not being facetious. I'm being humorous. Whatever happened to the customer's always right?"

"You're not a customer. For that, you'd have to step inside the shop."

"That's where you're wrong." Dan sounded triumphant, waving his mobile phone in the air. "For an hour, I've browsed Carlo's website on the internet and was going to plump for the blue-based purple. Ultraviolet. Colour of the year, apparently, but I might just write to Carlo and tell him he lost a sale because one of his over-zealous security guards was harassing me."

"Carlo's doesn't have a website, sir."

"Oh." Dan turned the ignition key, rewound the window and gunned the accelerator, leaving the smug security guard to savour his little victory.

Driving home, Dan recalled what he'd learned. Ernie's wasn't an ordinary car wash. There were too many young attendants and not enough dirty cars. The warehouse was laden with security features, from the steel-shuttered doors to the six CCTV cameras trained mainly on them. However, two covered the entrance to the site. The Bank of England may need such security, but a humble car wash in a medium-sized market town?

Dan had also learned that Gheorghe almost certainly lived on-site in the prefabricated building, but what about those 9ft tall containers? They puzzled Dan the most. Yet, he conceded, there was no proof anything illegal or untoward was happening. His informal check with the police through his driver colleague Martin had yielded no concerns. There was no smoking gun. Not yet.

But Dan knew. He just knew.

18

Murph was deep in conversation with Alfie, an elderly man whose hearing aid sent a flock of seagulls whistling and squealing every time he turned his head. The conversation was profound, philosophical, almost on a par with world peace. The sort that made the waiting and interminable water drinking at the Barrett Bailey bearable. *Britain's most loyal and loving animal.*

A blind patient had triggered the debate. He'd gone into the treatment unit with a radiologist leaving his golden-haired guide dog in the care of a nurse. Former showjumper and farmer for over 60 years, Alfie advocated a case for the horse. Murph opted for the dog.

"It has to be a dog. Look at him," said Murph, leaning forward and grinning at the guide dog that gazed back at him with sad brown eyes. "Look at those eyes, so gentle and willing. My family always kept dogs when I was young – mainly Labradors and Retrievers Friendly and caring. That's why they make outstanding guide dogs. It's all about the temperament. Tolerant and trusting. Where else do you find such trust?"

"In a horse," Alfie spoke with a slow rural burr.

"Really?" said Murph.

"Definitely. I should imagine more so in

a horse. Equines are affectionate and loyal – they don't make demands. They value companionship and prefer to live together in a herd. Once a horse trusts you, it will do anything for you. Anything."

"It won't bring your slippers," said Murph.

"No, I expect not, but horses accept people who care for them as one of the herd. They'll defend their owners, and there are plenty of examples. There's a good reason why there are many riding schools for disabled children up and down the country. Spending time with and riding horses generates positive energy and self-confidence. That's a fact. They're used to help injured soldiers recuperate too. Huge hearts. Brave, intelligent animals. I love them, and so I should. I have six."

Bill emerged from one of the clinic rooms and hobbled over using a walking stick. He'd resumed treatment four days ago and was over the worst. The debilitating side effects had left him feeling drained and looking drawn. His natural Lancashire grit and humour were unaffected.

"What do you think, Bill?" said Murph. "Horse or dog. Which is the most loving?"

"Is this a trick question?"

"No." Murph motioned to Alfie. "We have a difference of opinion."

"I have the casting vote?" Bill asked.

"Yes, if you like."

"Has to be a dog, doesn't it?" said Bill. "I

can't say I'm a big dog lover, but I know some dogs pine for ages if their owner snuffs it. No wonder. Some people treat dogs like children, buying them presents, talking in silly mum-and-dad speech, putting paw prints on birthday cards and that sort of rubbish. Yes, it has to be the dog. Come to think of it, not only is a dog more loving than a horse, it's more loving than most men's wives, and there's a way to prove it."

"Never," said Alfie, shaking his head and disturbing another flock of seagulls.

Murph looked puzzled.

"Prove it!" Alfie pursed his lips.

"Simple," said Bill. "Lock your wife and dog in the garage for an hour. When you open the door to let them out, see which one licks you all over and wants to go for a long walk."

Alfie chuckled. Murph smiled.

A nurse put her head around a door. "Mr Murphy, please."

Murph drained his water and shuffled in for treatment. Minutes later he emerged, joined the others and they headed off. Jaz's phone rang a few miles from Lexford. She dug inside her handbag, pulling out purse, tissues, all manner of womanly essentials, and stored them on her lap, Dan looking on in amazement as the pile grew.

On the seventh ring, Jaz found her phone and clicked to connect. "Hi, Mum."

Within seconds, Dan knew something was

wrong. He caught a look of anguish on Jaz's face, a faint tremor in her voice.

"Calm down, Mum, it'll be all right. He won't have gone far. I'm on my way – I'll be with you in twenty minutes or so. No. Not yet. How long has it been? Stay there and try not to worry. See you soon." Jaz ended the call.

"Problem?" said Dan.

"Dad's gone missing. Been away more than two hours now. He must have slipped out of the house when Mum was taking a shower. She's checked with all the neighbours. They haven't seen him. She's thinking of calling the police."

"That's probably a good idea," said Trish, who knew of Jack's diagnosis from one of her long talks with Jaz. "They pull out all the stops when someone vulnerable goes missing."

"I know," said Jaz, appreciating Trish's attempt to comfort her. "It happened once before, and he turned up next door but one. He can't have gone far. I would like to check a couple of places first before we call the police."

"Where?" asked Dan.

"There's the park where Dad used to take me as a child to feed the ducks." Jaz smiled at the memory. "There's a bronze statue of a nineteenth-century local MP, and every time we passed, Dad would give me a handkerchief and tell me to rub the MP's boot. All the other kids did the same. It's been a tradition for years. The boot's all shiny now and something of a town attraction."

"And the second place?" Dan asked.

"His allotment. He used to dig and plant there and brought home bags of onions and potatoes and delicious strawberries. They were divine."

"Okay, we'll check those places first," said Dan.

"Oh, Dan. You don't have to do that."

"It's not a problem. I want to."

Jaz didn't protest further.

The others offered to help, but Dan insisted on dropping them off reasoning that Jack would need a seat in the MPV when they found him. Dan and Jaz headed to Three Jays, made Joyce a cup of tea and told her where they intended to search.

"Yes, good idea," said Joyce. "I'm worried he'll do or say something and get into trouble."

"Please, tell me he's wearing his lanyard card and wrist bands," said Jaz.

Joyce nodded.

"I make sure every morning. It's the first thing I check when he dresses. You know that, Jasmine. I never forget." She cast an imploring look at Jaz, who instinctively took her hand in support.

"What does the lanyard card say, Jaz?" said Dan.

"It's like a plastic credit card but maybe a bit bigger." Jaz demonstrated with her hand. "It has a picture of Dad, his address, telephone number and a message, 'My name is Jack, and I suffer from a neurological disorder.' The wrist bands say the same thing."

"Don't worry, Mrs Sharkey, Jack should be easy to find." Dan's attempt to put Joyce's mind at rest with an upbeat smile failed.

Jaz and Dan went to check the allotment first. Jack had spent many happy hours there. Late into summer evenings, he would sip a mug of tea, munch on a couple of biscuits and marvel at the sunset, while moaning to his gardening neighbours about his football team. Recently, the allotment became too much, physically and mentally. Jaz and Joyce kept the area as tidy as they could but were losing the battle with weeds. Creeping bindweed, nettles, and honeysuckle made the plot look overgrown and unkempt.

Parking up, Jaz and Dan headed to the shed at the front of the allotment. Dan peered through the window. A gardening fork and spade caked in dry mud hung on hooks. Seedboxes, compost bags, and bottles of liquid fertiliser sat in the corner likely covered in cobwebs. A heavy padlock secured the door. There was no sign of Jack.

"Hiya, Jaz!" The friendly call came from a man in green wellies and brown overalls emerging from the shed next door. "Not seen you down here in ages."

It was Jack's old mate Archie. The pair had enjoyed some fine old football ding-dongs down the years – shared the odd tot of whisky too.

"Hi, Archie, you haven't seen Dad, have you?"

said Jaz.

"Haven't seen Jack down here for years, but funnily enough I saw him a couple of hours ago. I was driving here, and he was walking the other way, up Gladstone Street towards the park. I nearly stopped to say hello. He looked a bit unsteady on his feet to tell you the truth."

"Thanks. Say hello to Mavis. Got to go."

There wasn't much traffic on the road. Jaz and Dan reached Lexford Park within minutes. Like the river, the park was one of the town's most attractive assets. Pristine lawns separated by long lines of rhododendron bushes provided a vibrant display of colour when in bloom. A refurbished bandstand and quirky Victorian café restored to its former glory and selling scones, buttered tea cakes, and ice creams took pride of place alongside the shiny toe of the politician's boot.

Jaz passed with a fleeting glance and headed for the duck pond. "That's where we came when I was little," she told Dan, pointing to the wooden bench under a willow tree where Jack would watch her feed stale bread to the ducks on the pond. "I thought he would be here. I was sure of it." Jaz's bottom lip trembled, and a misty film filled her eyes. "What now? We'd better phone the police."

"Is there anywhere else, Jaz? Think. Anywhere he went regularly? A shop, the library … what about a pub?"

"Dad wouldn't be seen dead in a library. He used to say there wasn't any book short enough to suit him. There's a pub called The Anchor down by the river, a short walk from here. Years ago, he would call in for a pint with Archie and some of the other men from the allotment.

"Right, let's go," said Dan, putting a supportive arm around Jaz as they hurried back to the car.

Minutes later they pulled into the pub's car park and squeezed into the only parking place. The holiday season was underway, and the cloudless sky and warm breeze had attracted a gathering. Dan took a moment to scan the scene, a habit from his days in danger zones in foreign parts.

Half-a-dozen motorbikes leaned neatly on their side stands outside the front door. Four barge-style narrow boats hugged the bank on the river, and some of the occupants drank or ate bar snacks at picnic tables on the grassy slope, which had become the pub's overspill area. Five children scampered between wooden tables, giggling and tugging on a helium birthday balloon destined for take-off anytime soon. No doubt, tears would follow.

Inside the pub, Dan stood on tiptoes, craning his neck to see over the heads of people either drinking or ordering from the bar. All the tables in the lounge were full – no sign of Jack. Then, Dan spotted him sitting on a stool at the bar in the far corner, in an area separated from the main lounge, primarily used by darts players. A half-empty glass sat in front of him. Two young men wearing shorts and tee-shirts took turns to throw darts. Dan presumed the four men sitting on a wooden bench by the window were bikers. *Was it the neck tattoos, and leather jackets despite the warm weather that gave them away?* Two older men also sat at the bar.

Dan turned his head. "He's here, Jaz. Good call."

"Thank heavens," Jaz sighed, relaxing her shoulders.

The couple negotiated a winding, single-file path through the drinkers, Dan taking the lead with Jaz a pace or so behind. Halfway across the lounge, Dan detected an air of animosity between Jack and one of the older men. The man had a drinker's beer belly and the broad, muscular shoulders of a bricklayer. He'd stopped mid-conversation, risen from his stool and was jabbing a finger at Jack.

"Something's kicking off," said Dan.

The man grabbed Jack's jumper by the neck, scrunched it in his fist and snarled in his face. "Say that again, and I'll turn your lights out, you fucking idiot."

"Load of bollocks," said Jack.

"Right." The man yanked Jack off his stool and drew back his arm to deliver a punch.

"No, don't, he's not well!" In his haste to intervene, Dan lunged forward and knocked a pint of beer from one of the tables.

A customer tried to steady Dan but only succeeded in pushing him into two more drinkers, spilling beer down their shirts and trousers. Dan's warning failed to register amid the din of the bar. For a moment, his world resembled a slow-motion clichéd cameo from a Wild West saloon when his foot caught in the leather strap of a woman's handbag and he toppled over. As he went down among a forest of legs, he sent another table of drinks flying and saw the man's fist on a flight path towards Jack's nose. As Dan's head smashed into the wooden floor, he hoped Jaz couldn't see what was happening to Jack.

Bright lights. Blue, yellow, and white. All went quiet and distant as if someone had fiddled with the volume control on Dan's hearing. He could sense stale beer mixed with dust, taste coppery blood at the back of his throat. He tried to shout *Stop*, but his brain refused to respond.

Then an angel came – a Blue Angel.

One of the bikers sprang from the wooden bench with surprising alacrity for a burly Scotsman, lunging with perfect timing to deflect the man's punch with a steely forearm. In the same movement, he grabbed the man around the neck, dragging him backwards with a choking grip and easy aggression that suggested he was no stranger to barroom brawls.

"Pack it in, pal," growled the biker, whose

long pointed beard complemented the skull and golden wings on his tattooed neck. "He's nothing but an old man."

"He's nothing but a fucking idiot," spluttered the man, eyes bulging, face reddening as he gasped for breath, struggling in vain to break the biker's hold.

"Dad!" screamed Jaz.

"He's barred," bawled the landlord, emerging from behind the bar to a scene of carnage.

Overturned tables, spilt beer, broken glasses and a bloody-nosed Dan struggling to his feet, clutching his forehead and a lump sprouting on his head from the smash. The biker loosened his grip on the man who still seethed, neither he nor his boozing companion had further violence in mind with the other bikers milling around.

"I think you'd better leave before I call the police," the landlord warned.

Jaz put a protective arm around Jack, who seemed oblivious to the chaos around him as well as disinterested why his daughter had suddenly decided to join him for a drink. She led him to the door through a crowd of disapproving drinkers and spied his lanyard peeping out of his back pocket.

"Oh, Dad," she muttered.

When they were outside, Jaz said she wanted to wait for the biker, spotting his beard and tattoo as the gang emerged. She waved, and he sauntered over.

"I can't thank you enough. I'm Jaz."

"Billy the Bastard at your service."

"Oh," said Jaz, taken aback.

"That's bastard as in Bastards, Lunatics, Undesirables and Eccentrics or if you prefer, the Blue Angels Motorcycle Club."

Jaz smiled. "God knows what would have happened if you hadn't stepped in," pointing to the lanyard in Jack's pocket and explaining that he suffered from a neurological disorder.

"No problem, you don't have to explain. Happy to help," said Billy.

"Have you any idea why that man wanted to punch Dad?"

Billy said he'd heard raised voices and witnessed the altercation develop while nursing an orange juice and planning the next bike route with his mates.

"Two guys at the bar were having a heated debate about football. Every time one of them was halfway through a sentence, your dad butted in and said, 'Load of bollocks'. After the fifth time, I realised he seemed a little, shall we say, vulnerable. But the guys were pissed up, and one of them lost it and went for him."

Jaz nodded, informing Billy that victims of Pick's Disease often became fixated on conversations around them and can be vulgar and even obscene in their responses.

"He can't help it," she said.

"I've heard worse," chuckled Billy, stroking his

beard, "but do me a favour and don't spread it around that I did a good deed. I have a reputation to protect."

"I won't. But I'm glad you did."

Billy and his biker friends pulled down the visors on their helmets, tweaked their throttles and rode off into the countryside. Jaz and Dan bundled Jack into the back of the MPV. As Jack sat back, he looked up and spotted Dan's deformed forehead and his shirt soaked in beer and blood.

"You're that ugly bloke, aren't you?" Jack said.

Jaz chuckled. Dan didn't.

19

Jaz was waiting at the end of her driveway when Dan called to pick her up on Monday morning. She felt dreadful. Not physically, more ashamed and embarrassed.

She'd telephoned twice over the weekend to apologise to Dan for Jack's escapade. She also wanted to know if he had any side effects from the mild concussion sustained in his attempt to save her Dad from the angry man's wrath. She'd implored Dan to go to A&E for a check-up, but he was adamant – there was no way he was donating four hours of his life to medical science.

"It's a bump, Jaz, don't worry. I've had worse, believe me."

He sounded convincing, but in reality, Dan had popped painkillers all weekend and postponed a couple of bike rides, a sure sign he was not in the rudest of health. The lump on his forehead was now a yellow and purple bruise, and he had that slightly foggy feeling in his brain that often accompanies a head injury. On the other hand, when he caught sight of himself in the mirror, and like most action men, he enjoyed bearing the marks to prove his involvement in an altercation, how he'd rushed to the aid of someone less fortunate.

"Oh, glory, are you sure you're okay?" Jaz looked concerned as she slid into the MPV and saw the full rainbow effect of Dan's contusion.

"I'm fine. How's your dad?"

"Not good. Mum called the GP over the weekend. Dad's getting worse – he's irritable and agitated all the time. Mum's arranged an appointment for Wednesday to have him reassessed. It was the first slot available, and she must be worried because I know she hates troubling the doctor."

"Tell me if you need help or a lift anywhere," said Dan.

"That's kind of you, but I'm sure Mum and I can cope."

Murph, Bill, and Trish were all keen to hear about the search for Jack. Trish had called Jaz over the weekend and knew much of the story but Jaz filled in the gaps. Both Murph and Bill were impressed at how quickly Jaz and Dan located Jack.

Trish, on the other hand, was impressed by Billy the Blue Angel. "He sounds like my kind of guy. Strong, decisive. Public spirited. Good with his hands. Clad in leather and a biker to boot. I wouldn't mind a ride in the countryside with him."

"Now, now Trish," said Bill. "A bit of dignity, please. There are gentlemen present."

"Where?" said Trish, looking over both

shoulders amid much laughter.

Bill, as usual, was intent on having a bit of fun. He winked at Trish. "What I want to know is where was Dan when your dad was in his hour of need, Jaz?"

"You know very well where I was," said Dan, anticipating Bill's sense of humour.

"Oh, that's right, you had a ringside seat. Under the table. Are you sure you don't have a problem with the demon drink, Dan? I can give you a number if you—"

"There's a lay-by up ahead with your name on it, Bill. I could let you out there."

Over three weeks, the thrust of the MPV's banter had mutated from polite and respectful, if a little irreverent, to warm and cosy, onto its current stage that sociologists would describe as cutting without offending. A precious gift in a group dynamic, Dan mused, swinging the MPV into the grounds of the Barrett Bailey and parking alongside another Honeycomb car. Light rain fell as the friends scrambled out. Dan's colleague Martin was at the back of his vehicle, struggling to untangle the safety belt caught in the metal spokes of a wheelchair.

"Come on, come on, stop messing about, there was nothing wrong with it before," griped a woman of ample proportions, her large moon face caked in make-up. Dyed brown, tight-permed hair matched her demeanour. She'd swung one of her bandaged legs out of the car, the dressing getting soggy in the falling rain.

"I'm sorry, Mary, the belt's tangled in the wheel. I won't be a moment." Martin spoke with the practised patience required for the most demanding of Honeycomb passengers, a rare occurrence.

Mary's irritation was evident. "Oh, not good enough, just not good enough. Have you never done this before?"

Martin left the question trailing on the breeze, Dan went to help, and Jaz and Trish looked on curiously. Dan eased the belt clear of the spokes, while Martin released it from the knot formed during the journey and wheeled the chair around to the passenger side. He heard a couple of muffled grumbles from inside the car and couldn't be sure, but was that 'amateurs' he heard?

Martin ignored Mary's remonstrations. Taking a deep breath, he did as he always did with difficult patients, who for all he knew suffered from nerves and apprehension or the disorientating effects of medication. He summoned a tone of excruciating gentility.

"There you are. All sorted, Mary."

Mary eased her bulk into the chair, and Martin pushed her towards the double swing doors of the oncology department.

"No, no, leave the chair alone," scolded an impatient Mary, tapping Martin on his right hand. "I can do it myself. Just tell me where to go.

Come on, man, tell me where to go."

"Oh, let me. Please, let me." Trish hissed.

Martin turned around to wink his agreement, although the comment went soaring over Mary's head. Giggling, Jaz pulled Trish away, and the pair went to sign in at the automatic digital reception. Mary wheeled herself to her next altercation/appointment with those assigned to help her. Dan and Martin parked and with hunched shoulders against the gathering rainstorm headed for the hospital. The MPVs all had a golf umbrella bearing the Honeycomb logo, but neither Dan nor Martin would use one. It was a man thing.

"Umbrellas are for wimps," was the philosophy Martin expounded. "You have to be seriously wet to use them."

The men took a detour to their favourite coffee shop, bought steaming full-fat lattes in lidded cartons and carried their purchases to the drivers' room. On the way, Martin asked Dan if there was any news on Ernie's.

"No," said Dan, deciding to omit that Carlo's security guard rumbled him casing the joint from the furniture store car park. Even to Dan that sounded more from the realms of Enid Blyton than John le Carré.

"There was another hoax call to the cops from that address," said Martin.

"When?"

"Friday, I believe."

"Who was it? What did the caller say? Did the police investigate? Did they speak to Gheorghe?"

Imagination racing ahead of reality, the questions tumbled out of Dan's mouth as fast as adrenaline coursed through his veins.

"I bumped into one of my old police mates in the pub on Saturday night," said Martin. "He said the new call was identical to the first. Noise in the background. Silence. Then what sounded like children's squeals of laughter followed by the phone disconnecting. A patrol car went to check, and the officers chatted with the manager, the fat guy I presume. He said he had no idea who'd made the call but that the office was always open and often unmanned. The staff seemed to be working normally. The officers were satisfied that the call was a hoax and left after suggesting the manager keep the office locked at all times when empty."

"Thanks, Martin. It does sound like kids," Dan acknowledged, sounding convinced. He wasn't.

Jaz and Trish were out first. Bill was out quickly although he was frailer by the day as he inched his way down the corridor with his now permanent walking stick. The MPV would have been away in record time if Murph didn't have to visit the pharmacy to collect a prescription. Medication to control nausea he suffered each morning.

Jaz and Trish busied themselves, adding to *The Hay Wain* jigsaw now two thirds complete.

A weary Bill sat beside farmer Alfie and his whistling hearing aid.

"How are those horses of yours?" said Bill.

"Eh?"

"Your horses, all okay?" Bill turned, giving Alfie the advantage of seeing his lips move.

"Funny you should ask that. We had to put one of them to sleep this weekend. Had a nasty fall in the field. Broke a leg, poor thing. I imagine he was in agony."

"Could it not have gone to the horsey hospital?"

"No, hardly ever works," said Alfie. "Horses with broken legs rarely survive. I had a beautiful grey stallion a few years ago, Cloudy Bay we called him. He snapped his leg frolicking in the field. Bone shattered into a hundred fragments." He paused as if savouring the memory of a long-lost friend before continuing. "A horse's bones are light compared to its body, see, which makes setting them difficult. Can't keep them still for the bone to heal, and even if you could, there are so many complications. Laminitis. Infection. Blood circulation problems. I'd have paid whatever it took to save old Cloudy Bay, but nothing could be done.

"So how do you dispose of them?"

The question was somewhat macabre, but nothing much disturbed Alfie's equanimity.

"The son-in-law uses an agricultural digger to dig a trench at the bottom of the field. I dump them in there. He's done that half a dozen times down the years. I would have them cremated, but it's two-hundred-and-fifty quid a time. The crematorium sticks a few in together, so you never know if you have the right ashes. Bugger that."

"Will they dump you in the trench too when you pop off?" said Bill, a question only he would ask.

Dan looked up from his magazine and raised his eyebrows. Jaz and Trish broke off from the jigsaw to listen in.

"No. I'm going on top of the hill in the same field," said Alfie. "It's all done and dusted. My local church wanted twelve-hundred quid for a plot in their grounds – daylight robbery. I'm not paying that. I went down to the council and signed all the forms so it's all right and proper and I've put a bench up under a tree so I can have a bit of company now and again."

Mouths and eyes opened wide. There was something honest, bold and admirable about Alfie's funeral arrangements.

"That's a down-to-earth way of looking at it." Bill didn't apologise for the intended pun.

"Don't worry, I'm not planning to go for a few years," replied Alfie.

The conversation was the sort you wouldn't hear in Hendos petrol station or Trish's call centre. Murph emerged carrying a white bag crammed with boxes of tablets and bottles of medicine.

Dan went to fetch the MPV, waving to Martin as he left. "Don't forget to give Mary our love."

20

As the MPV passed the Lord of the Fries on the way home, Jaz piped up. "I don't like talking about death. I never did, even before this."

"Neither do I. It gives me the creeps," said Trish.

Alfie's words had made an impression.

"It's the only thing certain for all of us, Trish," said Bill.

"I know, Bill, but I've never seen a dead body. I've seen lots on TV but never live."

"Good one," said Bill.

Trish gave him a puzzled look before realising what she'd said and collapsed in a fit of giggles.

Murph cleared his throat and cleaned the spectacles balanced on his chest, this time with a tissue rather than his tie. He was the nearest the group had to a cleric and was about to preach though he preferred to view it as considered analysis.

"The problem is that people think talking about death will bring their demise closer," he said. His hushed tone and serene manner lent the words a measure of gravitas. The others listened intently. "The prospect frightens people. The silly thing is that people prepare for the birth of a baby for months. They plan, think of names, buy clothes and toys, it's part of daily life and conversation. Everyone wants to share the joy. Yet we whisper about death as if murmuring might not awaken the Grim Reaper."

"After these last few months, we more than anyone, know that doesn't happen," said Jaz.

"Sorry, Jaz, I didn't mean to be condescending. I know we have all confronted the prospect of death, and there's nothing like cancer to make you sit up and value life more. Cancer makes you aware of how short life is. Makes you concentrate on what's around you every day and appreciate the things and people you love. At least that's what I think."

The words were the most Murph had spoken since singing *Islands in the Stream.*

"Oh, that's a lovely thing to say, Murph," said Trish.

Dan mentioned a group in the United States who'd formed the Death Café club. The members had regular get-togethers, dissecting every aspect of death over tea and cake.

"Sounds a bit morbid," said Murph, "and some people might find it disturbing but if joining a group and talking about the end helps to break down one of life's great taboos what's wrong with that? We all want and deserve a good life, but I think it's important we all have a good death too."

"So do I," said Bill. "My grandfather died peacefully in his sleep."

"That's nice," said Trish.

"Unfortunately, his passengers died screaming in terror."

Trish's air raid siren went off on cue, and everyone chuckled. No subject was sacred from Bill Murdoch's jokes.

"How do you fancy going for a car wash?" Dan asked Jaz when he'd dropped off the others.

"Pardon?"

"More to the point, how good are you at taking pictures on your mobile phone?"

"Not bad. I love my phone – I upgraded a few months ago. The new camera is fantastic, a wide-angle with a larger sensor, loads of pixels and great for facial recognition and separating the image from the background."

"Jaz, I haven't a clue what you're talking about, but you have convinced me."

Dan pulled over and parked outside a row of shops just off Lexford High Street. Two elderly ladies stood gossiping outside a newsagent, one of them pointing to the Lexford Journal billboard mounted on the pavement.

CAT KILLER STRIKES AGAIN

The headline referred to the spate of recent suspicious cat deaths in Lexford. The death toll stood at seven and counting. Next door was a Chinese takeaway, Wok This Way, which was open but empty, apart from the bored owner who sat on a stool behind the counter. Late lunchtime trade in the height of summer, even when the sky was charcoal grey, was far from brisk. With the schools shut, much of the town was away on holiday.

Dan wound his window down to let in air, then began to reveal his reservations about Ernie's car wash to Jaz. He told her about Barcelona Boy and Gheorghe and the beatings he suspected the car wash boss meted out regularly. He described the suspicious minibus leaving the warehouse and the two unexplained hoax calls.

He mentioned his chats with Cathy Wheeler, how she was his most trusted colleague and friend, and how her contacts in the National Crime Agency were assisting with her special investigation into drug and slave gangs. He left out the bit about Jimmy Collins and her warnings about a sinister crime syndicate.

"Why don't you go to the police?" said Jaz.

The question was fair.

"I have done through Martin." Dan wasn't convincing. "The police aren't interested in a boss who whacks his staff now and then, or a couple of telephone calls from kids. They're too busy chasing cat killers." Dan nodded at the billboard and Jaz smiled.

"Okay. What do you want me to do?"

"Sit and snap as we go through the car wash. Make it look as if you're watching a video or something. I'm interested in the shipping containers at one end of the site and anything else that looks interesting."

"Ooh, this is exciting," said Jaz. "I feel as if I'm a private detective. Like Robin Ellacott."

"Who?" said Dan, his face blank.

"She's Cormoran Strike's assistant in the TV detective series."

Dan shook his head.

"You must have heard of it, Dan. *Strike*, that's the name of the series. Based on Robert Galbraith's novels, although JK Rowling writes the books. You know, Harry Potter. You've heard of Harry Potter, surely."

"Of course, but I wouldn't know Robin Whoeversheis if she knocked on my door."

"She's a smart detective and good looking too. And there's no chance of her ever knocking on your door."

Dan didn't know what to make of Jaz's last comment. He gave her a quizzical look.

"I'm just saying," she shrugged, breaking into a mischievous chuckle.

Dan slid the MPV into traffic. It took a few minutes to reach Ernie's just off the High Street at the far end of town. There were two cars in front – quite a queue for that time of day. Five young lads fussed over the vehicles. The oldest Dan recognised. The others looked nearer to 14 than 18, difficult to tell under hoodies or baseball caps.

The first car started its path through the wash cycle, and the second, a bright yellow

Volkswagen Beetle splattered in white dust, moved forward. Jaz raised her phone and started snapping, smiling and occasionally giggling to give the impression she was enjoying an intriguing video game. It wasn't much of a stretch as she could spend hours, approaching addict status according to her mum, on all manner of gaming apps.

The Volkswagen moved on, and Dan moved too. He wound his window down, and the eldest lad came over. Dan sensed a slight nod of recognition but couldn't be sure.

"I'll take the master wash." Dan handed over a two-pound coin. The master wash was the intermediate version – application of soap to the alloys, mudguards, and windscreens. The boys would then scrub the dirtiest parts of the car by hand. Dan thought the wash would provide ample time for Jaz to take photos.

The lads went about their work and Jaz was impressed with the speed and precision. It wasn't astrophysics, even ordinary physics. They wielded sponges, rags, and brushes but did so with focused zeal. Moments later, the reason for their apparent dedication appeared in the doorway of the office. Gheorghe watched closely, a stern look on his unshaven face, an unlit cigarette dangling from his lips. Jaz recognised him from Dan's description and subtly turned her phone to frame him in her shots.

Jaz half-hoped things might kick-off as they'd

done twice when Dan was alone. She was eager to gather evidence, but all was quiet. Gheorghe disappeared into the office and Dan, at the direction of the eldest lad, eased the MPV onto the washing track, engaged neutral and killed the engine. The mechanical wash cycle began. When the brushes engaged, and the water plumes drenched the car, Jaz leaned across to show Dan a sample of the pictures.

"They're perfect, Jaz. Don't forget the containers on your side as we come out."

There was no chance of that. Jaz was in the zone. The car emerged from the water tunnel, and she picked up a copy of *the Daily News* to mask her phone from observers. She fired a burst of pictures of the containers, warehouse, and exit gates. As the car drew level with the safety sign, Dan turned the key in the ignition, and the MPV swung around in an arc, out of the gates and filtered left towards Meadow Drive.

"That was great fun, Dan," said Jaz, flicking through the portfolio. "I've never been through a car wash before. I took a hundred and forty-two shots. Is that enough?"

"Crikey, Jaz. Fantastic! Can you send them via email or WhatsApp?"

Five minutes later they pulled up outside Jaz's house. It was mid-afternoon, and Jaz had promised she would walk around to sit with Dad for a couple of hours while Mum went shopping.

"Sorry, Dan, the file's big and the signal around

here is weak. I can't get these pictures to go, and I'm late for Mum."

"I'm sure they'll go eventually. Try again later."

"But I thought you needed them straight away."

"Ideally, yes, but I'm sure they'll keep a little longer."

"Here, take it," said Jaz, thrusting her phone towards Dan. "Download the pictures onto your computer and return the phone tomorrow morning. I don't need it tonight. Anyway, I'd only play games for hours. I'll talk to Dad instead."

"If you're sure."

"Yeah, no problem." Slinging her handbag over her shoulder, Jaz eased out of the MPV. She headed down the path with a jaunty skip. "Don't read any messages. Scout's honour?"

Dan gave a theatrical version of the three-fingered Scouts salute. Jaz chuckled. Was it her role as a private detective that she was enjoying so much or being Dan's partner? She hadn't decided. But something was different. Willingly, Jaz had separated from her mobile phone for an entire night. That was a first.

21

Dan filled up with petrol and decided to stretch his legs. He parked the ambulance car in its designated overnight spot and walked back to his apartment.

He stopped on the bridge spanning the River Lex and leaned on the stone balustrade, taking in the view and enjoying the afternoon sun. A row of pretty thatched cottages formed an agreeable backdrop to his left. The imperious Lexford Parish Church spire speared the sky to his right. The tree-lined river rolled on serenely, half a dozen swans hitching an elegant ride on the slow-moving current. *A picture-postcard spot.*

Dan's mind meandered. *What was the collective noun for swans? A group? A gaggle? A herd?* A blast from The Verve interrupted his random musing. He reached for his phone – Cathy Wheeler.

"Hi, Cathy."

"Where are you?"

"Watching the swans on the river. What do you call a group of swans?"

"A whiteness, I think."

"Really?" Dan's tone suggested he wasn't convinced. "A whiteness should apply to cricketers, but I suppose it works for swans."

Three swans reared up, flapping their wings.

"Wow, what a beautiful sight. Three of them are taking off."

Dan watched the three birds splashing down the river, skimming the surface with clumsy webbed feet before taking to the air – symbols of elegance and beauty.

"Fantastic."

Cathy's tone mimicked Dan's enthusiasm, but her message was not so uplifting.

"You do know in Scotland three swans flying together is regarded as a sign of disaster, Dan?"

"In that case, good job I'm in Lexford and not in Scotland. You're not trying to tell me something, are you?"

Cathy switched to a more business-like delivery. "I thought you might be interested to know the latest on my investigation."

"Yes, go ahead." Dan was eager.

"The NCA is convinced Jimmy Collins is behind the national crime network exploiting the young and vulnerable. Police arrested six Iranian nationals on a Kent beach at the weekend who'd negotiated the congested shipping lanes of the English Channel in a dinghy. Three of them were teenagers. Each paid four-thousand pounds for the ride and Border Force investigations tracked the source of their journey to known associates of Collins."

Cathy told how a 16-year-old boy, carrying a quantity of cannabis and heroin, died from a suspected drug overdose in the stairwell of a tenement block in a small town. Continuing investigations concluded he was a Romanian national. Sad, although nothing extraordinary.

Detail, not revealed publicly but divulged as a favour by her NCA contact had prompted Cathy to ring Dan. "The drugs were wrapped in a plastic Hendos supermarket bag." Cathy paused to let the information sink in.

"What's unusual about that?"

"*Hendos*," Cathy emphasised the name. "We're not talking about a national concern, with thousands of shops throughout the country. Hendos is a small, regional chain, with no more than a dozen outlets. Most of them in Lexfordshire and Essex, more than two hundred miles from where the boy died. I thought you'd like to know – could be something and nothing."

"Yeah, but it could be *the* thing," said Dan as the potential significance of Cathy's discovery hit home.

Dan's mind raced ahead. His imagination placed the dead boy in one of the seats of the silver minibus he'd seen leaving Ernie's from his vantage point in Carlo's car park.

"There's something else," said Cathy.

"Go on."

"Collins has been spotted in London. Or at least there've been possible sightings of him in vehicles he's known to be associated with."

"Is that unusual?"

"Yes. He does all his business from his

hideouts in Northern Ireland. He rarely leaves. He's known as the Bin Laden of Belfast because he has so much influence, but no one has ever clapped eyes on him. If he's in London, there must be a reason. Most likely it's to do with him cranking up or streamlining his business interests. Either way, if he's on the move, you can bet that isn't good for someone."

Dan thanked Cathy for the information, although he'd already computed none of it was evidence that Ernie's was anything but a bona fide car wash. *One plastic supermarket bag did not make a summer.* But it did reinforce his suspicions. As Dan headed home, he spotted the three swans flying overhead, tracking back down the river. Despite the warm sun, a shiver sliced down his spine as Cathy's words echoed in his mind.

A sign of disaster.

22

Jasmine Sharkey was a woman of many talents, a trait Dan Armitage had perceived over the past weeks. Unfortunately, photography wasn't one of them. Not with a phone hidden behind a newspaper and images obscured by a monsoon battering the lens. Two-thirds of Jaz's snaps resembled the swirl of murky water in Dan's washing-up bowl. Her thumb played a starring role in the rest.

Disappointing Dan concluded, munching through a mozzarella burger. His mood worsened when a blob of ketchup escaped and dribbled down his blue shirt. "Shit!"

Spooning up the mess, one of the clearer photographs caught Dan's attention as he licked sauce from his finger. He wiped his hands and returned to his laptop, clicking on the image – a side-on view of the shipping containers, the side including the improvised cut-out door and window. Every time he'd visited the car wash, a shutter masked that window. This time it was open. Half in shadow and behind a set of makeshift bars, a face stared out. A face Dan recognised. He zoomed in, energy rushing through his body. He whistled through his teeth. The picture was grainy, watery, partly indistinct but unmistakably, the image was Barcelona Boy, football cap worn back to front.

Why had the older attendant lied? Why had he said Nico, as he'd referred to him, had returned home? What else lay in those containers?

Dan pondered ringing the police, but there was no evidence of any wrongdoing – merely the sighting of a young lad with a foreign accent who'd taken a recent beating. Dan flicked through his contacts, hovered over Cathy Wheeler's number and decided against calling her. *What was the point?* Their conversation that afternoon had been interesting, and he wouldn't be surprised to see Jimmy Collins turn up on the national news flanked by NCA officers. Still, there was nothing new in what she'd told him. Apart from the Hendos bag, and that was a flimsy connection.

Thrusting Jaz's phone into his back pocket, Dan scooped up his jacket and cycling helmet. On his way out, he grabbed a torch. If there isn't enough evidence, do what he'd done as an investigative reporter. Go looking for more. Dan was that kind of guy. By nature, easy-going, but tenacious to the point of obsession when solving puzzles and overcoming obstacles.

The time was 9.20 pm when Dan reached Ernie's – after sunset, but not pitch black. A half-moon was rising and with few artificial lights to compromise his night vision, Dan could make out the topography of the site. Dan rode down the side street, which took him behind the car wash. He parked his bike against the high metal railings, 20 metres away from the side door into the warehouse and out of sight of the building he believed was Gheorghe's living quarters.

Standing back, Dan surveyed the site. The railings tapered to sharp points – no chance of climbing them. He walked along, hoping, but not expecting, to find a break in the fence. There was none. He turned left when he reached the outer perimeter and took the torch from his pocket. Dan knew from his reconnaissance there were no CCTV cameras trained on this part of the site and risked switching on the torch for a few seconds, sweeping the beam across the back fence. A gate – made of the same vertical rails as the fence but inside a metal frame, which meant it was scalable. If only he had something to stand on.

Dan looked around. Nothing. Then he remembered his bike. Retracing his steps, he wheeled the bike back to the gate, leaning it against the metal and jamming one of the pedals inside the railings to form a makeshift scaffold. With his right foot on the other pedal, he prised himself up until he could stand on the seat with his left. He climbed to the top of the frame, straddled the gate and dropped to the ground on the other side.

"Dan Armitage, not bad for a forty-nine-year-old," he muttered, breathing a little heavier but feeling proud of his manoeuvre.

The warehouse would be his first port of call. Dan was about to jog over the grassy verge when he heard a bolt sliding and the wooden side door open. He crouched and peered through the gloom, watching a man emerge. From the broad silhouette and curly hair protruding from his cap, Dan recognised the bus driver he'd clocked while in the furniture store car park.

A helicopter whir and a wail of sirens caught the man's attention. Dan assumed there must have been a shunt on the notorious Lexford bypass less than a mile away. In recent weeks, the area was the scene of several nasty accidents involving teenage drivers under the influence of legal highs. The man walked to the front of the warehouse, looked up into the night sky to watch the helicopter's beams and sucked a long drag of nicotine into his lungs, blowing the smoke out in one long plume. Dan had his chance. He tiptoed to the side door behind the man's back and stepped inside, heart racing.

In the pitch black, Dan heard a low, distant hum from deep inside the building and smelt a faint, sweet aroma. He turned on his torch, keeping it dipped and cupping his hand around the lens to radiate softer light. He was in a long corridor running almost the length of the warehouse with four doors leading off. Dan tried the handle of the first door and entered a considerable garage space containing three silver minibuses parked nose to tail. Petrol, oil, and industrial cleaner permeated the air. A shape in the corner, covered in a dusty brown tarpaulin, caught Dan's attention.

Dan threw back the canvas, revealing the front grill of a red Mercedes. He shone his torch on the registration plate: ERN 1E. *He'd found Ernie's car, but where was Ernie?* Dan fished Jaz's phone from his back pocket and took a picture, his mind hammering in time with his heart. No matter how he pieced the story together, Dan couldn't find a happy ending for the one-time well-respected owner of Lexford's premier car wash.

He retraced his steps to the corridor. After checking the bus driver remained distracted, Dan followed the low hum to the back of the building. He reached the last door leading off the corridor and turned the handle. It was surprisingly heavy, opening into a vestibule flooded in artificial light. Dan switched off his torch, craned his neck around the door and eyed a sea of green in an area half the size of a football pitch.

"Holy Moses." Dan breathed, overwhelmed by the scale of the horticultural operation before him.

Dan wasn't a gardener. He didn't understand why some plants needed ericaceous compost and others could do as well on good, old-fashioned grit. If you pushed him, he might have known the difference between a daisy and a hydrangea, but he might not. His nose twitched and sniffed the air, heady sweetness filling his nostrils. Dan looked upwards. The sophisticated panoply of lights and sprinklers rigged from the roof left him in no doubt. *A cannabis farm par excellence. A garden of illegal weed.*

"Holy Moses," Dan repeated, selecting the phone's camera mode and lining up the endless rows of plants in the frame.

Detecting movement behind him, Dan clicked the shutter button and turned his head. He picked out the blur of a broom handle hurtling towards him and Gheorghe's greasy hair and permanent stubble. Dan tried ducking but wasn't quick enough. If he hadn't been wearing his bicycle helmet, Dan's brain might have splattered against the warehouse wall such was the force of Gheorghe's swinging blow.

Part of the handle deflected off the helmet, the remainder smashing into Dan's nose and cheekbone. He heard a shout, but the voice was slow and drawn out. Dan fell to the ground, struggled to balance on one knee then slumped over onto the cold, stone floor. His brain shut down.

Breathing in perfumed air and gargling on fresh blood, Dan went to sleep.

23

Jaz grabbed her handbag, slipped on her jacket, and answered the front door, expecting to see Dan. She saw the postman instead.

"One to sign for." The postman handed Jaz a couple of brown envelopes and a parcel.

Jaz knew what the package was – the perfect present for her Mum's birthday. A two-piece gift set comprising a bracelet strap watch and heart chain bracelet. She'd spotted the jewellery three months before and dallied on overspending. When the summer sale halved the price, Jaz didn't hesitate. The postman thrust a device under her nose. Jaz signed her name with her forefinger, loving the warm feeling inside as the gadget brought happy memories of the drawing toy she adored as a child.

The postman smiled. "Have a good day."

"Thanks. You too."

Jaz closed the door and fumbled for scissors in the hallway cabinet. She'd chosen the wrapping service and wanted to make sure the gift was presentable. She needn't have worried – the pink paper embossed with 'Best Wishes' and 'Happy Birthday Mum' in alternate squares was perfect. A matching gift tag to add a special message was a bonus.

Jaz looked at the wall clock: 8:10 am. Dan was late. *Strange.* In the past three weeks, there'd been a couple of occasions when High Street traffic during school term had delayed him a few minutes, but schools weren't open, and Dan was a punctual man. She went into the front room to watch from the window, rummaging through her handbag for her mobile phone. *Of course, she'd given it to Dan the night before, which meant she couldn't text him.* She couldn't call on her landline either, his number was in contacts on her mobile phone, but she could call her mobile phone from the landline.

Jaz dialled. The phone rang six times before diverting to voicemail. She frowned, hung up and absently twiddled the strap of her handbag. For several minutes, Jaz repeatedly looked at her watch, fingers drumming and foot tapping as apprehension grew. She was about to ring the transport charity organiser when the landline rang.

She answered, expecting to hear Dan's voice. It was Trish.

"Haven't you left yet?"

"Obviously not or I wouldn't be talking to you, would I?" Borne of frustration Jaz's voice contained a touch of sarcasm. "Dan hasn't turned up."

Trish noted the concern. "He's probably slept in."

"I doubt it. Come rain or shine he's up at five

every morning. He cycles, collects the papers and delivers them to his neighbours. When you have a routine like that, you don't sleep in."

"What then?"

Jaz asked Trish for Dan's mobile number and said she would call. If she couldn't get a response, she would contact the charity organiser. When Dan didn't answer after several attempts, Jaz phoned the transport helpline number. The man answering spoke in a shrill voice, and Jaz had to hold the phone away from her ear. Still, his manner was caring – he couldn't have been more apologetic.

"That's odd, Miss Sharkey," he squeaked. "Don't know what's happened there. Dan's reliable. Could be he's broken down, but he hasn't called to let us know. You stay there and don't worry. Have yourself a nice cup of tea, and I'll ask another driver to take you to Barrett Bailey. Should be with you in the next half hour."

Jaz relayed the information to Trish and waited until the standby driver turned up. Jaz told Martin she was worried – Dan's absence was out of character. He assured her the charity had sent someone to Dan's flat and there was probably a simple explanation. Jaz felt better. Martin's tone had that effect, conveying authority and composure. He'd been a damn good policeman. The pair set off, picking up Murph, Trish, and Bill on the way, Dan's whereabouts being the main conversation.

"Maybe he's been speeding again, and the police have taken him in for questioning," said Trish.

"The police have more on their plate than chasing ambulance cars," said Martin.

"They pulled us over before," said Trish.

"Really?"

"Yes, really, and the officer was a proper jumped-up little Hitler too," said Trish.

"Steady on – I used to be a traffic cop. I do remember Dan telling me about that, come to think of it. Condescending twerp, wasn't he?"

"More like you've scared Dan off with all that talk about climbing mountains, Trish," said Bill.

Trish fixed Bill with an icy glare, which reminded him that subject was off-limits, for the best part of a year at least.

"Sorry," mouthed Bill.

The car reached the Barrett Bailey, and each passenger headed off for treatment. Jaz was first out, and this time didn't wait for Trish. Instead, she hurried back to the drivers' room and searched out Martin, enjoying his usual latte.

"Any news on Dan?"

"You've only been gone fifteen minutes, Jaz."

"I know, but it took forty-five minutes to get here. That's an hour since you picked me up and nearly two since I raised the alarm."

"Alarm's a bit strong, Jaz. Dan's a grown man and can take care of himself, but if it helps, I'll call HQ."

The news was inconclusive. One of the Honeycomb staff had knocked on Dan's door, and there was no answer, but Mike's wife let herself in using a spare key she held for occasions when Dan was away. Nothing was amiss.

The report worried Jaz more. She'd known Dan for three weeks but had given his disappearance much thought. If anyone had asked her to describe him in three words, without hesitation, she would have answered. Dependable. Loyal. Resourceful. If given a wider choice, she'd add, selfless, kind, fearless. A sharp sense of humour would be a good call too. A man of substance and character with four vulnerable cancer patients under his care doesn't go missing without reason.

"Martin, Dan's disappearance might have something to do with Ernie's car wash," said Jaz.

"But the police have looked into that and found nothing of concern. Dan knows, and I thought he'd accepted."

Jaz told Martin about the visit to Ernie's the day before. About the photographs and Dan's worries. For the first time, Martin looked troubled.

"Damn! I hope he hasn't done anything stupid."

24

On your death bed, it's said that hearing is the last sense to go. For Dan, it was the first to return. He could hear talking, recognise the rhythm and meter of a sentence, but the faint words, apparently from the end of a long corridor made no sense. Was the language Italian, Spanish, Portuguese? Maybe French?

Dan's brain hurt. So did his nose and cheekbone, and his pride. He wanted to go back to sleep, but someone kicked his right leg. Another kick, harder this time. Dan tried to prop himself up on his right elbow, but it gave way, and he fell back, banging his head on the unforgiving floor.

"Shit!" Dan sucked in a lungful of air, the stench of ammonia filling his bloody nostrils. *Urine.*

"Meester? You okay, meester?"

The voice was young, with an accent that was difficult to place. Part Italian, part Slavic. *Romanian?* This time, Dan succeeded in rising on his elbow and opened his eyes, despite the pain in the right, which was deep purple and wanted to stay shut. He peered across to the corner of the room lit by a single soft pink light bulb and smiled at the figure. *Barcelona Boy, Nico.*

Dan tried to stand, but a leather belt around his waist restrained him. The belt connected to a short chain, linking to an iron ring bolted low down into the wall. The contraption allowed sufficient movement to keep circulation flowing but barely enough to kneel, let alone stand. A similar restraint shacked Nico, albeit with a longer chain.

"Meester, you okay?"

Dan nodded. "How long have you been tied up here?"

"Two weeks, maybe more."

"Since Gheorghe beat you?" Dan raised his arm and mimed a flailing broom handle when Nico didn't understand.

"Da," said Nico, who looked younger than his 15 years.

The youth's composed demeanour in such dire circumstances immediately impressed Dan, and Nico appeared to recognise Dan as the man who'd intervened to save him from Gheorghe three weeks before.

Dan looked around the room, the same shape and size as a shipping container. A shutter covered the barred window, and he presumed the ladder leading from a hatch in the ceiling connected the lower and upper container. Shoehorned into one corner were three small bunk beds, another three into the opposite wall, the sides clad in a double layer of thick, soundproof boards. *No use screaming for help.*

Next to Nico was a large bucket, accounting for the overpowering stench of ammonia. The stains on the floor suggested repeated knocks or kicks to the bucket from the container's occupants.

"Who lives here, and where are they?" said Dan.

Nico spoke limited English, but with gentle coaxing, Dan was able to piece together parts of the boy's story. Raising both hands and flexing his fingers twice, Nico indicated another 20 workers lived in the adjoining containers. The boy revealed that he'd arrived in the UK with his parents and older brother, Andrei in 2015 when Romanians and Bulgarians became exempt from UK immigration controls.

The family struggled to find permanent work or a place to live, and neither Nico nor Andrei attended school. Desperation set in and after months of moving around, they secured work and accommodation at half a dozen car washes in Lincolnshire, toiling for £5-a-day, scraping together a living. At least they were able to stay together and augment their wages by working in the fields. Six months earlier, Gheorghe had turned up promising permanent work for Nico and Andrei if they moved to Lexford. Nico's parents believed a move would be a fresh start for their children. Nico paused at the mention of his parents, misty, sad eyes, computing the bleakness of his predicament.

The reality was Gheorghe had successfully

wrenched Nico and Andrei from the protection of their family. They were now under his control. Nico believed up to 40 other young immigrants, from Europe, Vietnam, Albania, and Africa worked and lived out of the shipping containers at various times.

"What do they all do?" said Dan.

"Some work in the green place. Some go on buses. Others clean cars."

Dan remembered his last conversation with Cathy Wheeler. How she'd told him drug gangs forced vulnerable teenagers, many of them illegal immigrants, to run to all parts of the country, targeting towns in rural areas thus far overlooked by big city dealers. He also recalled the three words the spokesman for the National Crime Agency used to describe the syndicates involved. *Violent. Sadistic. Ruthless.* He touched his swollen eye, and the thought occurred that right now, he could vouch for all three.

The door flung open, and Gheorghe and the bus driver came in. An aroma of stale sweat mixed with tobacco and industrial cleaning fluids hit the air. Gheorghe stood over Dan, his vast bulk magnified in the confined area. Enormous girth, planks of wood for shoulders, and dangling fists like lump hammers. In one hand, he clutched the broom handle. Low, menacing.

The driver, or notably what he carried by his right side, caught Dan's attention. A Glock G45 pistol, with full black frame and a compact slide. Dan froze, the gun confirming the desperate nature of his dilemma. Renowned for reliability, Glock pistols were a favourite of the military and Dan had seen many varieties on his assignments. His mind flashed to an abiding memory of an Afghan soldier pressing one to the head of an Al Qaeda terrorist. Dan had turned away, but the metallic click of death followed by the bruising explosion too often disturbed his sleep.

Gheorghe's sick, evil smile revealed a set of nicotine-stained teeth. One of his chipped front teeth formed a dark aperture when the two rows met. Strangely, when he spoke, his tone wasn't menacing, the lilt bordering on gentle.

"You like my car wash?" Gheorghe said to Dan. "You come many times, yes? I think you must like me."

"You're so cuddly." Dan didn't hold back. "If I admired fat weirdos who beat up kids, you would be my number one."

Gheorghe's smile became a snarl. Using the broom handle, he prodded Nico in the chest. The boy slid backwards on the floor and brought up his knees as he cowered in the corner.

"What are we going to do with you both?" Gheorghe said.

Dan attacked, using his most assertive voice. "People know I'm here. I've told the police about this place and sent pictures. You won't get away with what you're doing. They're probably on their way right now."

Even as he spoke, Dan realised he sounded like a clichéd kidnap victim from one of those ubiquitous police dramas of yesteryear. In his mind, he was thinking about something completely different. If only he'd told someone where he was, contacted the police, called Cathy to divulge his most recent suspicions when he had the chance. If only he had sent pictures. Why didn't he think of that? The first rule of investigative reporting. Back up your evidence. *If only.*

Gheorghe smiled again and shook his head. "No one is coming," he said, dangling Dan's and Jaz's phones. "You have sent nothing. Nobody knows you're here."

Dan's heart sank. His mind raced, weighing up the likely course of events. Gheorghe and the bus driver knew he'd seen the cannabis farm. He suspected workers in the other rooms off that long warehouse corridor bagged and weighed harder drugs – cocaine indeed, heroin perhaps. This outfit was not a small operation. The infrastructure was sophisticated, and that fleet of minibuses doubtless travelled considerable distances transporting drug runners, almost certainly teenagers. Manufacture and distribution with all bases covered – the perfect illegal business model.

There were cameras, lots of them, but no overt guards at the site, which had perplexed Dan at first. Now, he realised why. In a medium-sized town such as Lexford, 24-hour guards at a simple car wash would arouse suspicion. Without them, Gheorghe and company could hide in plain sight. The odd extra teenager on view would simply merge into the bigger picture.

But it was the gun that curdled Dan's blood. He was under no illusions. The pistol changed everything, and its presence prompted him to calculate the financial stakes at this site alone to be in the millions. What was the only glitch in the entire production line right now? *Dan Armitage.* Who was the idiot who'd stumbled in after performing a circus act on his bicycle to straddle the perimeter fence? *Dan Armitage.* Who knew enough to blow this money-spinning can of cannabis to oblivion? *Yes, Dan Armitage. That would be you, too.*

No, whichever way Dan weighed up the presence of the Glock, the prognosis wasn't good. *I'm fucked*, is what Dan was thinking.

"What happens now?" is what Dan said, surprising himself with a calm delivery.

A ringtone sounded, and Gheorghe cracked another nicotine grin as he thrust a meaty fist into one of his pockets, pulled out a mobile phone and accepted the call. He stepped outside the doorway, at the same time motioning to the driver to keep watch over Dan and Nico.

Dan shut his eyes and strained his ears to focus on the muffled conversation in rapid

Romanian. He searched for the slightest clue. A name or a place. A time maybe. Anything that might help extricate himself from this deepening hole.

He understood none of the words but immediately detected urgency. Gheorghe's demeanour was accepting and respectful, almost submissive. It was apparent he was taking orders, not giving them. The chat lasted no more than two minutes. During that time, Dan's sharp antennae for news homed in on one word – 'Curatatorie' – repeated several times as if Gheorghe sought confirmation.

Then Gheorghe mentioned a name and Dan felt a chill, sitting upright as he heard the name again.

"Meester Collins."

25

Murphy's Law decrees anything that can go wrong will go wrong and does at the most inconvenient time, which explains why bread falls buttered side down. Why appliances work when the repairman calls, and why, after Murph and Bill had slurped two litres of water apiece, their machine broke down when Jaz was desperate to leave.

"How long are they going to be?" said Jaz, trying but failing to keep frustration from her voice.

"I don't know. I'm not psychic, said Martin. "Depends on the problem, but hospital staff can filter patients to other machines. It shouldn't be more than an hour. Why not grab yourself a coffee and relax?"

Jaz threw Martin an evil look. Relaxing was the last thing on her mind. She picked up a magazine, flicked through the pages then slid it back onto the table, glancing at her watch – 11 am, and the drivers' room was filling up.

Trish wandered in and sat beside Jaz, who was now absently filing her nails. "Still worried about Dan?"

Jaz nodded. "I know we haven't known him long, but he wouldn't go missing without telling someone, Trish. He wouldn't."

"I agree, but what can we do? We've tried ringing his phone, and someone's called at his house. He hasn't been missing long. Let's finish the jigsaw. Take your mind off it."

Jaz shook her head and folded her arms, leaving Trish to search out the final pieces of the jigsaw. Jaz wasn't in the best frame of mind.

Two women sat down near Jaz, one with a sing-song accent laden with curdled vowels Jaz recognised as English Midlands. The woman launched into a whine, plainly an extension of the conversation shared in the waiting room with her companion.

"As I was saying, Eileen, I've cancelled my sixtieth birthday party. I wanted all the family and friends around, but how can I do that now? I'll have to cancel plans for my twenty-fifth wedding anniversary too. What else can I do? I've got nothing to celebrate now that I have cancer."

Any other day Jaz would have kept her mouth shut, but she was in no mood for self-indulgent snivelling and that woman's nasal whining grated like a dentist's drill.

"Oh, shut up! Just shut the ... up."

Jaz couldn't believe she'd said the words. Loud and laced with venom. Trish looked around, mouth gaping. This was her territory. Essex girl badinage, except she would have added the expletive and not paused. Jaz – sweet, intelligent, considered Jaz, did not belong here. Then Trish remembered the quiz and how Jaz had taken down the battleaxe from The Rage of Aquarius. *Go, girl.*

"What?" wailed the perplexed woman.

"You heard me." Jaz stood up, fixing the woman with a look teetering between pity and contempt. She raised her voice so everyone could hear. "Stop feeling sorry for yourself. Everyone here is in the same situation, and I dare say many are worse off than you."

"Of course, you have something to celebrate. You have your sixtieth birthday and twenty-fifth wedding anniversary. They mean something to you, your family and friends or should do. Why let cancer steal your happiness? You don't have to think about cancer every day. You can have a day off on your wedding anniversary or your birthday. Stop giving in to it and stop whining. By the way, many happy returns for your birthday, whenever it is."

Jaz didn't wait for a reply. She turned, stomped out of the room and headed down the corridor. Trish looked at Martin, who raised his eyebrows and shrugged. Muttering as they went, the two women shuffled outside to wait for their taxi.

Jaz returned looking composed and refreshed after a brisk walk around the Barrett Bailey perimeter. She'd stopped at the main entrance to admire the imposing bronze statue of Elizabeth Barrett Bailey. She'd seen the image through the car window many times on her way in and out of the hospital but had never given it a second thought, never asked who Barrett Bailey was. Jaz read the heading on the plaque – Elizabeth Barrett Bailey's name and dates, 9 April 1840-17 June 1928.

After reading the short biography, a warm glow coursed through Jaz's body and a determined smile spread across her face as she appreciated the achievements of one of Britain's true pioneers. Qualified in Britain as a physician and surgeon. Supporter and benefactor of a range of pioneering hospitals staffed by women. Suffragist. Dean of Lexfordshire University Medical School. One of Britain's first women school governors. First woman Mayor of Lexford. First woman magistrate in Lexfordshire. *What a life, what a woman.*

Instantly, there was purpose in Jaz's stride as she nipped back to the drivers' room. Gone was the frustration and helplessness she'd felt on the journey to the hospital. Now, Jaz radiated renewed confidence and strength infused by a brief encounter with an extraordinary woman who'd died almost a century before.

"Look, Jaz, all done." Trish pointed to the jigsaw. "They can ship this one down to A&E and put a different one in its place."

"Well done, Trish. I need to make a call. Can I borrow your phone?"

"Yes, I suppose so." Trish handed her phone to Jaz.

"Be back in five minutes." Determined, Jaz surged down the corridor.

Trish turned to Martin, and this time she shrugged.

When Jaz returned, Bill and Murph still awaited treatment and the logjam caused by the broken machine meant there was a packed drivers' room. Patients ready to go but transport unable to leave because of stragglers. The room was noisy with the babble of conversation and the motor of an air-conditioning unit struggling to cope with the constant opening and closing of the exit doors.

Jaz slid in on a bench seat next to Trish, who was flicking through a newspaper she'd bought. No Dan meant no free copy of *the Daily News*.

"Let's do the quick crossword," said Jaz, reaching in her bag for a pen and handing back Trish's phone. "That should wile away twenty minutes."

The crossword kept the friends entertained until a plump woman in her seventies pushed her way through the throng of drivers standing in the cramped waiting area, followed closely by her son. The pair sat on the two remaining seats. The woman spoke with a smoker's rasp, the man sported a neck tattoo and LOVE branded on the knuckles of his right hand.

"Whoever said this place was the best in the country with state-of-the-art technology needs their eyes testing, mate." The woman spoke to her son, in a tone and at a level suggesting her words were for public consumption. "We've been here nearly two hours and haven't seen a doctor. Then they tell us the machine's broken and we'll have to come back tomorrow. National Health Service? More like *No. Health. Service.*"

The woman spat out the last three words, emphasising what she deemed to be her sharp wit.

Jaz caught Trish's eye. They had the same thought. *Not more whiners.* The NHS saves countless lives every day and employs loyal, caring, compassionate professionals operating under enormous pressure. Most people understand that. So why do a few prefer to damn the entire concept after experiencing nothing worse than a dodgy coffee at the hospital kiosk?

Jaz's glance to Trish turned into a warning glare, followed by an index finger to the lips and an insistent, "Shh." She had already caused a scene that morning but knew her outburst would be nothing compared to the verbal conflagration if anyone lit Trish's fuse.

"It's a shithole, that's for sure," said the tattooed man.

On the verge of remonstrating, a couple of drivers looked around. An uneasy sense of impending confrontation filled the air.

A taxi driver, wearing a white turban, put his head around the door and spoke in a heavy accent. "Taxi for Taylor."

"That's us," said the man, rising to his feet and grabbing his mother's arm.

"At least this one speaks the lingo," said the irritated woman.

The drivers looked at each other, shook their heads and Trish put out an arm to help the woman to her feet, catching the woman's eyes for a moment.

Trish gave a sweet smile. "See you next Tuesday."

"Not bloody likely," replied the sour, confused woman.

Bill and Murph walked through the door, and Martin scurried off to bring the car to the pick-up point. He took the scenic route back to Lexford, missing out the dual carriageway, driving amid a land of big fields and rolling terrain, where swifts dived and darted overhead and farmers constructed huge fortress shapes out of hay bales. He had to stop three times. The delay with the broken machine meant Bill and Murph had replenished their water intake more than usual and Murph, in particular, was feeling the pressure.

On the third occasion, Bill announced, "I'll keep you company this time, Murph. I don't think I'll make it all the way home either."

As they waited, Jaz mulled over the details of a fractious morning. When the journey resumed, she asked Trish for an answer to something that had perplexed her for a while. "Trish, what does

'See you next Tuesday' mean? I've heard you say it quite a few times since we met, sometimes to people you don't know, and I have no idea."

"Really, Jaz. You don't know?"

"No."

"What about you, Bill? Murph?" Trish asked.

The men pulled faces and shrugged.

Trish laughed. "Come on. You're winding me up. You must know."

"Honest," said Jaz. "I heard you say it to that obnoxious woman today and thought you couldn't possibly know if she's coming back for treatment next Tuesday. And I remember you saying the same thing to that policeman, the one who stopped us for speeding."

"Okay, how can I put this?" said Trish, a giggle in her voice. She pinched her chin in a contemplative fashion. "Think what letters of the alphabet do the first two words sound like, then add the first letters of the last two words. What have you got?"

"Synt?" Murph asked.

Trish cackled. "Not quite, Murph. Try again."

"I've got it," said Bill. "Trish Parker, you should be ashamed of yourself."

Jaz was still confused. "Is it not ladylike?"

"Oh, yes, very ladylike," Bill chortled.

The car slowed as Martin approached traffic lights on his way into Lexford. "I'm not surprised Dan has gone missing," he said. "You lot are completely bonkers!"

26

Dan woke up, shivering. He had no blankets and despite the summer night, a cold draught sliced through the sliver of a gap in the roughly-hewn frame of the closed window. It must have been three or four in the morning. Maybe later.

For a moment, Dan didn't remember where he was. Then the bleak reality of the night before crushed his foggy brain. He mulled over the details. When Gheorghe had finished his telephone conversation, he'd craned his head around the door of the container and beckoned the bus driver to join him. He'd slammed the door, extinguishing the only light. Not a word to Dan. Not even a glance or a sneer in his direction. Dan had noticed there was no handle on the inside of the door. Why would there be in a shipping container or a prison cell? Take your pick.

The container wasn't pitch black. A haze of borrowed light, mostly from floodlights at the main entrance to the site seeped through the ill-fitting shutter. Dan had waited for his night vision to kick in, enough to detect movement. Then he'd asked Nico to translate the gist of the telephone call. The boy had been too far away to hear distinctly. He'd cowered in a corner, away from Dan and farther away from Gheorghe.

"Have you heard of Meester Collins?" Dan had said, assuming a similar accent to help the boy.

"No."

"Okay. What does curatatorie mean?"

"No understand what you say."

"Curatatorie," Dan repeated, changing the pronunciation.

"Ah. In English, it's what you call a cleaner."

"Shit." Dan shut his eyes and controlled his breathing.

Dan and Nico spent the next hour talking about the boy's family and his life back in Romania. Dan worked out that Nico's brother Andrei was the older attendant at the car wash, the one who'd told him Nico had returned home, doubtless in a bid to protect him. Dan suspected that he was also the culprit responsible for the hoax calls, probably in an attempt to rescue his brother. Nico had two younger sisters, but they lived in Romania with grandparents. They were in school and wanted to be nurses. Nico yearned to be an engineer, designing cars.

"Like Formula One," Nico told Dan. Grinning, he'd made the shape of a car with his right hand and simulated it gliding around an imaginary track, with a passable impression of an accelerating racing car engine. "I see on television, but I like speed." Nico's face had a mischievous twinkle. "I like noise. Big noise. I want to make these cars."

Inevitably, considering the permanence of his Barcelona cap, the chat drifted towards football. Within minutes, Dan concluded what Nico didn't know about European football, particularly the English Premier League, wasn't worth knowing. The chat switched to baseball, then basketball. Soon, Dan was out of his depth, Nico again displaying a comprehensive knowledge for one so young. It wasn't the knowledge that entranced Dan, more Nico's exuberance. Chained up like a dog for weeks, beaten and abused, yet he spoke with hope and ambition, retaining a beguiling charm that shone through his limited English.

The conversation changed to the possibilities of escape. This time, Nico was gloomy. His shackles remained in place because his incarceration, under threat of worse, helped Gheorghe keep Andrei and the rest of the young workers in line. Andrei brought food and water each day, accompanied by the bus driver or Gheorghe, which left no opportunity to talk or plan.

Dan tugged at the leather belt around his waist. Solid, unyielding, and, he determined, no amount of wriggling would make a difference. The lock at the front was like a clasp on an aeroplane seat belt except this one required a key. The chain connecting the belt with the metal ring bolted to the steel wall only confirmed Dan's fears. Freedom would need the key, a sturdy knife, or a sledgehammer. With that realisation, Dan settled back against the wall, and through sheer exhaustion coupled with effects of concussion, had fallen asleep.

A sense of foreboding filled his dreams. Curatatorie and Meester Collins churned through his mind. In the circumstances, Dan understood what a cleaner was, and it had nothing to do with the car wash. The cleaners coming Dan's way were the ruthless villains Cathy Wheeler had warned him about, the ones he'd promised to avoid. Hardened criminals hired to clear up any mess or dispose of obstacles, human or otherwise, threatening the profitability of the business.

"The Kray twins," Cathy had said.

In his dream, Dan saw the bus driver's black Glock G45 looming towards him and felt the barrel pressed against his forehead, so hard it cut a fine red circle in his skin. *Cold and metallic.*

"Do you feel lucky, Dan?" said a voice, sounding nothing like Dirty Harry.

The voice was familiar – a soft Middle-Eastern accent. No menace. In slow motion Dan saw a finger pull the trigger, the shooter's face fixed in a permanent grin, flesh and skin burned to the bone, shrouded in a mask of death. *Faz.* Then the snorting and whistling of three flying swans. But he was still alive and felt relief and respite and a soaring sense of well-being. Then the cycle started over. *Again and again.*

That was why he was shivering. It wasn't the cold; it was anxiety. The PTSD he'd denied but had come to recognise. The PTSD Lance had urged him to have treated, that Jaz had reignited with her questions. If he'd been back in his flat, Dan would have fiddled in his drawer and searched out a spliff. Instead, he resorted to a technique he'd learned in Syria when bombs dropped, guns fired and all he could do was curl under a table and hope it was not his unlucky day.

Dan started counting, rhythmically muttering under his breath, first, naming five things he could see, which wasn't easy in the darkness of the container. Bucket, ladders, door, window, Nico. Four he could touch – belt, metal, hair, skin then three he could hear – breathing, aeroplane, stillness. He cheated a little on the last one, but stillness rang in his ears. Anyway, who was checking? Down to two things he could smell. That was easy. Shit, piss. Finally, one he could taste. That was easy too. Blood. The coppery taste at the back of his throat that would stay until he took a drink of water to wash it away.

Dan had read about the counting technique in a survival pamphlet sourced by *the Daily News.* The Human Resources Department had issued leaflets to all staff required to undertake foreign trips, probably to comply with insurance responsibilities. The technique primarily alleviated panic attacks, and Dan had employed it on several occasions in Syria.

"I've yet to make it all the way to the end without becoming less anxious," the writer of the pamphlet insisted in the footnotes.

It was true. The method worked – Dan could vouch for that. Slowly, he felt calmer and warmer. The door clanged open, and the bus driver's silhouette loomed in the doorway. Dan sucked the gushing current of air deep into his lungs. After spending a night close to the contents of that bucket, the air tasted sweet and fresh. For a few moments, a shaft of early morning sunshine flooded the container, and Dan saw the extent of the dirt and grime in which Gheorghe forced the site's young workers to live.

On the wall opposite, Dan glimpsed a mural in a wide-angled frieze, fashioned in crayon and pencil, depicting various scenes. A boy on horseback, a boy at the wheel of a motor car, three dogs at feeding time, a girl with hideously over-applied make-up and a big man wielding a stick, baseball fashion. Dan wondered who'd drawn the pictures. A talented artist, but what did they mean? Did the figures tell a story, similar to the cave paintings of Neanderthal man, or the doodling of someone desperately relieving the boredom of these four walls?

The driver took two bottles of water from a

bag, rolled one to Dan and the other to Nico. Dan twisted the top and guzzled, three long slugs swilling away dust and blood at the back of his throat. He wiped his mouth with his sleeve and looked up to see Gheorghe pushing his way into the container carrying the broom handle.

"Stefan, you're needed in the warehouse," Gheorghe snapped at the bus driver, who immediately obeyed.

Gheorghe turned to Dan. "Good night?" he asked smirking and nodding at the bucket. "You like my hotel?"

"Room service isn't up to much, and you can tell the maid she's missed a spot or two of shit. But I suppose that's easy to do in a place like this." Dan's dilemma hadn't stemmed his sarcasm.

"Funny. You are very funny, Meester who?"

"No, I think you'll find it's Doctor Who?"

"It doesn't matter what your name is," said Gheorghe, oblivious to or perhaps underwhelmed by Dan's attempt at humorous bravado. "You will be staying with us today, and then you go for a little ride later. I don't think you will find that quite so funny."

Dan's mind whirred with all manner of extreme fears. However, he weighed it up, 'a little ride' could mean only one thing, and it wasn't a taxi cab to the nearest police station. Gheorghe turned to leave and stepped halfway outside the doorway.

"At least let the boy go," shouted Dan. "He's

just a kid. He's done nothing wrong. He can't do you any harm, and he's no use to you here."

Gheorghe spun around, fixing Dan with a hostile glare. "That is where you are wrong, meester. He is the most important person here. Because of him, the rest know what will happen if they don't do what I say."

27

When Trish arrived home from the Barrett Bailey, she prised herself out of the back seat of the MPV and was waving goodbye when Jaz opened the front passenger door. "Fancy a coffee?"

"Yeah, sure." Trish looked puzzled.

"Okay, I'll let you make one," said Jaz, waving to Martin and banging on the car roof to signal he could drive away. Martin had dropped Bill off, and only Murph remained.

"Hope you don't mind, Trish, but I wanted a word," Jaz said.

The women walked up the short driveway, and Jaz stood back to study the stylish three-storey semi-detached house. She'd seen the property from the car but hadn't taken much notice. Estimating that the place dated to the early 1900s, the house was in a smart area not far from Lexford Park, but on the opposite side to her parents.

"Nice place," Jaz smiled, which Trish took as code for, "How on earth can you afford this?"

"Oh, I only rent the bottom floor," said Trish, "and for how much longer I'm not sure."

Trish turned the key and entered a communal hallway. An impressive chandelier and stairs to the right led up to two more apartments. Trish fumbled with her keys, opened the front door, and Jaz walked into a beautifully appointed room she wasn't expecting. Lacquered oak flooring, expensive burgundy leather sofa lounging on a luxurious cream rug and an inviting log burner set into an inglenook fireplace.

A recent makeover had transformed two rooms into an open-plan living space, one end featuring a mahogany table with a silver candelabra as a centre point and six chairs with ornate backs and plush cream upholstery.

"It's gorgeous," said Jaz, surveying the walls adorned with Impressionist prints, among them Monet, Renoir, and Van Gogh.

"Don't sound so surprised."

"Sorry, Trish, it's just I expected something a bit more, well, modern maybe."

"You mean, blingy."

Blingy was exactly what Jaz meant. The elegant décor was at odds with the tottering heels and garish nail varnish. Three gold rings on Trish's right hand, an ankle bracelet, and gaudy line in headscarves didn't match the apartment's cultured sophistication. Nor did the moving admittance of Trish's car-crash life.

"Too many people believe the stereotypes about Essex girls," said Trish. "Sure, we like a bit of fun, and I'm no good at quizzes or crosswords. I was hopeless at school exams, can't speak a foreign language, hell, I'm not always that great at English. That aside, in other ways, we ladies are as smart as anyone else. I bought a couple of houses for a song in the 90s, and after renovation, renting for ten years then selling for a tidy sum, I was able to pay for all this."

"Good for you."

"Let's have that coffee." Trish headed into the small but well-appointed kitchen. She made two mugs of instant with water too near the boil, and the couple sat on contoured wooden stools letting the steaming coffee cool on the kitchen worktop.

"I need you to help me find Dan," said Jaz.

"Okay," said Trish, a little diffidently.

"I would have asked Bill and Murph, but Bill is struggling at the moment, and poor Murph can't go anywhere these days without having to visit the loo. It's down to us, Trish."

"I thought it was down to the Honeycomb service or the police," said Trish.

"They don't realise. Dan must be in danger – he wouldn't have gone missing without contacting us. He has my phone as well as his own and has had a terrible accident, or his absence has something to do with that car wash. It could be too late if we wait for the police to get interested."

"Okay, count me in," said Trish with trepidation.

Jaz leaned over and squeezed Trish's hand. Trish had been looking forward to an hour or two dozing in front of afternoon television to ward off fatigue caused by daily radiotherapy. The nap had become a regular occurrence these past weeks, but sleep could wait for once. After drinking coffee, the women grabbed their handbags and Trish grabbed her car keys. Jaz didn't own a car and Trish hadn't driven for months following the advice from her consultant that driving was unsafe while undergoing treatment. There was every chance the insurance was currently invalid. You would have thought Trish would know that working in a call centre selling insurance. However, such details rarely worried Trish.

"Let's start with the hospital," said Jaz.

Twenty minutes later, the ladies pitched up at Lexford Infirmary in Trish's red Renault Clio. Rather than heading straight to A&E and demanding to know if doctors had treated or admitted anyone named Dan or Armitage, the couple avoided a data protection jobsworth and hurried to the oncology department. During many visits for surgery and chemotherapy, Trish had made friends with a nurse called Ellen, a fellow Essex girl with a bubbly personality and similar air-raid cackle. She was on the day ward, helping patients requiring infusions. The infirmary possessed no radiotherapy machines, but routinely administered chemotherapy.

Trish and Ellen threw their arms around each other and caught up with girlie small talk before

Trish explained the reason for the visit.

"Sit right there," said Ellen, pointing to a clinical line of plastic chairs in the waiting room. "Be back in no time."

Minutes later she burst through the double doors crossing her arms horizontally in front of her. "I've been through all the lists with my mate from A&E, and no one called Dan or Armitage has been through here."

Jaz wasn't sure whether to be relieved or disappointed. She and Trish thanked Ellen for her assistance and returned to the car.

"Where now?" said Trish.

"Dan's place."

"How do you know where he lives?"

"I asked Martin when he mentioned the Honeycomb people had been to check on Dan's flat."

"Yes, but they found nothing."

"Maybe, but let's see what we can find."

Late afternoon and the rush-hour traffic was building up in Lexford, not helped by a burst water main, which had flooded the High Street, causing gridlock. The car crawled across the bridge over the river, and the women spent an hour inhaling petrol and diesel fumes before turning into the road housing Dan's upmarket apartment block, Paltrow Court. They took the lift to the second floor. Jaz knocked at number 20, and as expected, there was no answer. She tried number 21 – again no response. She headed along the corridor to number 19, relieved when the door opened. Learning of Jaz and Trish's mission, Mike's wife, Julie, beckoned them inside, telling the pair what they already knew. One of Dan's colleagues visited, and Julie let him into Dan's flat with her spare key. There was nothing to suggest anything was out of place.

"When did you last see Dan?" asked Jaz.

"Yesterday morning. No, wait, I saw him last night. I'm not sure what time. Between eight or nine maybe. He was going out on his bike."

"I see," said Jaz, encouraged by this sighting.

"I thought it strange because Dan tends to ride early in the morning. Always drops a newspaper in on the way back. I heard his door shut then caught a glimpse of him from the panoramic window as he cycled towards Lexford town centre."

"Did you hear or see him return?" asked Jaz.

"No."

"Can you describe Dan's bike?"

"I can do better than that."

Julie motioned to Jaz and Trish to follow her into the utility room – a road bike leaned against the worktop. Black, sweeping white trim and the brand name written on the frame. SPECIALIZED. The words Roubaix Sport were also prominent and a distinctive yellow bottle cradle clung to one of the vertical bars.

"This is Mike's bike," said Julie. "He bought his at the same time as Dan. They're always talking bikes and got a discount for buying two identical models at the same time."

Jaz noted the make, colour and trim, thanked Julie for her help then hurried back to the car with Trish.

"Next stop Ernie's," said Jaz, feeling better already, if only because she was doing something constructive rather than worrying.

"Won't it be closed now?" said Trish.

"We'll find out."

Reaching Ernie's around 7:30 pm, the pair found the gates shut. Trish drove past the main entrance and turned left into the next side road running along the perimeter.

"Slow down and go all the way around if you can," Jaz urged.

"Yes, boss."

Jaz gave Trish a sharp glance then surveyed the entire site through the metal railings as they edged along the road. With cloud cover, the dusk gathered fast. One of the site's security lights illuminated the main entrance, but there was no sign of activity. The place appeared locked up for the night.

"Stop."

"What?"

"Stop!"

Trish braked, and Jaz pointed to a gateway in the metal railings where there was a gap in the razor wire. Leaning against the gate was a black bike with white trim.

Jaz peered through the gloom and read the brand name. SPECIALIZED. "I knew it," Jaz said with a triumphant trill.

"What now?"

28

Dan tried to stay positive. Waiting came with his job. Interviewees who didn't turn up. Press conferences delayed. Improvised explosives requiring detonation before a journey could continue. Waiting had become a routine part of life.

This time was different. This time Dan was waiting for the inevitable, and he didn't know how to change the situation. He and Nico had exhausted their conversation. There were only so many football teams Dan was prepared to discuss and Dinamo Bucharest, the boy's passion alongside Barcelona, wasn't one of them.

Stefan had tossed in two more bottles of water. Both Dan and Nico swigged the liquid then the boy settled in the corner, slow, easy breathing culminating in sleep. Dan listened to the rhythm, mulling over two things – his past and whether he had a future. Resting his chin on his knees, he thought of Annie. He remembered how they'd met at a Christmas fresher's ball, chatting about music and mutual friends when Annie looked up, giggled and pointed at a large sprig of mistletoe.

"It would be rude not to, wouldn't it?" Dan had said. He took Annie in his arms, kissing her slowly and gently for what seemed like the rest of the evening.

After that first kiss, the couple were inseparable, Annie even supporting Dan from the touchline every Wednesday afternoon as he played football for the art department at Manchester University. Dan did his part, turning up without fail when Annie was the star turn, as she always was, at the debating society. He remembered her devouring his sweet and sour chicken stir fry. How impressed he was when she mixed Mojitos, Margaritas, and Rum Caipirinhas without consulting a cocktail recipe. Dan also remembered how sad films moved Annie to tears, recalling their time together as if it were yesterday. A perfect fit – so passionate and natural.

Dan hadn't experienced such a comfortable, warm relationship with a woman since Annie. At least, not until he met Jaz. His mind drove down another avenue of daydreams, reliving the last weeks in Jaz's company. The emu incident and quiz confrontation. The search for her dad and the story of her past. A feeling of joy and optimism surging through his veins, yes, even when she called him an idiot. He wanted to cling to those memories. He had to. If he didn't, he knew he would immerse himself in darkness and negative thoughts. Such as how he'd become Lexford's version of Mr Bean, vaulting that perimeter fence in a cycling helmet, and walking headfirst into a broom handle before an assignation with Jimmy Collins's henchmen.

Dan's mind was in turmoil as the door opened. Not flung back as it had been by Stefan and Gheorghe, instead, eased ajar with a tentative prod. Dan looked up, half-expecting Stefan to hurl another water bottle his way and couldn't believe who he saw.

"Jordan."

Dan rubbed his eyes, focused again, and the pock-marked face, long, lank hair and shifty expression stared back. Adrenaline exploded deep in Dan's sympathetic nervous system, cogs whirred in his disbelieving mind, and his heart hammered as he fought against the belt restraining him. He tried to reach, perhaps throttle if he could, this young man he'd never trusted.

"Jordan. You're one of them. You sad loser. You're one of them."

"Dan?"

Even in Dan's state of turbulence, the inflexion of disbelief in Jordan's trembling voice was unmistakable.

"What are you doing here? Why are you tied up?"

"Never mind me. You first. What the hell are you doing here?"

"I was looking for Jaz."

"Jaz?"

"Yes Jaz, the lady from the petrol—"

"I know who Jaz is, creep. Why are you looking for her here?"

"Because this is where she is. I've been following her."

"What?"

"I've been tracking her on my phone."

Jordan removed the phone from his pocket, and a pulsing blue line lit up the display screen pinpointing Jaz's device at Ernie's car wash.

"You've bugged Jaz's phone?" said Dan. Are you stalking her?"

Dan launched himself at Jordan, this time managing to grab his arm and send the phone flying before wrestling him to the floor.

"You're a nasty, good-for-nothing pervert," spat Dan. He tried to punch the back of Jordan's head with his right fist and pressing his skull into Jordan's left ear with such force, a piercing yelp echoed around the container.

Jordan jammed a forearm under Dan's chin, attempting to stem the attack and felt his skin burn as it scraped across the rough stubble. They strained against each other, sinews protesting, bones cracking, grunting and gasping for breath, clinging so tight they resembled surreal lovers in a clinch. For a few seconds, the fight was even, but as they rolled in the toxic detritus, Dan began to gain the advantage. Despite giving away more than 20 years, he was wider, heavier, stronger, fitter.

Close to exhaustion, Jordan let out a scream

of desperation, tears running down his cheeks. "Dan, Dan, you don't understand! I love Jaz. I love her, Dan."

"So do I. I love Jaz!" Dan roared back, spit and blood rolling down his chin, the realisation of what he'd said tumbling into his consciousness.

It was out. There was no putting that sentence back in the box.

Shaking with emotion, Dan and Jordan glared at each other, faces so close they inhaled each other's hot breath and spittle.

Gasping, Dan pulled Jordan's head against his. "Okay, Jordan, okay."

"I'm not a pervert, Dan, honest. I just wanted to look after Jaz when she got sick."

"Okay, Jordan. I believe you."

Slowly, the pair disentangled, and Jordan went on to tell Dan how Jaz had asked him to help set up her new phone before starting her cancer treatment. As resident amateur IT expert at the petrol station, Jordan was eager to assist. Armed with her password, he'd taken the opportunity to synch her phone with his, which took less than the four minutes she was away from the check-out making coffee. Jordan had tracked Jaz's every move since.

The coincidences all began to make sense. How Jordan knew Dan was Jaz's Honeycomb driver when spotting him buying petrol. Jordan turning up at the White Horse quiz and why he was outside Dan's apartment when Jaz left her phone in the MPV. Now, the phone tap had brought Jordan to Ernie's car wash to find Dan in his hour of need. *The Lord certainly moves in mysterious ways.*

"Where is Jaz?" said Jordan, bruised and bewildered and for the first time taking in the stinking squalor of the container and the plight of Dan and Nico.

Sitting in the corner, Nico stared, displaying no emotion, just the puzzled expression of a child accustomed to violence and confrontation.

Dan said he didn't have a clue where Jaz was but had borrowed her phone the night before. "Never mind. Do you have a knife to cut this strap?"

Jordan pulled an object from his back pocket. Dan had never met anyone who carried or at least admitted to carrying a Swiss Army knife. He grabbed the object, scrutinising the blunt blade, tiny corkscrew and other gizmos. Dan concluded that if he had two days to unpick the seam of the leather strap, plus a decent torch, the gadget might have come in useful.

Right now, a motorbike and an ashtray came to Dan's mind. He thrust the knife into his pocket and told Jordan about the beatings, the drugs warehouse, the gun and how Gheorghe had imprisoned Nico for weeks.

"Listen, Jordan. You need to call the police. Tell them where we are and about the gun."

"Where's my phone?" Jordan looked around

the dark reaches of the container, panic in his eyes.

"I sent it flying when I went for you. To your right, I think."

Jordan dropped to all fours and crawled along the floor, a glimmer of fading light from the gap in the open door pointing the way. He came across a couple of empty plastic bottles, a shoe, a discarded spanner and a sticky mess in a corner – a spillage, which had been there a long while. Finally, Jordan grasped his phone and jumped up. Now he could show Dan he wasn't good for nothing. He pressed the fingerprint recognition button, the device burst into life and Jordan jabbed 999. Nothing. He tried again and again – still nothing.

"Oh, no! There's no signal."

"Calm down. You should get a signal outside. Tell the police to get here, quick. We're relying on you."

Jordan turned to go, stopping when he heard disc brakes of a powerful vehicle engage and the crunch of tyres on the gravel outside the container. He looked at Dan. The pair struggled to see each other.

Dan pointed upwards. "The ladder, Jordan."

A heavy door slammed.

As Jordan climbed, he heard boots on the steps outside the container door. The door flung open, and Gheorghe and Stefan strode in. Gheorghe turned on the low pink light, and two other men followed. Around 40, stocky, with an athletic gait, one of the men stood more than 6ft tall. He wore black trousers, a black leather jacket, a round-necked grey and black hooped jumper and dark glasses with black frames – Darth Vader came to Dan's mind. The man had dark hair, and his jaw's slight overbite gave him a stern demeanour. The eyes were small and close together. *The eyes of a killer?* Dan thought so. He looked the type who could handle himself.

The other man, in his fifties, was shorter and paunchy with pale features and thin, receding red hair, combed forward. Cream trousers and white shirt emphasised the man's pallor, and he'd fashioned a crisp knot in a cream and brown striped tie. A light brown overcoat and brown leather gloves suggested he felt the cold even on a summer's night.

"This is the problem, Meester Collins," said Gheorghe, directing his words to the pale man and pointing at Dan, who was kneeling on the floor, looking up.

Jimmy Collins leaned against the ladder and took a packet of cigarettes from his pocket. Slipping off a glove, he lit up, taking a long, slow drag. He exhaled a cloud of smoke and spoke in a soft, high-pitched Belfast accent. "I've seen bigger problems crawl out of a plum."

Dan thought he'd never seen anyone look or sound less like a gangster.

Collins fixed Dan with eyes devoid of sparkle

or compassion. "What's a fine-looking man like yourself doing nosing around here? Who are you?"

Dan saw little point in fabricating a story and told the truth, or at least an edited version. He gave his name and confirmed what he did for a living. Not the war correspondent bit, just that he worked for a charity, transporting cancer patients to and from hospital. He left out his knowledge of Collins's crime empire and his suspicion that Ernie's was a central player in a slave gang ring. Instead, he described how he'd witnessed Nico's beating, his concern for the teenager and further worry when he thought the lad had disappeared. Dan said he'd turned up at the car wash after work hours and scaled the perimeter fence to see if he could find Nico. That was all.

"And now you have found him," said Collins, flicking ash and smiling over at Nico. "If you don't mind me saying, that's a public-spirited thing to be doing, looking out for a young boy. Surely it is. I'm impressed. I admire you, but here's the thing. Your actions give me a wee problem. See, why would a man searching for a poor, lost, beaten-up kid be inside my warehouse taking photographs, recording the security cameras and my site from every angle? They aren't good photos, it's true, but there are enough to fill a family album."

Dan's heart sank. *He'd trawled through Jaz's*

phone. "It's a new phone. I was trying out the camera," he lied.

"Of course, that would be it. I wish I could believe you, but that would be taking me for a fool, you agree?"

"I don't think you're a fool," said Dan, who'd concluded the presence of Collins meant two things.

First, Ernie's was a small but vital part of his empire, ideally situated astride the motorway networks to run drugs, illegal immigrants, and prostitutes to all parts of the country. Second, the chance of him walking out of Ernie's was sliding from slim to non-existent. Knees numb, Dan tried to control his aching bladder as the bleakness of his predicament registered. His throat was dry, his head spun, and an ugly churning squatted in the pit of his stomach. Taking a deep breath to stem the panicked feeling, Dan fixed Collins with an insolent glare.

"I think you're a gangster." Dan's voice was calm. "Not the sort with a code of honour, who only shoot and maim other gangsters muscling in on their patch. More the kind preying on young children, turning kids into slaves and girls into prostitutes."

A calculated gamble. Dan had witnessed insurgents pleading during interrogations in Afghanistan and Iraq, heard stories of civilians begging for their lives at the hands of terrorists. It never induced compassion. Dan didn't want to die but reasoned no one gained respect or won reprieve by showing weakness.

"What am I saying? You're not a gangster. You're a petty criminal who deals in dodgy car washes and seedy nail parlours. Pushing drugs. Do you never think of the lives you're ruining?"

Collins's thin lips tightened and for the first time, his eyes smouldered, but his voice remained soft and calm. "That's a nice speech, Dan. Truly, it is. But we knew you weren't taking photographs for fun. You were taking them for evidence. NCA. Police. Newspapers. Television. You could represent any media. I don't care. What I do care about and know is that you have cost me a lot of money and inconvenience."

"I wanted to take care of Nico, that's all," repeated Dan.

"What do you think we've been doing? He can stay with us for as long as he likes."

Dan bristled. "You mean he can run drugs and work for next to nothing. What sort of life is that?"

Collins savoured a long drag of nicotine and dropped his cigarette to the floor, grinding the butt into the rest of the trash. "Tell me, Dan, have you ever taken drugs? Maybe once, perhaps when you were a student? A little cocaine? The odd bit of weed?"

Dan licked his dry lips. For a moment, he averted his eyes, and Collins detected a hint of doubt. The memory of the spliff that had eased his anxiety after the horrors of Iraq invaded his dreams played through Dan's mind. Crucially, he proffered no denial.

Collins laughed. Cold. Callous. "I thought so. Supply and demand, Dan. People want what I sell. That doesn't make them bad people. What I sell is good, clean stuff – no dodgy gear. We don't do that. It's a living. Pure and simple. A lot of people wouldn't have jobs without us."

Dan was incredulous. *This situation was surreal.* Was Collins trying to justify his exploitation to a man shackled to a wall in a stinking container? A man with no chance of escape!

"I think we have done enough talking," said Collins.

Dan shivered even though his hair stuck to his forehead with sweat. He ran his parched tongue around cracked lips, a warm trickle of fear running down the inside of his thigh. He believed he knew what was coming next.

Collins reached inside his jacket for another cigarette and spotted the dark void in the ceiling. He sensed movement above him, the scrape of a foot? A puzzled expression played across his face, and he mouthed, "Johnny" to his minder, motioning him to check out the upper container. Collins was moments away from discovering Jordan and his phone. Dan couldn't let Johnny extinguish his only hope and had seconds to decide.

As Johnny headed for the ladder, Dan pulled Jordan's Swiss Army knife from his trouser pocket. Blindly, he flicked open a couple of the tools and lunged upwards from his kneeling position. The minder anticipated the blow and tried to swerve the impact, but Dan got lucky. The knife ricocheted off Johnny's downward jab, diverting inwards but continuing upwards. The combined force and precision of the screwdriver and nail file embedded in Johnny's groin. Collapsing to the floor, the man screamed as never before.

29

Trish's crisp tone reverberated around the Renault, "Bollocks." Accustomed to the pithy delivery, Jaz looked across at her search party partner and smiled. "Honest. I'm sure that's right, Trish. Could have been more."

"Come on, how big would a wardrobe have to be to hold that many pairs of shoes?"

"They lived in a palace, Trish. Malacanang Palace. It wouldn't be a wardrobe like in your house or mine. Probably a huge corridor."

"Like the Dartford Tunnel, you mean," Trish said, exaggerating for effect.

The girls sat in Carlo's car park overlooking Ernie's, not far from the spot where Dan observed the car wash days earlier. No smart-aleck security man this time. Carlo's had packed up for the night, and doubtless, the security man was home watching some omnipresent TV quiz show. Jaz and Trish made a wise decision against vaulting the perimeter gate for a snoop around and chose to stick about until dark. The conversation had turned to shoes, mainly because Trish was wearing her highest heels and the thought of scaling that fence highlighted their obvious impracticality. That the couple were cancer patients, had compromised immune systems, no hair and were weakened by a course of debilitating treatment didn't come into consideration.

Trish admitted to owning 50 pairs of shoes and thought she detected a disapproving look from Jaz. "Including flip-flops and slippers," she added hastily.

Jaz owned ten pairs, which led to her telling Trish about the time she'd flown to Marikina in the Philippines as part of her job with the FCO. On a spare afternoon, she'd whiled away a couple of hours at the shoe museum, housing hundreds of shoes owned by Imelda Marcos, the former first lady of the Philippines, renowned for her extravagant lifestyle. Jaz remembered reading the exhibit information card stating that Imelda's wardrobe held 2,700 pairs of shoes when protestors stormed the palace after her husband's fall from power.

"There was also a card with a famous quote from Imelda," said Jaz.

"What did she say?"

"They went into my closets looking for skeletons, but thank God, all they found were shoes, beautiful shoes," said Jaz, pleased with herself for memorising the quote word for word.

"I hope we're not looking for skeletons."

"Don't even joke, Trish."

A throaty engine driving at speed up to Ernie's gates interrupted the idle chat. A black 4x4 BMW with tinted windows, the type of motor used in presidential motorcades or, Jaz mused, drug drops. The engine revved and headlights flashed until electronic gates swung open and the vehicle surged forward, pulling up outside the containers where two men waited.

Jaz and Trish saw one of the men open the passenger door. A man climbed out followed by his black-clad driver. All four disappeared into a container. "What do you think, Trish?"

"Looks like something out of *The Godfather*."

"Oh, don't. Do you think Dan's in there?" Jaz wore an anxious frown.

"Let's find out." Trish turned the key in the ignition and switched on the Clio's lights. Dusk was fading.

Quite what Trish thought she and Jaz were going to do was unclear. Perhaps screech into Ernie's, bang on the container door and order the brutes to hand over Dan and his bike or else they'd feel the sharp end of her stilettos. That could easily have been Trish's plan. If so, it was fortunate that as the car began to move, the women heard three bangs on the roof. Dressed in dark blue jeans, black jackets and peaked caps with a black and white band, two men appeared – one at the driver's side, the other at the passenger window.

A tingle of trepidation tinged with intrigue rifled through Trish's body and her first thought was to slam her foot down on the accelerator. Instead, she pushed the button to wind down the window. "What's your game, pal?" Trish said, wondering if she and Jaz had wandered into one of those night-time car park assignations she'd read about.

"Are you Mrs Parker?"

"Who wants to know?"

The man flipped open a leather wallet displaying an embossed crown emblem, his name, warrant number and the words, National Crime Agency.

"Yes, I'm Mrs Parker. How do you know my name?"

"We checked your car registration on the police database. What are you doing here?"

"Looking for a friend," Jaz shouted across Trish.

"And who might that be?"

"His name's Dan Armitage and …"

The officer frowned, cupped his jacket collar around his ear and spoke into a mobile phone attached to his headphones.

Jaz and Trish couldn't follow his conversation, but 'Armitage' surfaced several times above the indistinct chatter. There was a pause, which the friends took to be the officer waiting for confirmation. Eventually, he leaned on the car window frame into Trish's car.

"Don't be alarmed," he said, leaving Jaz thinking was there any phrase more likely to induce a state of alarm? "We have reason to believe Mr Armitage may be in the premises below. He could be in danger, but we have everything under control."

Jaz and Trish heard the whir of a helicopter then a car pulled up on the far side of the car park. Four men tumbled out wearing black jackets bearing the National Crime Agency's insignia, two in the front carrying semi-automatic carbines with holographic sights attached and two behind with pistols in their holsters. Dread consumed the occupants in the Clio.

Jaz elbowed Trish. "Now, I'm scared. It's like being in one of those hostage films when everything kicks off near the end."

30

The butt of the Glock 45 pistol smashed into Dan's skull. Stefan delivered the blow, leaving Johnny tearful and curled up in the foetal position near Nico, paralysed by pain the like of which he'd never experienced.

Dan slumped over, then rose to his knees as Gheorghe's boot landed in the pit of his stomach. Dan felt an overwhelming crack, a wave of heat and nausea as though something or someone was ripping his guts from his body. He turned to the light, blood seeping from a head wound. Collins's pale face came into soft pink focus.

"You know ... violence is rarely ... the best option," Dan slurred, as he cleared his brain. "You can still walk away, Mr Collins. We could all live to tell the tale."

"That's what worries me." Collins stubbed out his cigarette on the ladder frame and flicked it away. "And, let me remind you, Dan, you started the violence."

"No. You beat me to it by twenty years or more."

"I think we've seen and heard enough here."

"What happened to Ernie?"

The question had been troubling Dan for some time and caught Collins by surprise.

"Ah, Ernie. Nice chap. He ran a good, clean business – all above board. He looked after his cars – that Mercedes of his was immaculate. Unfortunately, Ernie was a lot like you, Dan. He didn't see the big picture, had no imagination. I made him a generous offer, truly I did. Too generous. But Ernie was not for selling."

"So you killed him."

"I wouldn't put it quite as blunt," said Collins, swaggering in the apparent ubiquity of his power. "Let's just say two worlds collided, and Ernie's planet went the way of the dinosaur. E for Ernie. E for Extinct." Collins chuckled. He liked that analogy. "But enough of this small talk."

Collins motioned to Gheorghe, and a smug smile played on the big man's lips. Gheorghe turned to Stefan and beckoned with his fingers for the Glock 45. With a slap, the butt of the gun landed in his palm. Gheorghe stood over Dan slowly raising the barrel, intent on savouring the moment. A kaleidoscope of unconnected thoughts danced in Dan Armitage's mind. He remembered Nico's beating, the first time he'd faced this bully down. Dan knew that the Romanian relented because of a police threat and the fear that any investigation would compromise the secrecy of the operation. That would have exposed him to the cruel wrath of Collins.

Dan thought of all the war zones visited, all the tight spots in which he'd found himself, all the precautions taken and how stupid he'd been to sleepwalk into this mess. He remembered Faz and immediately felt guilty. Recalled Annie and that vibrant, exciting time in his life when the two of them believed they had a lifetime together and everything seemed possible. Dan focused on Jaz and how she would have called him an idiot, reflected on what might have been and felt an ache combined with a warm glow inside. Waiting for the inevitable, Dan hung his head.

Gheorghe lifted the barrel, his trigger finger increasing pressure. Collins and Stefan braced themselves for the loud shockwave at discharge.

Pop ... pop ... pop.

Three loud shots in rapid succession reverberated around the container. Gheorghe dropped the gun, and it clattered to the floor. Perplexed, he turned to his right to see Nico pointing a black revolver, the barrel, smoking. *Johnny's revolver.* When felled by Dan's Swiss Army thrust, Nico had removed the weapon from the minder's jacket. Three shots – payback for the beatings and abuse he, Andrei and the other car wash kids had suffered at the hands of Gheorghe these past six months. Nico stared ahead. Dead eyes. No expression of shock or remorse on his face. Just a matter-of-fact robotic stare, as if in a trance.

Gheorghe staggered backwards clutching his chest and stomach, a seeping red patch staining his light-blue shirt. He slumped to the floor, gurgling and wheezing, his right foot twitching at an odd angle. Stefan grabbed the gun from Nico. As he turned to face Collins, he saw a figure jump or fall, he wasn't sure, from the void in the ceiling and land on Collins's shoulders. The Irishman went down as Jordan wrapped his right arm around the man's neck.

"Good for you, Jordan," shouted Dan.

"Shoot the bastards, shoot them!" screeched Collins.

Stefan swung the gun around. He looked towards Dan but wanted to free Collins before dealing with him. Stuck fast and choking, Collins struggled against Jordan's grip. Stefan took a couple of paces towards Jordan to fire off an accurate shot. From three feet away, he pointed the gun at Jordan's right leg, the only part of his anatomy visible.

Terrified, Jordan's eyes opened wide. Still maintaining his hold, he braced himself against the impact. "No, don't. Please. No!"

There was a thunderous bang, the container shook and filled with smoke, and the stench of cordite overwhelmed. Four black-clad figures carrying semi-automatic weapons burst through the door.

Dan couldn't hear. It was as if he were swimming underwater in an alien world, looking in on events over which he had no control. He could have been alive he could have been dead. He wasn't sure. The smoke from the stun grenade cleared, and Dan's head throbbed. Realising he was alive he didn't know whether to laugh or cry. Dan did both, shoulders shaking, chest heaving as he sobbed and chuckled. The armed-response squad secured Collins, disarmed Stefan and dragged Johnny down the steps of the container and out into the night. Two officers grabbed Jordan by the collar and pulled him in the same way. Disorientated by the explosion from the assault team's stun grenade, Jordan had also damaged his right ankle in the jump from the ceiling void.

"No, he's a good guy, he's one of us," shouted Dan, a sentence he didn't expect to say that night.

The officers ignored Dan and yanked Jordan outside.

"Dan Armitage?" The chief officer holstered his pistol.

Dan blinked away blood running from his head wound. "That's me."

"We need to free you, get you to the hospital and then a briefing, okay?"

Dan nodded.

The chief glanced across at two more officers who'd piled into the container to untether Nico. The boy looked straight ahead into the distance, saying nothing, eyes and mind anywhere but in the maelstrom of his living hell for the past three weeks.

"Go easy on him. He's been through the mill.

He's only a kid, but he saved my life for sure," said Dan.

When Dan was free, he rose to his feet and swayed for a few moments, searching for balance. Shrugging aside an officer who tried to help, he limped outside. After inhaling clouds of ammonia for more than 24 hours, the enveloping fresh air felt divine. Fussing paramedics surrounded Dan, stemming the bleeding to his head. They checked his vital signs and made sure he was safe to move before insisting on wheeling him on a trolley to the waiting ambulance.

Edging to the ambulance, Dan refused. "I got myself into this mess. I'm damn well going to walk out of it."

With a police helicopter overhead and sirens splitting the night air, Dan could barely think. Near the entrance to Ernie's, huddled with a small group of onlookers behind police tape cordoning off the area, Dan saw Jaz. The words he'd yelled at Jordan flooded his brain. *Oh God, did I say I love Jaz?*

Dan's head thumped to a violent beat, blood and sweat stinging his eyes. His mind gyrated with possibilities laced with yearning and excitement but constricted by PTSD, a lifetime without Annie and a fear of rejection, which he had never admitted, not even to himself. The memory of his words surfaced again. *Yes, I said I love her. What now?* Dan called Jaz's name, but the commotion devoured his shouts. He waved his arms, undeterred by the searing pain in his ribs and chest.

A paramedic attempted to lead Dan away, but Dan fended him off. His eyes met Jaz's, and he could no longer hear the helicopter or see blue lights flashing. The couple gazed at each other, Dan allowing himself to bathe in the warmth and intensity of Jaz's eyes, letting her gaze caress him, soothe his aching wounds. He saw Jaz's lips mouth his name, a concerned look sweep across her face before stress and dread drained away, instinct took over, and she ducked under the tape and sprinted towards him.

A police officer outstretched an arm to stop her, but Jaz sidestepped him losing a shoe in the process. Her eyes shone with relief and joy and seconds later she was in Dan's arms, hugging him with such force he thought he might pass out as another sharp spasm rifled his ribs. Neither of them spoke. Instead, Jaz sobbed, while Dan's shoulders heaved. The couple clung to each other, their body heat making both feel safe and secure until two paramedics gently prised them apart.

Even then, Dan's hold lingered on Jaz's shoulders as he looked deep into pale blue eyes. Smudges of purple mascara mixed with tears reminded him of the time in the ambulance car when he'd revealed her panda eyes in the vanity mirror and they'd laughed until they hurt. In the catch of the next moment, something profound and emotional stirred within Dan Armitage. He had never felt more alive. He bent down and kissed Jaz tenderly on the lips, snuggled against her cheek and whispered in her ear. "I love you, Robin Ellacott."

Jaz giggled and looked up at Dan, hair, matted with blood, right eye closed, nose split in two places. Overwhelmed by the tension and anxiety of a traumatic night, she said the first word that came into her head. "Idiot!"

31

A police officer ushered Jaz back behind the tape to where Trish stood. Dan clambered into the ambulance.

"I thought I told you to steer clear of Jimmy Collins," a familiar voice reproached.

"Cathy! What the hell are you doing here?"

"Trying to look after you and may I say, that is not an easy job."

A paramedic eased Dan onto the ambulance trolley.

Cathy Wheeler sat in one of the passenger seats and pushed her spectacles to the top of her nose, notebook and pen poised. "Okay, tell me all about it. What went on in there? You look a complete mess."

"Thanks. Shouldn't I be telling the police first?"

"You're a journalist, Dan, what do you think?"

"But how did you know?"

"Jasmine phoned. She was worried when you went missing. She thought your disappearance was out of character and when she realised the local police weren't interested she called *the Daily News* looking for me. She sounded a bit chaotic as you'd borrowed her phone, so she didn't have any contact numbers. Apparently, you told her all about me. Said I was your most trusted colleague and friend, or something like that. I'm flattered, I suppose.

"As soon as Jaz mentioned the car wash, I remembered our conversation. You know, when I told you what a nasty piece of work Collins and his cronies were, to stay away, and you said you would run a mile if you bumped into them or words to that effect."

Through all the blood and bandages, Dan managed to look sheepish. "I know, Cathy, but I was only going for a quick nose around. I wasn't banking on running into Jimmy Collins in Lexford."

Cathy gave another reproachful look. "I called my contact at the National Crime Agency, the one I've been working with for the special investigation. When I mentioned Collins, he was interested. The Agency was searching for Collins in London but began monitoring routes into Lexford and spotted one of his vehicles on the motorway. They didn't know he was inside but decided to chuck up the works just in case. Helicopters, armed response team. Impressive."

"Thank Christ they did."

"No, thank Jasmine."

"And you."

"Too right. I would have looked a real muppet if they'd descended on a car wash and found nothing but a bucket and brush."

Dan accepted two painkillers and a cup of

water to swig them down, a medic cleaned the wound on his head, and the ambulance driver took off for Lexford Infirmary.

"Look, Dan, we haven't got long. *The Mail*, *Sun* and *Express* are on their way, and I need to stay ahead of this and make the main edition with the real story," said Cathy. "I know one man was shot dead and another four are in custody. What happened?"

The cabin paramedic put out her hand in a protective fashion. "I don't think he's in a fit state to be answering questions."

"Oh, yes he is," said Cathy, who'd posed as his 'other half' at Ernie's and persuaded one of her NCA chums to turn a blind eye to her trip on the ambulance.

"I'm all right," said Dan.

In the time it took to reach Lexford Infirmary, Dan told Cathy what he'd learned. The cannabis farm, hard drugs warehouse, the drug runners and his suspicions about prostitution rings, slave labour, and child abuse. Dan described the moment he thought he was going to die and gave a sketchy account of Nico's story. How Gheorghe held the boy captive, tethered him for three weeks and how Nico saved his life. He also told Cathy that Collins admitted killing Ernie Watkins.

"It's a great story, Dan, but how will the cops put Jimmy Collins away? It's your word against his. At the moment they have him placed at a crime scene, but he didn't kill anyone or shoot a gun as far as I know. He was wearing gloves so won't have left fingerprints, and you can bet your life his name and bank balance isn't traceable to that car wash or anything to do with Ernie. He'll pay off his men to do a spell in jail like countless times before."

Dan looked deflated. "He was boasting about the whole operation. There must be something to tie him to Ernie."

"Not when his thousand-pound an hour brief arrives. The fact that he showed up at all tells you Ernie's was important to his operation, but he'll concoct a fairy tale, get bail, skulk off into the night and there's every chance he might not come to court."

"What about Jordan?" Dan sat upright as the ambulance turned into the hospital grounds.

"Who's Jordan?"

"Long story Cathy, but Jordan's another person I need to thank for saving my life. He was lying low in the upper container and jumped on Collins when shots fired."

"So he would have heard everything? Maybe seen it too?" said Cathy.

"He must have."

"Where is he now?"

"No idea."

This time the paramedics insisted on wheeling Dan into the hospital. He did not protest. His head throbbed, as much from Cathy's inquisition as the open wound, his stomach burned, and his ribs were tender to the touch. Cathy accompanied Dan into A&E, passing herself off at reception as his next of kin. She sounded convincing as she knew his date of birth, address and much of his medical history. She even knew his blood group, AB positive, uncommon in the UK. The foreign desk at *the Daily News* had flagged up the information in the event doctors required the details on one of Dan's assignments.

The hospital declared a 'major incident', and the emergency department manager cleared as many patients as possible. The place teemed with armed police. The reason quickly became apparent.

Johnny was in Cubicle C, receiving treatment for what a hospital spokesperson would later describe, euphemistically, as a crush injury. Nico was in Cubicle A, awaiting a physical examination, overnight observation and assessment by the paediatric consultant, a psychiatrist, and social services.

Paramedics wheeled Dan into Cubicle E. Two nurses took over, drawing the curtains and attaching him to a heart monitor. A junior doctor arrived searching for the best location to insert a cannula. When the medical staff left, Dan lay back and closed his eyes. Cathy was about to go to file her story when a new patient arrived in Cubicle F.

"Thank you, doctor. It feels a lot better."

Dan's eyes flew open – he knew that Dalek voice. He rose on his right elbow.

"That's Jordan." Dan jabbed a finger towards the adjoining cubicle so Cathy could be in no doubt.

Two policemen stood outside Jordan's cubicle. His details and story still required corroboration and the NCA were taking no chances. Out of police view, Cathy stuck her head around the curtain. Jordan was alone.

"Come on, Dan," said Cathy, urging him off the trolley and helping him unclip the electrodes sticking to his chest.

She held the curtain back, and Dan slipped into the adjoining bay. Jordan sat in a wheelchair with his right lower leg in a splint.

"Dan." Jordan's tone was one of surprise.

Dan put his finger to his lips and motioned behind his back for Cathy to join him. "Jordan, this is important. After you climbed the ladder, could you hear the conversation in that container?"

Jordan nodded.

"Did you see what happened?"

He nodded again, and Cathy couldn't contain her excitement.

"What about the little red-haired Irishman? Did you hear what he said about Ernie?" Dan asked.

"Yes. I couldn't get a signal on my phone, so I

did the next best thing." Jordan dug into a pocket of his combat trousers and removed a phone, so slim the police check had missed it when dragging him out. "See." He pressed the video mode button.

Jimmy Collins's head filled the screen then the camera panned back to him talking at Dan who was on his knees. Jordan had filmed the entire encounter. He hit the volume button and the soft tones of the Irishman, along with Dan's voice, were unmistakable.

"Unfortunately, Ernie was a lot like you, Dan. He didn't see the big picture, had no imagination. I made him a generous offer, truly I did. Too generous. But Ernie was not for selling."

"So you killed him."

"I wouldn't put it quite as blunt. Let's just say two worlds collided, and Ernie's planet went the way of the dinosaur. E for Ernie. E for Extinct."

Cathy clapped her hands. "This is it, Dan. The smoking gun we've been looking for. It could put Collins away for life."

She desperately wanted to take the phone away to watch the video in its entirety but realised that might compromise the evidence. There couldn't be any suggestion of tampering. A defence lawyer would seize on any impropriety at a later date. Instead, she grabbed Dan's head in her hands and kissed him on the lips.

"Got to go," Cathy said. "Look after yourself and make sure Jordan keeps that phone safe for the police. By the way, don't believe what Collins said. You've got loads of imagination. Too much. It's what got you into this mess."

With that she retraced her steps, drawing back the rear curtain to leave via Dan's cubicle before calling her NCA contact to inform him of the treasure on Jordan's mobile.

Jordan looked at Dan with scared, mournful eyes. "Dan, you won't tell Jaz about tracking her phone, will you? Please, don't say I'm a pervert."

Dan placed his hand on the young man's shoulder and gave a squeeze of encouragement. "You're not a pervert, Jordan. I shouldn't have said that. You're a brave lad and helped save my life. You will need to tell the police how you came to be at Ernie's place but as far as I'm concerned, your secret's safe with me. Honest."

32

Bill and Murph weren't happy. The morning after the night before, Jaz was getting an earful from her fellow male passengers.

"Why didn't you phone us?" said Bill. "It's like we attended the rehearsals then missed out on the opening night."

"Yes," Murph agreed, "we could have offered assistance in the search for Dan."

Martin had done his pick-ups at the usual time, and the friends were heading to the Barrett Bailey, Jaz and Trish still buzzing from the events of the previous night as was Lexford. Facebook and Twitter were awash with the goings-on at Ernie's. The incident was the main news on local radio. Reporters interviewed eyewitnesses, meaning anyone who'd leaned out of a window and seen the hovering police helicopter. To reassure residents, a police spokesman outside Ernie's car wash promised a more visible police presence in the town.

Shootings weren't commonplace in Lexford. Martin was about to pull out of town when he saw the billboard outside the newsagent:

ONE DEAD IN LEXFORD SHOOTING

"Stop, Martin. Let's grab a *Daily News* and see

the report," said Trish.

Martin pulled over, and Jaz jumped out. She bought three newspapers – *The Sun, the Mail* and *the Daily News*. Armed only with sketchy information police had released and the uninformed speculation of onlookers, *the* Sun and *the Mail* consigned the story to an inside page lead. *The Daily News* splashed the story across the front page.

The main headline screamed:

DRUG BARON NABBED BY COPS

A strapline above provided more information:

ONE DEAD AND UK'S MOST WANTED MAN ARRESTED AFTER SHOTS FIRED

There was a fuzzy library picture of Jimmy Collins climbing into a car alongside the headline. Above the main body of the story, Cathy Wheeler's 'Exclusive' stood out, her name in bold capital letters. Across the bottom of the page was a white-on-black blurb, promising more drama on the inside pages:

THEY PUT A GUN TO MY HEAD – Pages 4-7

Jaz opened the newspaper, and a large picture of a smiling Dan driving a jeep jumped out at her. Dan had posed for the photo a few years ago while on assignment and Jaz deemed it rather flattering. He looked like an action man. The emotive headline spread across two pages zoned in on the moment Dan thought he was going to die. Media buzz phrases such as 'Gun Terror' and 'Police Raid' peppered the sub-heading. No one could accuse *the Daily News* of underplaying the events of the night before.

At Trish's urging, Jaz turned the page again. There was more – two pages analysing how UK gangs exploited thousands of vulnerable children, foreign and domestic, every year. Another picture of Cathy Wheeler sat at the top of the left-hand page accompanied a credit for the special investigation that had lasted almost a year. There was no mention of Jordan's video, and Cathy was meticulous not to include anything about Collins that could prejudice any forthcoming trial.

"Bloody brilliant," said Bill, leaning over Jaz's shoulder and pointing to the caption under Dan's picture:

Dan Armitage ... a man who can

"It must have been terrible for him with a gun to his head. Imagine what would go through your mind," said Murph.

"I'd prefer not," said Bill.

"If anyone can handle that sort of situation, it's Dan," said Trish.

"There are worse things than guns, though, Trish," said Bill.

"Such as?"

"As the saying goes, give a man a gun, and

he'll rob a bank. Give a man a bank, and he'll rob everyone."

"I've never heard that saying."

"It's not wrong, though, is it?"

Trish shook her head.

The animated chat continued throughout the journey. Bill and Murph wanted to devour every detail, impressed when Trish told them she and Jaz arrived at the furniture car park overlooking the scene of the crime before the police.

"It was all down to Cathy Wheeler," said Jaz. "She has contacts in the National Crime Agency who listened and acted immediately."

"Yeah, Jaz, but it was you who worked out where Dan was likely to be," said Trish. "You phoned Cathy, although it was my phone you used, so technically I should get some credit."

"You sound like Thelma and Louise," said Bill.

"Hardly," said Trish. "They were running from the law and had shot someone. We were trying to persuade the police to come to us to stop someone being shot."

The car turned into the Barrett Bailey, and the group split up to go to different treatment rooms. As always, Jaz and Trish were first out. They decided they had time to indulge in a luxury ground coffee at the concourse coffee shop, rather than the usual instant type on sale at the kiosk. Trish did the honours, buying a mocha for herself and a latte for Jaz. Settling in a soft leather armchair next to Jaz, Trish dropped a sugar cube in her coffee and stirred the drink lazily with a spoon.

"Jaz, what did Dan say to you?"

"What do you mean?"

"You know. When you first saw him and knew he was alive – when you ran and threw your arms around him. When he kissed you full on the lips. Remember? You can't have forgotten. What did he say to you?"

"Oh, Trish, it was all a blur. I thought someone had shot Dan. He appeared to have major trauma to his head, and I was scared witless. I could see the blood, but I didn't know how bad the injury was. The police were trying to get me back behind the tape."

"You're avoiding the question, Jaz. What did he say?"

Jaz gave Trish a sheepish look, picked up her cup and set it down again. She could sense Trish had passed frustration long ago and on her way to infuriation.

Trish took a slurp of coffee.

"Okay," said Jaz, inhaling a deep breath. "He said he loved ... loved ... loved Robin Ellacott."

"Who the fuck's Robin Ellacott?" spluttered Trish, spraying mocha from her mouth, and leaving a fine mist hanging in the air.

The elderly couple at the next table cast a disapproving glance. Trish threw one back.

Jaz reached for a serviette and wiped stray coffee from her handbag. "A private detective working with Cormoran Strike, you know, the guy on the telly with one leg who solves crimes. She's the leading lady in the series."

Jaz explained how she'd told Dan she felt like Robin Ellacott when taking photographs at Ernie's car wash. They made a good team – a good investigating team.

"I think Dan was just teasing, just being funny," said Jaz. "It was all very emotional. Come on. He'd just had a gun pointed at his head."

"Jaz, did he say, 'I love Robin Ellacott,' or did he say, 'I love you, Robin Ellacott'?"

"Does it matter? I think it was the second one."

"I thought so. That means Dan was saying, 'I love you, Jaz' and using Robin Ellacott as a pet name between lovers. Something you had shared intimately in the past that only the two of you knew about."

"Are you sure?"

"I saw that kiss, and it wasn't the type you often see between private detectives, either real or fictional. Honestly, Jaz, sometimes you're a real klutz."

"What does that mean?"

"Stupid, Jaz, stupid. Awkward. Slow on the uptake. Fancy me telling you what a word means. You're one of the cleverest people I know, but where relationships are concerned, you are a klutz. Open your eyes. Dan's been in love with you since the first day he picked you up. I could see that. We could all see that."

"Oh."

Suddenly, Jaz felt invigorated and apprehensive. It had been a long time since her unsatisfactory entanglement with David. Since then, she'd kept men at arm's length or parried their advances, sometimes with direct, even cutting humour, like her persistent suitor at the petrol station. Putting up defences can become a way of life. The scars of a broken relationship can remain tender forever.

Trish could see the angst and vulnerability in Jaz's face, but wouldn't let this moment pass without knowing. "Do you love Dan?"

Tears welled in Jaz's eyes. She fidgeted for a tissue in her coat pocket.

"I don't know, Trish. I'm confused." Jaz's fingers ran through her blonde wig. Her voice was weak and scratchy. "We've only known each other for a few weeks. He's a great guy, kind, generous, and he makes me laugh."

"So does Bill," said Trish. "He's all of those things too."

Jaz ignored the interruption. "I care for Dan, but with everything going on, the chemo, feeling sick, not knowing what's going to happen, not knowing if I'll need more treatment, not knowing what the outcome might be …"

Trish raised her hand. Her voice was loud, the tone, strident. "Stop! Right now. Stop blaming cancer, Jaz. Stop wearing the cancer mask to hide your real feelings. It isn't fair on Dan, and it isn't fair on you. It's not fair on the rest of us who have cancer and no one to go home to, who cry into our pillows every night because we have no one to share things with. You're a grown woman, Jaz. You're intelligent and good looking and, for fuck's sake, DO YOU LOVE DAN?"

Mouths agape, the elderly couple at the next table put down their coffee cups and fixed their eyes on Jaz. Two other couples on nearby tables did the same, while the young waitress in the coffee shop, carrying a tray of empty cups and food wrappers, stopped in the middle of the room. She looked over her shoulder, waiting for Jaz's answer.

Time stood still.

Jaz dabbed her eyes. "Yes," she said, blowing her nose and giggling through tears. "Yes. I think so, Trish. I think so."

The young girl moved on, the elderly couple smiled at each other, and the lady even motioned to clap but didn't.

Trish raised her painted-on eyebrows and said one word. "Halle-fucking-lujah!"

Jaz inhaled deeply, feeling as if she'd jumped out of an aeroplane after much reflection. With an open parachute and untold elation, she floated to Earth not knowing where she would land.

33

Jaz waved through the window as the MPV turned into the main entrance of the hospital and drove past the statue of Elizabeth Barrett Bailey for the last time. "I'll miss this place."

Today was Friday, and Martin was in the driving seat. Doctors at Lexford Infirmary had insisted on admitting Dan for two nights of observation. Trish and Jaz visited, but Cathy Wheeler had been there with two officers from the NCA, so they'd spent little more than five minutes at his bedside. Enough time for small talk. Not enough for meaningful conversation. Dan had promised he would be up and about to see them finish treatment, but doctors had banned him from driving until he was clear of the double concussion inflicted by Gheorghe's broom handle and the butt of the Glock 45.

"I won't miss it," said Bill.

"Thanks a lot, Bill," said Trish.

"It hasn't been that bad, has it, Bill?" Murph asked.

"You lot have been okay I suppose, and this Honeycomb service is fantastic, I couldn't have got here every day without it. But I've still got gremlins downstairs, and it's wearing me down day after day. Doctors warn about the side effects and insist they have to give you the worst scenario. Some days I've felt as if that's what I've been going through, the worst scenario. I've started having hot sweats at night, and before you say it, I know you ladies know all about them."

"Poor Bill," Jaz sympathised.

"I'll miss you, Bill. We'll all have to visit you," said Trish.

"Don't forget, Trish, it's number fifteen," said Bill.

"I thought you lived at seventy-five?"

"He does," Jaz said. "He's joshing with you."

Martin stopped the car, and his passengers climbed out and went their separate ways. By happy coincidence, and mainly because a malfunctioning machine delayed Jaz and Trish, the four finished at the same time. Fortuitous as that meant ringing them out together, apart from Bill who still had sessions remaining. His nasty diarrhoea period had put back his treatment. He was fond of telling everyone it was a bit like Picasso's Blue Period, except that his was a different colour and lasted longer.

The four friends were a motley bunch. Bill now walked with two canes, and Murph shuffled along one step above stop. Trish held a white perforated 3D mask of her head and face. Used to keep her head firmly in position while undergoing treatment, the mask was a macabre, redundant souvenir of her time at the Barrett Bailey.

"Would you like to take your face home," the nurse asked.

"Yeah, I think I'll put it on the wall."

"Oh, that would work. Have you noticed it looks different whichever side you view it?"

"Are you saying I'm two-faced?"

"No," the nurse giggled, "but it might scare the kids at Halloween."

Trish laughed and with her free arm leaned over and hugged the nurse. There was something of a demob atmosphere. The others milled around the wall-mounted bell, and the nurses and radiology staff gathered in the corridor. Bill watched from the adjoining waiting room.

"Prostrate problem is it?" said the big lady sitting next to him.

"Prostate," corrected Bill.

"That's what I said. Prostrate, like my husband. He's got a prostrate problem too."

"How terrible, you mean he can't lie on his face?" said Bill, who'd woken up in an argumentative vein and decided to enjoy the mood while it lasted.

The lady looked Bill up and down as if he were simple. Manically, Bill smiled back.

The bell rang. Trish and Jaz hugged the nurses nearest to them, Murph smiled with an appreciative nod, and the trio walked down the corridor, gathering good wishes and milking applause as they went. The tradition of ringing a bell had begun in hospitals treating the sickest children, but an observer at the Barrett Bailey had been astute enough to realise people of any age appreciate goodwill and fond farewells.

Reaching the end of the corridor, Trish was ready to push the double doors through to the drivers' room when they swung open from the other side. There stood Dan, white bandage on his head, face a mass of purple and yellow bruises. His right eye was half shut, and a crusted red scab separated his nose into two distinct halves. Due to pain from three cracked ribs, Dan held himself awkwardly, but his eyes twinkled, the smile wide and welcoming.

Jaz gasped. "What are you doing here?"

"I told you I would be up and about to see you all finish your treatment. One of the other drivers gave me a lift over. I wasn't going to miss the finale."

"It's good to see you, Dan," said Murph.

"It's good to be here, even if I'm walking slower than you, Murph."

Dan fished in the inside pocket of his jacket and pulled out a slim black box with a silver motif. *A jewellery gift box* was Trish's immediate thought. Her heart skipped, and she looked across at a wide-eyed, open-mouthed Jaz.

"Jaz, I have something to say to you, and I have something for you," said Dan.

The nurses formed a semi-circle of laughter and goodwill, looking at Dan expectantly.

Jaz's mind whirred so fast she could hardly

hear what Dan was saying. Her eyes flitted from his face to the black box in his hand. The hairs on the back of her neck tingled, her heart leapt, and she struggled to catch her breath. The intelligent, rational Jaz knew it was impossibly soon and hardly the place for a grand romantic gesture. Dan was not an impulsive kind of guy, and she wasn't a love-sick teenager, but Trish had filled her head with possibilities and opportunities. Jaz's brain buzzed with a mess of emotions – torn between reality, yearning for the love and life that always eluded her.

"Jaz, if it weren't for you, I dread to think where I would be now," said Dan. "Cathy told me what you did, how you came looking for me and wouldn't give up even when the local police didn't seem interested. How you phoned her and pleaded with her to call her NCA contacts. I will never be able to thank you enough. I had a lot of time to think in that dark container, and I know I owe you my life. You are incredibly kind and caring. You are beyond special, Jasmine Sharkey. The sweetest, most extraordinary person I have ever met. Thank you."

Dan handed the black box over. Jaz glanced up at him and smiled, fumbling with unusually clumsy fingers. The lid gave way, and there it was. A black phone. Her black phone. The one she'd loaned Dan after she'd taken photographs at the car wash, the one that led Jordan to Ernie's. The motif on the box was the crown emblem of the NCA.

"The police have finished with it now," said Dan. "I know how precious your phone is to you, so I thought I'd get it back as quickly as possible."

Jaz's ears filled with thunder and her bottom lip trembled. She knew it was ridiculous, but in that fleeting moment of expectancy, a tiny part of her craved a gesture of commitment. She burst into tears, so many feelings colliding and exploding in her brain. She covered her face with her hand to try to hide her reaction, then rushed through the double doors and out into the car park. Trish swiftly followed, brushing roughly past Dan, who stood with arms open wide and a bewildered expression.

Trish dug him in his tender ribs and hissed, "Daniel Armitage! I need to talk to you."

34

Trish arrived early – organisation wasn't her best skill, but this meant so much. She'd booked into a small bed and breakfast in the North Wales village of Llanberis and spent the last hour pacing the car park across the road from the Snowdon railway station. July 20th, 10 am – almost a year since Trish's treatment at the Barrett Bailey ended.

The headscarf was gone and in its place, a short mop of curly, grey-flecked, dark hair. Trish's natural black eyebrows had regrown, appearing darker than before, and gave her a striking appearance. She'd returned to her job and looked fit and toned, helped by the swimming and walking regime of the last eight months after receiving the all-clear from her consultant. She still required regular check-ups and her local doctor had advised her to take things slowly, but Trish had never been good at taking advice or waiting.

"Where are they?" she muttered, perching on the boot rim of her Renault Clio with the tailgate open. She pulled on walking boots and stuffed the bottoms of her combat trousers inside her socks.

Trish stood and craned her neck to peer at the

mountain rising imperiously, connecting with a deep blue sky punctuated with fluffy white clouds. A tick on her bucket-list awaited. The car park was almost full, but Trish had reserved a space next door with a folding chair, clipboard and pen. She'd repelled several would-be parkers with a curt wave, a flash of her Hendos loyalty card and a blatant fib.

"I'm doing a survey for the National Trust. Sorry, we need this space."

Minutes later, she saw Dan's white Audi turn into the car park. She jumped up and down, waving both arms above her head. A cheery wave returned from the passenger window. *Jaz.* Trish pointed to the 'reserved' space, and Dan pulled in.

"Hiya!" Excited, Trish ran to Jaz, enveloping her in an affectionate hug. Dan received the same welcome. "I can't tell you how good it is to see you both," said Trish. "Come on, Jaz, let me see."

Jaz, whose own honey-blonde hair had grown back thicker than ever, although it was short and neat and, like Trish's, flecked with grey, stretched out her left arm and splayed her fingers. A gold, single diamond engagement band sat on her ring finger. Plain but classy.

Trish's eyes danced with delight. "When's the big day?"

"Not sure," said Dan. "But soon. You will be first to know, Trish."

"I should think so too. If it wasn't for me ..."

She let the sentence trail away on the breeze, but Dan gave her a knowing look.

After the tears and awkwardness of that last day at the Barrett Bailey, Trish had decided the chances of Daniel Armitage and Jasmine Sharkey ever getting together by themselves were up there with Murph walking on the Moon. They needed a push. From Trish. And Trish didn't do romantic clichés. Engineering dinners for two. Nights at the theatre or contriving to get one of them to spill a drink over the other, which seemed to end up with a couple in bed in romantic comedies, wasn't her style. Trish was direct, which was why she'd telephoned Dan the night after Jaz departed in tears and asked him the question.

"Do you love Jaz?"

"Have you been speaking to Jordan?" said Dan.

"Eh? No. What's he got to do with it?"

"Never mind."

"Give me a straight answer, Dan. Do you or don't you?"

Silence.

"Dan?"

There was a long pause, and for a moment, Trish thought Dan had disconnected. Then she heard a cough and a catch in his throat as if something were stuck and he was desperate to set it free.

"Yes, Trish. I think I do."

Another awkward silence.

"I'm not good at this sort of thing," said Dan.

"Oh, really, I would never have noticed." Trish didn't hold back. "Well, I've got news for you. Jaz loves you, too. Let's stop farting around and get you both together before I lose the will to live. That would be terrible timing! I'm expecting to get the cancer all-clear anytime soon."

True to her word, Trish arranged for the couple to meet two days later at The Anchor pub. No Blue Angels required this time, although the initial meeting was a little stilted. Dan leant forward, and Jaz pecked him on the cheek. There was an awkward pause before Jaz looked around at the half-empty bar and spoke.

"Should we be here? I thought we were barred."

"That's just your side of the family." Dan pointed to his bruises and bandages. "Anyway, who would recognise me looking like this?"

They shared a laugh. Dan bought himself a pint of bitter and a raspberry and mango soda for Jaz. The couple talked for the rest of the night, discussing anything and everything. Especially the parts Dan had been reluctant to divulge, such as his love for Annie and her sudden death. The loss of their child. His anger and sense of injustice. The ache and yearning he'd hidden for too long. It all poured out, and Jaz took his hand in hers and listened.

Ever since they'd been inseparable and when Dan's ribs mended, and his wounds healed, he had no doubt. He took Jaz to her follow-up appointments after three months and six months. When the consultant confirmed there was no sign of cancer, the couple celebrated with joyful tears and glasses of bubbly.

As they sipped, Jaz admitted that at last, she could rid herself of an analogy that had haunted her. "I read an article in a magazine, where someone likened having cancer to being trapped in a cage with a lion cub. At first, the animal was small, cuddly, relatively harmless, but as each week passed, the cub grew bigger and stronger until one day it had huge teeth and massive claws. A big lion, capable of devouring the person trapped in its cage."

A squeamish expression clouded Dan's face. "That's scary."

"And I haven't been able to shake that feeling of dread since reading," said Jaz. "That lion was *always* with me. At home. In the hospital. In the car. At the cinema. In my dreams. In the bathroom. Especially in the bathroom. I don't know why."

"But now it's gone. No more lion, yeah?"

Jaz smiled, and the couple clinked glasses.

"No more lion."

Dan had also helped Jaz and her mum through a challenging time with Jack, whose Pick's disease showed rapid progression. Jaz gave up her job at the petrol station. Jack's GP advised a care home, but mother and daughter were determined to keep Jack at Three Jays as long as possible. Jack had connected with Dan, who was happy to ignore and adept at deflecting Jack's more abusive comments.

Some things are meant to be. As if to prove the adage, Dan received a call from Thomas Henry, proprietor of the *Lexford Journal*. An old-school businessman, Henry had read with interest the blanket coverage surrounding the capture of Jimmy Collins and an award-winning local journalist's involvement.

"Come and work for us as Editor-in-Chief," said Henry. "You won't become rich, but I can promise two things. You'll receive my full backing in your editorial decisions, and you will make a difference."

Dan took 24 hours to mull over the offer. After a chat with Jaz, he rang Glyn Morris, Editor of *the Daily News*, to tell him he wouldn't be returning. The local newspaper had hired the Journalist of the Year. Quite a coup. Dan had given up dodging bombs for a living.

To make peace with his decision, two weeks later Dan drove Jaz down to Highgate cemetery on the anniversary of Faz's death. He showed her the plaque proclaiming his Lebanese comrade as 'An Eloquent Hero'. They stood hand in hand, looking at the urn holding desert sand, which Dan had collected from the battlefield. He told Jaz the full story, including the horrific details that had haunted him since. He confessed his nightmares, bouts of PTSD and his reluctance to attend counselling as Lance had done. They drove home from Highgate in near silence, both pondering the enormity and extent of what they'd discussed.

For the first time since losing Annie, Dan felt truly unburdened. That night he stayed at Jaz's house in Meadow Drive, and they made love for the first time. Not mad, passionate, physical sex but slow, sensual, rhythmical and caring. Afterwards, Jaz rested her head on Dan's chest and ran a finger down his bicep. She traced the raised edges of the four-inch-long silky scar tissue just above his elbow. He explained the scar was the result of shrapnel received when a roadside bomb exploded in Afghanistan 20 years before. At the time of the blast, he was standing talking to Faz, about 100 metres away.

"Any more bumps and bomb craters I need to take into consideration?"

Dan took Jaz's left hand and placed it at the top of his right buttock. He guided her soft fingertips and long nails around a swirling, knotty depression in his skin.

"Bullet hole?" said Jaz.

"No, a metal rugby boot stud when I played at school. I was eleven. Bloody hurt."

Jaz laughed. She felt safe, comfortable. Togetherness with Dan felt right. With a feeling of belonging and arms and legs entwined, the couple fell into a deep sleep.

The next day Dan took her to the old Gothic church of St Anne's in Broughton Conquest, the one he passed on his morning bike ride, whose hallowed grounds dated back to the Domesday Book in 1086. Wandering around the stone walls, they marvelled at the tower, and its octagonal turret then ventured inside to look at the brasses, memorial slabs and the arch in the wall of the south aisle. Here, was a recumbent effigy of Sir John Sewell, knight of the 14th Century, features still intact albeit minus his lower limbs.

Maybe it was the sacred atmosphere, the weight and thrill of the history encased in solid stone walls. Perhaps this was the perfect time and place. Whatever the reason, Dan's fumbling fingers pulled a small velvet box from his pocket. He opened it on the third attempt – no black phone this time. When she saw the diamond ring, Jaz gasped, a soft echo resounding around the otherwise empty church.

Dan had planned to get down on one knee, but in the nervous muddle, he forgot. He placed the box on his upturned palm and bowed his head. "Jasmine Sharkey, will you marry me?"

This time there were no tears, only a joyous whoop as Jaz threw her arms around Dan's neck and hugged him, knocking the box to the stone floor. "Yes, Dan ... yes. Yes!"

Jaz giggled as Dan slumped down on both knees alongside the knight to retrieve the box.

When he stood, Dan eased the ring onto the third finger of Jaz's left hand.

"Now it's yours forever," Dan said.

They held each other close, Sir John Sewell looking on. Wide-eyed and legless.

35

Jaz gasped for breath as she and Trish stumbled along a stretch of loose shale and slate. "Hold on, Trish, I'm not as fit as you."

The pair had passed the halfway point on the Llanberis Path up the mountain. They'd stopped a couple of times, taking in the spectacular view, but Jaz needed another breather. For the past year, the girls had stayed in touch – neither had heard from Bill or Murph.

"I do hope Bill and Murph turn up," said Trish, wriggling out of her rucksack straps, digging inside for a water bottle and gulping two long slurps.

Jaz and Dan followed suit and drank from their bottles, Jaz resting on a rock, Dan standing next to her. Trish inched to the edge of the path and looked down at a sheer drop of some 50 metres.

"Be careful," warned Jaz.

Trish raised both arms in the air and stood on tiptoes as if she were a high board diver. "Have you ever felt that impulse to jump, Jaz? To jump off the edge and feel yourself sailing like one of those falcons we saw earlier. I have. Swooping and gliding without a care in the world. Wouldn't it be wonderful?"

"Yeah, until you hit one of those rocks," said

Dan. "Then you wouldn't have a care in the world."

Jaz swigged water and took a bite from a chocolate energy bar. She paused to chew and swallow. "The French have a phrase for it."

"What do you mean?" said Trish.

"It's called l'appel du vide – call of the void – and it's precisely that feeling. The impulse to jump. People experience the desire in all sorts of high places – roofs, high-rise flats, bridges, cliff edges. It doesn't happen if you're on an aeroplane or enclosed behind glass or bars, only when you're unprotected. Like now, Trish. Please, come away from that edge."

Trish took a step backwards and turned to her left as the Snowdon steam train honked, chugging its way up to the summit on the rack-and-pinion railway. It was several metres away and packed with summer passengers. Trish waved, a few waved back. Jaz peered intently for any sign of a wide-brimmed, beige hat, wondering if Murph might have been one of the riders. He wasn't.

"Let's get cracking," said Dan, offering a helping hand to Jaz as she prised herself off the rock.

Slowly, they climbed for the next hour as robust, fitter walkers steadily overtook them. On a couple of occasions, walkers descending the mountain too fast slipped and slid on shaky ground, triggering a mini-landslide of small stones amid a volley of oaths and squeals.

All the while, Dan took pictures, fascinated by the Alpine topography, its rounded valleys and glacial landforms and the beguiling Snowdon lily growing from precarious cliff faces. He snapped half a dozen goats on a rock edge, expertly tiptoeing across terrain that would require ropes and grappling irons for two-legged mortals. As the trio ascended, Llyn Llydaw, a lake more than 50 metres deep according to Jaz's guidebook, reflected the scudding clouds.

The friends stopped again, and Jaz flicked through the guide she'd bought at the train station. She was enjoying learning about the mountain's history. "It's thought the summit is the tomb of a giant called Rhitta Gawr," she said.

"Who?" said Trish.

"In Welsh folklore at least. Says here, he wore a cloak of men's beards and was slain by King Arthur after taking his beard."

"What a bloodthirsty lot. Can't say I'm into all that folklore stuff," said Trish.

"How about this for a fact?" said Jaz, flicking the page. "On the first day the train opened to the public in 1896, it plunged down the mountain."

"Was anyone hurt?" said Trish.

"The guide says the crew jumped clear from the engine when it derailed. The guard applied the handbrake and brought the carriages full of passengers to a halt. He was the hero."

"Good on him," said Dan.

Jaz read on. "Oh, how sad. One passenger panicked, leapt from the carriage thinking it wasn't going to stop and died."

"And the moral of the story is …" said Dan.

"What?"

"Don't jump to conclusions."

Jaz smiled and shook her head.

"Come on, we'd better keep going," said Trish. "It's getting colder."

The reason for the change became apparent as a cloudy mist enveloped the climbers and sent the temperature tumbling.

"Ooh, that's not clever," Trish shivered, yanking a navy blue fleece from her rucksack and pulling it over her head and shoulders.

Jaz donned a thick cardigan and raincoat, and Dan wriggled into a sweatshirt, wrapped an anorak around his waist and tied the sleeves in a loose knot. They trudged on for another half hour. Damp, unwelcoming cloud persisted, obscuring their view of the summit although arrows and landmarks confirmed the peak was near.

"Do you think Bill and Murph will be there?" Trish said, for at least the tenth time.

"I hope so, Trish, but it's quite a journey for both of them," said Jaz.

"That's if they're still around," said Dan.

"You don't mean …" said Trish.

"Both have been through a lot. Neither are getting any younger and … you know what I mean."

The path narrowed. Up ahead the friends could see Hafod Eryri, the Snowdon visitor centre with its café and oak and granite façade. The pace quickened, and the trio reached the building five minutes after Trish's allotted meeting time: 14:05.

At Snowdon's crown, from Llanberis, the path forks. To the right, the rail station, visitor centre and café, the summit reached by roughly-hewn, helpful man-made steps to the left. All three opted for a visit to the café, reasoning that was where Murph and Bill would wait if they had made the journey. Inside, many train passengers and walkers enjoying a well-earned rest and light refreshments congregated. Some sat around tables close to the panoramic windows, cursing the rolling clouds robbing their eyes of some of the most memorable views in the United Kingdom.

Dan scanned the room, hoping, for Trish's sake, to spy a familiar face. Shoehorned into a corner, he spotted Murph, by chance, or maybe design, next to the toilets – hat in place, glasses, dangling around his neck. He wore that familiar, serene expression, a pot of English tea and china cup on the table.

"Hey, Murph!" Dan shouted across the room.

Murph replied with a wave of recognition. Pushing their way through the crowd, Trish got to him first and threw her arms around him, Jaz followed then Dan shook Murph's hand.

"It's great to see you. How long have you been here? Have you seen Bill? You haven't been to the summit yet, have you?"

Murph shook his head as if trying to unscramble his brain. "I've missed your machine-gun questioning, Trish. The answer to all of them, except the first, is no." He glanced at his watch. "I arrived about half an hour ago and was told I could only stay for half an hour, so I bought another ticket, just to see you, Trish."

"Ah, that's lovely," said Trish.

The group chatted for several minutes. Murph revealed his treatment hadn't been entirely successful. He still had elevated PSA readings, but the doctors hoped to manage matters over time.

"The doctor was kind and straight with me. He said he couldn't cure the disease, but that I was much more likely to die with it than because of it. At my age, I'll settle for that. He told me to take it easy and not climb any mountains, or anything stupid."

"Sorry, Murph," said Trish.

Like the others, Murph hadn't heard from Bill since the day they'd left the Barrett Bailey. After waiting another ten minutes, Dan suggested making their way to the summit for the obligatory photograph.

Trish wore a resigned expression.

"Okay, but I do hope Bill's all right."

The group trudged out of the café and up the steep stone staircase towards the top, a tough climb for Murph taking slow, ponderous steps walking with the aid of a cane. Dan supported Murph's arm to help him reach the summit, which housed a small stone-built viewing circle. An inscription informed climbers they'd reached the highest point in England and Wales – 1,085 metres above sea level.

Trish took slow, deliberate final steps, savouring her bucket list moment before bounding up the last step. "Wow, we made it. Brilliant!" she screamed, spinning around, arms in the air. "And what can we see? Fuck all!"

Everyone chuckled.

"But it was worth it, yes, Trish?" said Jaz.

"You betcha."

Dan began lining them up for a group photograph he planned to take with a timer as Trish felt a nudge in her back.

"Excuse me." A small, wiry woman with softly curled grey hair and a friendly face spoke. "Is your name Trish, or Jasmine?"

Jaz spun around.

"I'm Trish, that's Jaz."

"You don't know me. My name's Jean Murdoch."

"Bill's wife?" said Dan.

"Yes."

"Where is Bill?"

"He told me all about you and asked me to give

you this."

Jean handed Trish a white envelope. Trish's anxious face matched the clouds as it drained of colour. Bill had addressed the letter: 'To Trish, Jaz, Murph, and Dan – the best five-minute friends ever'.

"Oh, Jean," Trish's voice faltered. "This doesn't mean … does it?"

Jean's tone was sombre. She looked down, ran her tongue around her lips and took a deep breath. "When he became very ill, not long after finishing his treatment at the Barrett Bailey, Bill told me about Trish's bucket list wish. He made me promise to deliver this letter today, come what may. Said you made a pact to meet up here at two pm and that I could take the train."

Trish opened the envelope and drew out a note in Bill's spidery handwriting.

"Read it out, Trish," said Dan.

Pausing to compose herself, Trish cleared her throat and read:

Dear Trish, Jaz, Murph and Dan,

If you're reading this, you will know I am not among you. I'm probably topping the bill at the great Palladium theatre in the sky. I wanted to say a few words to congratulate you on reaching the top of the world, well, Wales at least, and showing the Big C who's boss.

I can't tell you how much I enjoyed those four

*weeks we spent travelling to the Old Bailey.
I know I moaned and whined, and shares in
diarrhoea medication must have gone through
the roof that month. In the end, I realised four
strangers had become four fabulous friends I
would thank and remember for the rest of my
life. Thank you for putting up with me and
helping me through the worst of times.*

*Trish. You have the softest heart and the
sharpest tongue. I love the way you cut through
the crap and tell it as it is, even if you never
understood my jokes the first time.*

*Jaz. You are one of the kindest, generous,
most intelligent women I have met. Emus
the world over should watch out.*

*Murph. Lord of the Flies Down. I'll
save you a seat by the toilets.*

*Dan. Good driver. Great companion. Marry
her, Dan. For God's sake, marry her.*

*Have a lovely day, and I only hope
your view is as special as mine.*

Love to you all. Hope I don't see you anytime soon.

Bill

Trish reached in her pocket for a tissue and blew her nose, tears ran down Jaz's cheeks, Murph stared at his feet, and Dan tried to swallow the lump lodged in his throat. Sad and uncomfortable, Jean shifted from foot to foot.

Then, from somewhere below, on the steps obscured by the swirling cloud, a familiar voice bellowed in a flat, northern accent.

"What's the difference between a golfer and a mountain climber?"

"Bill? Is that Bill?" Trish screamed, leaning over the summit platform, and peering into the murk below.

"You'd better believe it, Trish."

The friends strained to see, and there he was. Bill, balanced on two sticks, looking pale and gaunt but smiling, mischievous eyes twinkling.

Looking sheepish, Jean gabbled her apologies for the letter. "He wrote it when he feared the worst, at his lowest ebb. When the pain wouldn't go away, and he had horrible side effects from the medication. But when he started recovering again, he insisted I still had to give the letter to you and say nothing. That is how he felt, and you know what Bill's like – he has to make a grand entrance."

Dan bounded down the incline, put his left shoulder underneath Bill's right armpit and helped him up the last few steps to the summit. Trish and Jaz's tears turned to squeals of delight as they greeted Bill with hugs and remonstrations for his poignant letter-cum-practical joke.

"Now, let's take that picture," said Dan.

What happened next, Jaz would have called serendipity. Trish described it as a bit fluky but, at that moment, the cloud, commonplace in mountainous regions, lifted. Only for a minute or two, as if someone had drawn back the curtains. Sunshine burst through to bathe the group in a warm glow, and the temperature rose ten degrees. Shaped by the elements for millions of years, the view was magnificently wild and wondrous. Trish later reflected, when scrolling through the pictures, a beautiful, sweeping reminder of man's insignificance.

"It reminds me of what you once said on the way to the Old Bailey, Trish," said Bill. "About when the mist cleared after your cancer diagnosis, and you knew you had to fight for your life. Well, you've done it again. The mist has gone."

"You've all done it," said Dan, setting the timer on his camera positioned on the ledge of the summit viewing wall and joining the others.

Linking arms in a line and huddling up close with Jaz and Trish in the centre, the group peered into the camera lens.

"Go on then, Bill, what is the difference between a golfer and a mountain climber?" Dan asked.

"One goes, whack, shit, the other goes, shit, whack."

Between rapturous laughter and joyful tears, Dan's camera clicked. The friends didn't need words. Beaming faces thrust into the warmth of a sympathetic sun said it all.

How wonderful to be alive!

ACKNOWLEDGEMENTS

With love and gratitude to Carole and Michael for their help and encouragement.

Thanks to Pete Coulson for his interest and support, and to the volunteer ambulance drivers, unpaid and unheralded, who help transport patients to life-saving treatment.

Most of all, a heartfelt thank you to those who confront adversity every day and plough on regardless with courage, humour and hope. Truly, you are an inspiration.

All royalties from this book will be donated to the Primrose car service, part of the Bedford Hospital & Friends Charity, helping transport patients to radiotherapy treatment.

ABOUT THE AUTHOR

A journalist by profession, Frank Malley worked as a columnist and deputy sports editor with the Daily Express for 15 years. He was also chief writer with Press Association Sport, covering Olympic Games, football, and rugby World Cups, and top events in golf, tennis, and motor racing.

Shortlisted for Columnist of the Year in the Sports Journalists' Association awards, Frank began writing books after turning freelance.

www.frankmalley.com

If you enjoyed *When the Mist Clears*, the author would appreciate a quick review on Amazon, Goodreads, or your favourite book website. Reviews are vital – a few lines make all the difference.

ALSO BY FRANK MALLEY

The 13th Assassin

The Hit List

The Killing Circle

Codebreaker

If it Looks Like a Duck

Living on the Deadline

Simply the Best

Available in paperback and Kindle formats from Amazon.

Printed in Dunstable, United Kingdom